THE
GUILTY
MOTHER

BOOKS BY SAM VICKERY

One Last Second

My Only Child

Save My Daughter

Her Silent Husband

The Promise

One More Tomorrow

Keep It Secret

The Things You Cannot See

Where There's Smoke

Novellas

What You Never Knew

THE
GUILTY
MOTHER

SAM VICKERY

bookouture

Published by Bookouture in 2023

An imprint of Storyfire Ltd.
Carmelite House
50 Victoria Embankment
London EC4Y 0DZ

www.bookouture.com

ISBN: 978-1-83790-350-4
eBook ISBN: 978-1-83790-343-6

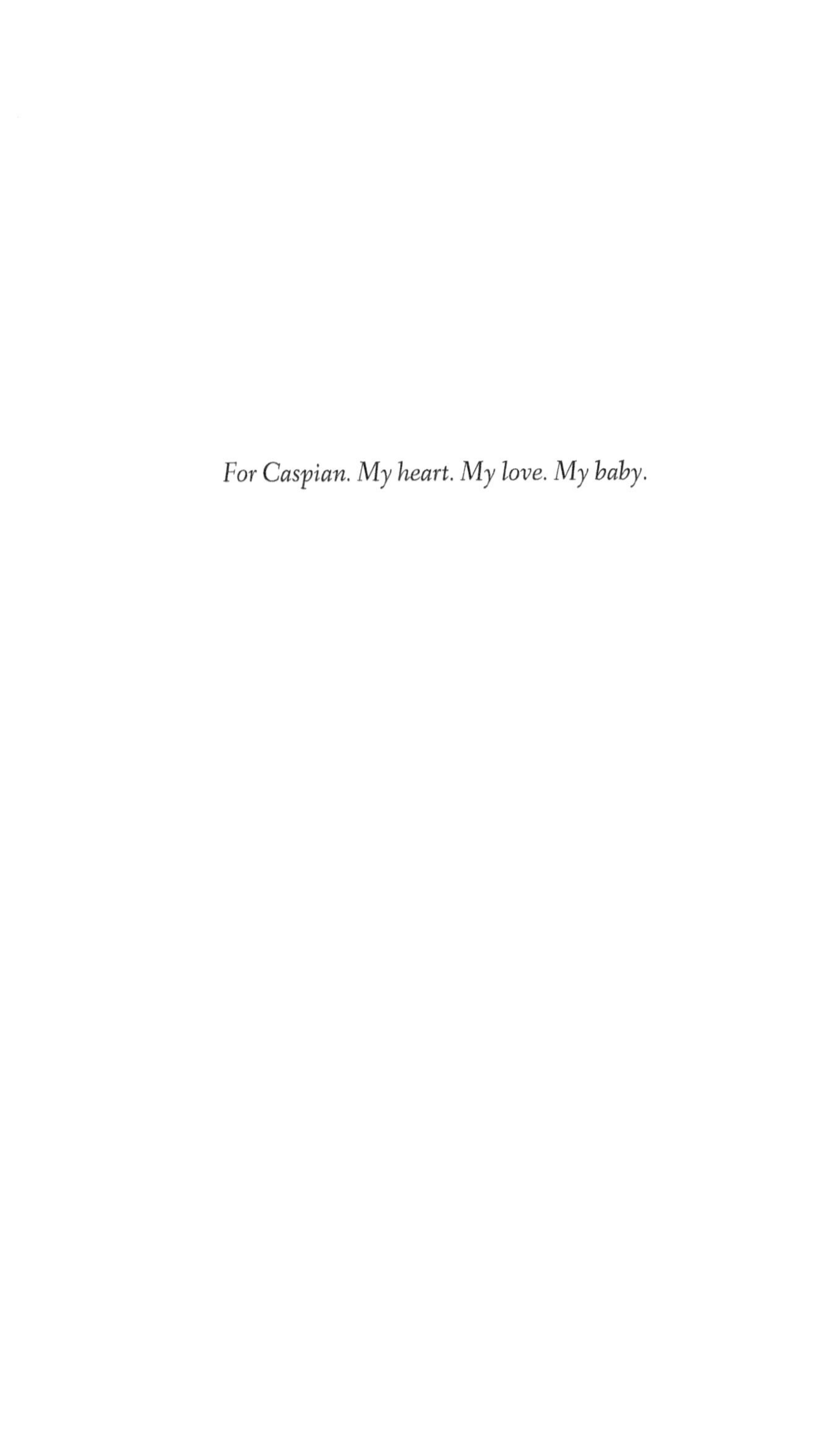

For Caspian. My heart. My love. My baby.

PROLOGUE

The thing about getting older is you start to believe the stories you've created for yourself. When you're young, you're still developing your character – the world is yours for the taking, a blank canvas for you to make your mark. You can be brave, clever, sexy, funny – whatever the hell you want. But as the years pass and you make certain choices, follow particular paths, you close more and more doors, though you never see them slam shut in your face. You begin to put yourself in a box, believe that the person you've become is set in stone – this unshakeable, unchangeable entity – and as each year passes, you grow more and more resolved in those beliefs.

I'm scared of heights.

I'm terrible at maths.

I'm beautiful.

I'm kind.

I would never hurt a fly...

It's only when something huge happens, an event so cataclysmic it rocks our world, that our belief in who we thought we were can be shattered. What we thought we were capable of becomes a distant memory as we charge forward, surprising even ourselves. It is then we come to see that the stories we told ourselves were just a comfort blanket. A safe series of lies to give us security in a world we don't always understand. That when pushed, we have the potential to become someone completely unrecognisable – someone who is capable of doing things we would never have dreamed of.

Does everyone have this darkness inside them, this intense feeling of loss and loneliness they can't begin to explain? Are we all just walking around curtailing our true selves for fear of what we might find if we search deep enough? I don't know. Perhaps it's just me. But as I stand in the pouring rain, watching the trail of blood run off the kerb into the gutter, knowing it's too late to take back what I've done, I can't help but wonder.

ONE

LISA

I knew it couldn't last for ever, this fleeting happiness, this feeling of everything being exactly as it should be, but in this moment, it didn't matter. For today, with my family sitting around the kitchen table, Holly and Jack teasing each other about the lumpy gravy they'd made – Holly always tried to add more powder to the mix after the water was poured and never learned that it made it stodgy and impossible to recover – and Mike opening a bottle of red, pouring a generous splash into my waiting glass, I was happy. Content. Able to squash down the anxieties that came with being a mother and pretend nothing could touch my little family.

It was a bitter pill to swallow when I let myself consider how rapidly their childhood was coming to an end. I wasn't ready for it to be over – to even contemplate the idea of my babies flying the nest, though friends were telling me their own children were making plans to do just that. I couldn't bear the thought of it. I still needed them with me. Needed moments like this, where we all could sit together enjoying a home-cooked Sunday roast, where I could press pause on the hurry of life for a little while and savour this quality time with my family. I wasn't ready to let them go.

I carried the dish of potatoes over to the table, and Mike jumped up, coming to help, taking the honey-glazed parsnips from the counter, the plate of perfectly cooked sliced lamb. He winked as he passed me, and I let my hand graze his hip, wanting to pull him close and hold him tight. To make him promise that nothing would ever change. That everything would be okay.

Shaking away the intrusive thoughts, I sat down, focusing on my children, their easy banter as they reached for the serving spoons. Jack piled his plate high, I noticed happily, but Holly only took one potato, one thin slice of meat. She looked up, our eyes meeting briefly, and I watched her reach forward, adding another potato to her tiny portion as if to ward off my concern before I had a chance to speak. I would have to keep an eye on that. She was already too slim for her height, and I was sure she needed more calories than she was allowing herself. Being the parent of a teenage girl was so much harder than I could have anticipated. I wondered if *my* mum had thought the same about me and felt a pang of sadness that I would never have the chance to ask, now that the breast cancer had finally beaten her.

I closed my eyes, irritated at myself for once again heading into this negative spiral of thoughts. It wasn't the time for them now. Not when I had so much to be thankful for. I took a sip of my wine and smiled at Mike as he came to sit beside me.

'This looks gorgeous, Lisa,' he said, kissing my cheek before reaching for the lamb, serving some to me before attending to his own plate. 'Kids, isn't your mum just the best cook in the world?'

'S'good.' Jack nodded, his mouth already full. 'Thanks, Mum.'

Holly nodded. 'Yep, delicious,' she agreed, though she'd barely taken more than a tiny bite.

I squeezed Mike's hand. 'Don't be silly. It's just a basic roast. Anyone could do it.' I glanced at the lumpy gravy the kids had made and hid a smile. I could have made it from scratch, but I preferred it this way – for them to feel like they'd helped. It was important.

'Not like you,' he insisted. 'I've said it before and I'll say it again. You should have been a chef, Pixie.'

I smiled, enjoying his flattery, though I knew he meant it. And maybe there was some truth in it, but cooking for him and the children had always been enough for me. I didn't want to turn something I did for pleasure into an obligation in exchange for a pay cheque. Besides, Mike had always earned enough to provide for us. I was content.

I picked up my cutlery, digging in, and had just put the first forkful to my lips when the doorbell rang and I felt my whole body stiffen. Mike's hand was already coming to my knee as if he expected me to jump up, though I couldn't have moved if I'd tried. I was frozen to the spot with fearful anticipation, and somehow I just knew this was it. I'd been waiting for this moment, the sound of a fist banging on the front door. If I weren't so terrified, it would have almost been a relief that the wait was over. Everything I'd been trying to pretend wasn't real, every dark thought that had kept me from sleeping, was about to become reality, and there was nothing I could do to stop it from happening.

'Who can that be?' he said, frowning. 'We're not expecting anyone, are we? I bet it's those bloody double-glazing salesmen again. They're just relentless lately. Jack,' he said, 'go and get rid of them, will you? If they ask if the homeowner is in, tell them we rent. That will get them to clear off.'

'Righto.' Jack jumped up, picking up a gravy-soaked potato from his plate with his fingertips and crushing it into his mouth before heading for the door.

'Eat up, Pixie,' Mike said to me. 'You've been on your feet

all day. The least you deserve is to actually eat your meal in peace. No point letting it get cold.'

'Right, yes... of course,' I murmured, though I made no attempt to lift my fork again.

There were voices, male, deep, in the hall, and Mike's frown deepened.

'They're coming in,' Holly said softly, her words echoing my thoughts.

'Bloody hell,' Mike said, slamming down his fork and getting to his feet. 'I should have gone myself. Too much to ask that he might send them packing, I suppose—' He broke off, his eyes widening as two men in suits came into the kitchen, followed closely by Jack.

'Sorry, Dad, they said they're police. I didn't know what to do,' Jack said, glancing from the two men to Mike.

The elder of the pair stepped forward, flashing an ID and looking across the laden table towards me. Ignoring my husband, he said, 'I'm DS McCormac. Are you Lisa Grey?'

I didn't respond. My heartbeat was thudding in my ears, my fork still clutched in my hand, drops of the gelatinous gravy dripping onto the pale blue plate below.

'What *is* this?' Mike demanded, his expression clouding with confusion.

'I'm ever so sorry to interrupt your meal,' DS McCormac said, turning to Mike now. 'These things are never convenient, I'm sure you'll agree.'

'Things? What *things*?' Mike said, and I could tell he was getting agitated, needing answers I wasn't sure they would be willing to offer. 'Has something happened?' he asked suddenly, and I saw him glance at me. I knew he was thinking of his elderly parents, afraid for them in the rickety old static caravan they'd moved to two years previously to be 'closer to nature'.

'Unfortunately, yes,' the detective said, clasping his fingers together for a brief moment. He turned back to face me, and I felt my stomach drop. 'Mrs Grey, I'm arresting you on suspicion of causing the death of Russell Fox by dangerous driving on the nineteenth of June. You do not have to say anything, but...'

His words blurred and faded in my head as I stared at his face, watching his lips move. I didn't speak as his colleague approached and guided me up from my chair before putting the cold metal of the handcuffs around my wrists. The sensation was shocking, the metal too heavy, jolting me back to the moment like a glass of cold water to the face.

Mike and Jack were arguing, yelling about the officers making a mistake, that Russell was our friend, our neighbour; his wife had told us herself that he had been killed in a car accident the previous weekend. Mike had spent the days following the accident in shocked silence, and a sombre mood had blanketed the house. They had it wrong.

I tried to open my mouth to speak, but nothing came out.

'Mum,' whispered Holly from across the table, and I turned towards her, seeing the pale, frightened face of my baby girl, her eyes glistening with tears as she sat terrified, the steam rising from her roast potatoes swirling before her.

'It will be fine,' I managed, though it came as barely a whisper. 'I don't want you to worry. It will all be fine,' I repeated as I felt strong hands steer me towards the door.

'Mike,' I called, suddenly remembering, 'the crumble's in the oven – don't leave it on!' I'd cooked it specially – it was everyone's favourite. I hoped they would still eat it. There was fresh custard in the fridge and ice cream in the freezer for Jack. He always said eating custard made him feel like an old man who'd lost his teeth, along with his drive for life. He was such a funny boy.

'Lisa!' I heard Mike call from behind me as I felt myself being propelled down the hall. I was glad I was wearing sandals. I'd left them on after I'd popped down the end of the garden to put the vegetable peelings in the compost bin. I wondered if I would have had to go barefoot if I hadn't.

'Lis,' he repeated. 'I'll fix this. I'll sort it, I promise.'

I nodded, trying to keep calm as I let myself be guided out of the front door, down the path and into the back seat of the smart steel-grey Audi parked at the kerb, Mike following close behind. I bent my head, unwilling to look through the window into the eyes of the man I was leaving behind.

'Lisa,' I heard him murmur, his voice childlike, pleading, as if I could somehow stop this from happening. As if I might have any say in my future.

I linked my fingers together on my lap, the cold metal of the cuffs digging into my wrists, and a moment later, the car was moving and it was almost a relief not to have his sad eyes fixed on my face through the glass, searching for answers I didn't have.

I leaned back against the seat, a feeling of absolute numbness settling over me, dulling my terror, though my fingers trembled in my lap. We were driving away from my family, my life, and as we passed through the streets I knew like the back of my own hand, I realised there was a chance I might never come back home.

TWO

VICTORIA

I stared blindly at the television, the news pouring out misery into the room, making the atmosphere all the more bleak. I was too numb to find the energy to reach for the remote and switch it off. Each morning since that awful night, I had found myself unable to resist turning on the TV, needing to fill the house with noise, voices, the silence too much to bear. I perched on the edge of Russell's favourite recliner, winding my long brown hair around my finger in an anxious rhythm, picking out each wave and curling it tight, enjoying the sensation as I pulled hard against my scalp. It was hard not to imagine him here now – the smell of fresh ground coffee in his favourite mug, the sports channel playing on the TV, his favourite way to spend a Sunday afternoon.

But he wasn't here. Instead, there was just this permeating silence, so strong that not even the monotone voices of the news reporters could squash it. Never in my forty-three years had I spent so much time by myself as I had in the past week, and I found I was lost, unsure how to fill the long days, wondering what my life was to become now that my husband was gone.

Not gone. *Dead*, I reminded myself. Never coming back.

Never. The thought sent a shock through me, and I felt my throat tighten involuntarily against a wave of emotion, panic, confusion. How could you spend more than half your life with someone only to wake up one day and know that you would never see him again? How was anyone supposed to just accept that as fact, deal with the knowledge that you'd never hear his voice, see him smile, never fight or laugh or touch him again for the rest of your life? It was so final, so real, and yet it still felt like a dream. A nightmare I wasn't sure I belonged in.

I hadn't been able to face any of the things I knew I should be doing. There was a funeral to organise. People still to call, to tell, but I didn't want to. His mum had been hard enough. What kind of cruelty is it to have to tell a woman of nearly seventy that her only son is dead?

Morag's howls of anguish had sent ripples of nausea through me when I'd picked up the phone to break the news, and it had taken all my strength not to hang up on her. We'd never been close, never seen her more than a few times a year as a couple, and Russell had rarely bothered to call home, but still, she was – *had been* – his mother, and now she was left childless, and all just months after her husband had keeled over out of the blue from a heart attack. He'd been strong as an ox, right up to the moment he dropped dead, and I knew Morag had been more shocked than anyone that he was really gone. She was alone now, just as I was, widowed and childless, though I hadn't bothered to highlight that point of connection between the two of us. It was too late for us to try and form a bond now – she'd made her feelings about me clear, though I'd gone into the marriage hoping to be a friend to her. In Morag's mind, I would always be the woman who had stolen her son from her.

I hadn't had the courage or the energy to call anyone else after I'd finished comforting her. It had occurred to me later that day that she hadn't thought to ask if *I* needed anything, if I might be struggling too, and though I wished she had, wished she'd taken control of organising the funeral, at least, I couldn't blame her. I had never had a child to lose, but I could understand the pain it must create to grow a person within your own body, nurture and love them, and then have to live without them.

I leaned forward, wrapping my arms around my knees as I watched the screen that dominated the living room, footage of some protest taking place in London, brightly coloured banners being carried by righteous-looking people of all ages. I admired their determination, though I was sure their efforts would come to nothing. Life wasn't that simple. I wished I could be as naïve as they were, believing their actions had power, but I was far too jaded for that.

A streaker wearing nothing but a colourful piece of cloth around her shoulders ran into view behind the stodgy-looking reporter, the camera too slow to pan away as she broke into an energetic stamping dance, and I let out a burst of laughter, then just as quickly clamped my hands over my mouth, disgusted at myself.

It was too soon to laugh – to smile even. It was only the shock that had made me do it. Just the shock of adjusting to this new world without him by my side. I pressed my hands tighter to my mouth, a warning, and when I was sure I had regained control of my emotions, I reached for the remote and switched off the television.

The house phone rang, startling me in the sudden quiet of the living room, and I stood, walking over to it on the sideboard, answering automatically, a habit I couldn't have broken if I'd tried.

'Hello?'

'Mrs Fox?'

I felt my heart stutter at the sound of the serious masculine tone at the end of the line. 'Yes,' I replied, the word catching in my throat.

'This is DS McCormac. I wanted to give you an update on the case.'

I gripped the phone, suddenly feeling the need to sit back down, not sure I wanted to hear what he had to say.

'Oh,' I managed, leaning heavily against the sideboard. 'Okay.'

I had been expecting this call. I knew they were looking into what might have happened. A hit-and-run was all I'd been told when the police had knocked on my door in the early hours of Sunday morning. I knew they would want to dig deeper and find out who had killed him. Who could have driven off and left him for dead.

'We've arrested a woman we have reason to believe was driving the car that hit your husband,' he continued. 'A neighbour of yours.'

'Who?' I whispered, gripping the phone tighter between my hands, my fingernails pressing hard into the polished black plastic. 'Who did you arrest?'

'A Mrs Lisa Grey. We'll be interviewing her this evening. Obviously I'm only letting you know as a courtesy,' he added, his voice turning sympathetic.

He'd been the one to tell me Russell was dead. I doubted he'd forgotten the way my knees had buckled, his reflexes not quite quick enough to catch me as I crumpled to the ground at his feet. I wondered how much he was bending the rules to make this call, or if it was just normal protocol.

'No charges have been brought as yet, and I'd appreciate it if this stayed between us for now,' he said. 'I'll keep you updated.'

I agreed, my head swimming as I ended the call and placed the phone gently back in its cradle, my imagination conjuring up the pretty, elfin face of the woman who had been my closest friend for twenty years, picturing the terror in her eyes as the police led her into a cell, locking the door behind her.

THREE

LISA

There had been a spot of gravy on Jack's collar. It shouldn't have mattered, all things considered, but it was all I could seem to focus on as I sat uncomfortably in the back seat of the car, trying not to look at the two policemen in the front. I could picture him now, standing on the doorstep, mouth ajar, eyes filled with terror, that little brown smudge on his white polo shirt.

It would stain, I was sure of it. He'd take it off later and kick it under his bed and who knew how long it might stay there. And as much as I longed to be a domestic goddess, I knew I'd end up fighting a losing battle against it until I gave up and threw it in the clothes bank at the end of the road. I'd never been great at these things, try as I might.

The police radio crackled, offering snippets of muffled conversations happening between other cars, though the two men in front didn't seem in any rush to get involved. They didn't speak, either to me or to each other, and I fought the urge to break the silence. What could I possibly say?

When I'd seen stories in the news of people getting arrested, or films where a woman was dragged away in cuffs, I'd always assumed it would feel surreal. Like a bad dream you might wake up from at any minute. But this was nothing like that. It was too real. Jagged and cold – *painfully* real. The smell of aftershave from the men sitting in front of me, the gentle bump as we drove over a speed hump. The sound of children screaming in delight as we passed the playing field, tiny legs clad in shiny nylon shorts running at top speed to reach the football first, their parents holding reusable coffee cups as they watched proudly from the sidelines. It was all so normal. None of it felt like a dream. Not even the fact that I knew I wouldn't be going home to my own bed tonight.

The realisation made me think of Mike – how scared he had looked as I was put in handcuffs, the helplessness he must have felt as he'd had to stand back and watch them take me away. I didn't know if I would have been able to stop myself from physically stepping between them, a human barrier, had it been Mike they had come to take. I would have fought. And when I inevitably lost, I would continue to fight. I would do everything in my power to bring him home. The passion I had for my family gave me strength. It made me able to take on the world, but Mike, as much as I loved him, didn't have that ferocity within him. He would be afraid. He would fight for my freedom, but he wouldn't know where to begin, and it would sap him of every last drop of energy. Where the fight would fuel me, drive me to try harder, to never give up, I knew just how much it would take from Mike. Would he be able to step up to the challenges coming our way? Would he manage to hold on to hope when it all felt insurmountable?

I looked away from the window as we turned the corner down a road I didn't recognise, and I realised we were driving into an underground car park. DS McCormac wound down his window and keyed a code into a pin pad, and the barrier lifted, letting us through. He drove towards a ramp and down a level, then swung the car into a space and got out without preamble, walking round the car and opening my door, reminding me to watch my head as I stepped out.

The car park was lit with bright, high-voltage strip lighting overhead, casting a glare over the gloss-painted pale grey floor and breeze-block walls. I squinted, rubbing the skin beneath the cuffs, feeling very small compared to the two men, who seemed to tower above me. I felt suddenly vulnerable, hyper-aware that I was completely at their mercy, cuffed and unable to do anything to defend myself. The cotton dress I was wearing felt too short, the cold breeze tickling my bare legs, and for the first time since they'd walked into my home, I felt a trickle of trepidation poking holes through the numbness that had stolen over me since my arrest.

I felt a hand come to my back, guiding me across the hard grey floor towards a door on the opposite side of the car park, and didn't resist. There was no point in making a scene now. It would only make things worse.

We went through the door, greeted by more unrelenting strip lighting from above, then down a long, narrow corridor, finally emerging into a reception room furnished with a wide welcome desk, dark green with protective glass barriers, a couple of blue plastic seats along the wall screwed into metal brackets on the ground. And big double doors leading to the world outside.

I cast a glance at the doors, part of me longing to escape, but I knew I would never do it. Instead, I turned to the desk, my face blank as I waited for what would come next. The second man who'd come to my home, whose name I hadn't heard, muttered something to DS McCormac before walking away, not even bothering to glance in my direction as he passed me. The woman on the desk smiled politely from behind her computer as I was guided forward.

She looked me straight in the eye, and I blushed, embarrassed at standing there in handcuffs. 'Hello there. Have you been arrested or in trouble with the police before?'

I cleared my throat. 'Uh, no. No, I haven't,' I replied.

'And can I have your last name please.'

'It's Grey.'

She typed it into the computer. 'First name.'

'Lisa.'

'And what brings you here today, Lisa?' she asked, her warm voice at odds with the situation. She reminded me of the receptionist at the nail salon Holly had persuaded me to go to last month on a girlie day out. I felt like this uniformed officer was about to show me her new selection of gel polishes. 'I—' I began, but DS McCormac cut in.

'Lisa has been arrested on suspicion of causing death by dangerous driving.'

I looked down at my feet, wanting to argue with him, to tell him he'd got it wrong. It felt crazy to just stand there and have them talk over me – *about* me – as if they already knew who I was. They didn't know me at all. They had no idea, no right to make such judgements about me. But I knew I couldn't say anything. I pressed my lips together.

Finally the woman stood up, and I watched, my stomach tightening, as she walked out from behind the desk. DS McCormac gave her a nod and strode off round the corner, leaving the two of us together, though we were far from alone, several other officers working, hunched over computers behind the main desk.

'You doing okay? You look pretty pale,' she said, frowning.

I shrugged, not knowing how to answer a question like that, given the circumstances. 'Could I have a glass of water please?' I asked, my voice coming out quieter than usual.

'Of course,' she said politely. 'Let's get those cuffs off you too, shall we?'

I nodded, trying not to show how relieved I was, and lifted

my wrists, watching her slide a small key into them, instantly loosening the tight metal before sliding them off. She clipped them onto her belt, then filled a plastic cup from a water dispenser beside the desk and handed it to me. I finished it in three gulps and handed it back to her.

'May I have some more?' I asked.

She nodded and refilled it once again, and I drank that too, feeling a bit better.

'Okay now?' she asked.

I nodded. 'Yes, thank you,' I replied, though I would have asked for more if I weren't afraid of her thinking I was taking her for a ride. I still felt so thirsty, my mouth dry and gritty, and I wondered if I was more nervous than I realised.

'Good,' she said, taking the cup and tossing it in the waste-paper basket. 'Then let me show you to your cell.'

'My cell?'

She nodded, gesturing for me to walk on, and I froze, my legs leaden and uncooperative.

'But... but I assumed they just wanted to talk... to ask me some questions,' I said, my voice coming out reedy and thin. I was desperate for her to believe that I had no idea why I was there.

'That's the plan. I doubt you'll be waiting long, but in the meantime, you'll wait in the cells.'

'But... can't I just sit here?' I asked, pointing to the row of seats along the wall. 'I won't be a nuisance – I'll keep out of your way.'

'I'm afraid that's not possible. Sorry,' she said, and I thought I saw a flash of impatience cross her pretty features. 'You *do* understand what's happening? You've been arrested, Lisa. Not just invited in for questioning. This is a serious business.'

She glanced over her shoulder to where a group of staff were chatting loudly about whose turn it was to make the coffee. She tutted, looking back at me. 'If you'd like, I can get someone to come and answer any questions you might have, but I'm afraid that for now, you'll have to come to the cell. I need to get back to the desk.'

I opened my mouth to argue, then closed it again, thinking better of it. I didn't want to piss her off before I'd even been interviewed. I didn't want her to think of me as the kind of person to make trouble. 'Okay,' I agreed softly, seeing that I had no choice. 'I understand.'

She smiled, clearly relieved. 'It won't be for long. They're just sorting a few things out.'

She motioned for me to walk ahead, then followed me down another shorter corridor and took a bunch of keys from her pocket, opening a door. I stood at the threshold, unable to move, aware that as soon as I stepped inside, I would be locked in.

I would have taken the handcuffs over this any day. The tiny room was bare, aside from a raised bench with a narrow blue plastic mattress placed on top. No sheets. No blankets. And as warm as the day was outside, it felt cold in here. The walls were stark white, and there was no window. It felt like a tomb.

'Just for a little while,' the policewoman repeated.

I stiffened my jaw and nodded, stepping forward. She didn't wait for me to change my mind before shutting the door firmly, locking it behind her.

I tensed my shoulders, unwilling to let myself panic, and spun on the spot, slowly taking in the bright white walls, the smell of disinfectant emanating from the wipe-clean sleeping mat. Then, feeling awkward and sure that I was being watched, I climbed onto the bed, sitting back against the wall, wishing I'd worn something warmer. Mike always joked that I would be chilly in the Bahamas, and he was right.

The thought of him made me picture us all around the table earlier today, the laughter from Holly and Jack, Mike's warm eyes as he watched me cook. The memory gave me courage. It gave me strength.

I didn't deserve to be here. They couldn't possibly have any evidence I was involved in Russell's death. I just had to stay calm, patient. I could cope if I just took it one minute at a time.

I breathed in deeply, forcing myself not to panic, then pulled my knees up to my chest, wrapping my arms around them, and leaned my head back against the wall, waiting for whatever I had to face next.

FOUR

VICTORIA

I stood at the living-room window, staring across the road at Lisa's front door, a sense of uneasy anticipation churning in my belly. Any moment now, Mike would come flying out the door, car keys in hand, as he rushed off to collect her from the station. Or perhaps the police would bring her home. I doubted it. I couldn't imagine them going out of their way to act as a taxi service, even if they were at fault. But she *would* come back – and soon. They would ask a few questions, establish her innocence, and she'd be told she was free to go. I was sure of it. Lisa was lucky like that.

And yet their front door remained closed, Mike's old Land Rover, the car he'd bought cheap for spares and repairs and spent countless hours working on until it was up and running, sat alone and silent on their driveway.

The car was Mike to a T. He frequently insisted on taking Lisa and the kids out on weekends to the back of beyond, down narrow potholed lanes, to go hiking or camping or on some other adventure. Rain, sun or snow, nothing would stop him if he had a plan in mind, and I'd often laughed, watching Lisa's stoic expression from my window as she'd clambered into the passenger seat dressed in waterproof trousers and wellies. She was a good sport about it, but I knew for a fact that if it wasn't for her desire to stay in town, where she could walk to the shops – feel part of civilisation, in her words – Mike would have sold up and taken them all to live in some ramshackle cottage in the middle of nowhere years ago.

Lisa, I knew, had always indulged his fantasy, but insisted privately that she'd never leave the convenience of town life. She'd grown up in Ashford, and as far as I could tell, she had little desire to move elsewhere. With the coast a quick car ride away and an abundance of gorgeous Kentish countryside in every surrounding direction, they'd stumbled on the best of both worlds.

I glanced at the clock on the mantelpiece, my hands fidgeting nervously in front of my abdomen as I realised that two hours had passed since I'd spoken to DS McCormac on the phone. It was coming up for four in the afternoon, and the thought that she might have to spend the night in a cell made me feel strangely nauseous. She would be so scared, so worried about Jack and Holly. And knowing her, she'd be racked with guilt for scaring them, rather than thinking of herself. If there was one thing I knew about Lisa, it was that she loved her kids.

The detective's call had served as the jolt to the system I needed. It had been seven days since Russell had been killed, and the entire week had been a blur. I had got out of bed at eight every morning, showered and dressed, done my make-up – a slave to my routine – but that had been it. All my energy was sapped by those few simple tasks. This was the first day I had even bothered to open the curtains.

Mike had knocked on Tuesday, asking to borrow Russell's stepladder, and I'd told him in the shortest way possible what had happened, refusing his offer to get Lisa to make some meals for me to heat up, sick at the thought of eating more than a piece of dry toast and a cup of miso soup. I'd closed the door, ending the conversation as quickly as possible, and returned to the armchair, where I'd let my mind switch off, protecting myself from the barrage of overwhelming emotions simmering millimetres beneath the surface. But while I had been in my safe little cocoon, hiding in the half-darkness of my living room, the police had clearly been hard at work.

I tore myself away from the window, pacing back and forth across the oak floor, not knowing what to do with myself. I felt so alone. I had nobody to talk to, though the feeling was admittedly one I was more than familiar with. I still felt like any minute now I would hear the sound of Russell's car pulling onto the drive, the metallic clink of his key as it slid into the front door. I would smile, pour him a drink, listen as he talked about work, sports, his latest purchase – usually some expensive and ostentatious piece of furniture that had me cringing inwardly. He always needed to unload his thoughts and tell me every detail of his day after we spent any time apart. He liked that I was a good listener. That I asked the right questions without detracting from his stories. But there was no car engine now. No key. Just a buzz of electricity and the far-off hum of a lawnmower from somewhere down the street.

Our own lawn was still neat and tidy, having been mown the previous weekend. Russell never let it get overgrown – he was fastidious about keeping it in immaculate condition, no matter the season, though more often than not he managed to convince me to do the gardening while he was at work. He reasoned it was cheaper than a gym membership and nice for me to get some fresh air rather than staying cooped up indoors, waiting for him to come home.

I froze, struck by the realisation that I'd been thinking of him in the present tense. It was still so fresh, so hard to wrap my head around the idea that he was really dead. I felt caught in the space between my life with him and whatever would come next, a surreal limbo I wasn't ready to escape, even if I'd had the slightest idea how to.

The memory of that night played over and over in my mind on an almost constant loop. I had been lying in bed, the sound of rain on the window, the mattress cold beside me where he should have been. In my half-conscious state, I'd seen the blue flashing lights illuminating the bedroom wall, and mechanically clambered out of bed, going to the window to look. There had been a flurry of activity on the corner beneath the big horse chestnut tree that stood there, too sheltered for me to see, but when the knock had rapped hard against the front door a good while later, echoing through the silence of the moonlit house, I had known what was coming.

I could still remember every tiny detail of the hour that followed. Pulling on my warmest dressing gown, despite the humidity left over from the summer storm, I'd done up each button slowly, then sat down on the end of the bed, sliding my feet into slippers, breathing slow and deep. The knock had come again, louder and longer this time, and I'd made my way down the stairs in the dark, my sweaty hands sliding against the banister, hesitating before finding the courage to unlock and open the front door.

I could have drawn a perfect picture of DS McCormac. His face was emblazoned on my mind, that awful look in his eye, the way he had swallowed hard before speaking, as if steeling himself for the job. He'd asked if he could come in for a chat, and if I'd been holding on to a shred of doubt, that sentence would have crushed it. They never say that unless there's something to fear, do they?

Last year, when there had been a break-in three doors down, the police had gone door to door and the first thing they'd said was, 'Nothing to worry about. We're just here about a spot of trouble in the area.' But DS McCormac hadn't said that, and I'd known. Everything that followed had only confirmed what I already felt, and I was sure I was still in shock now. My husband of twenty-two years was dead. I was a widow. I was alone.

I looked down at the ugly ornaments on the sideboard, half tempted to pack them away so as not to have to see them again. I picked up a pair of vintage brown leather binoculars, then glanced around, feeling guilty. I could almost hear his words echoing in my head. 'You don't appreciate good taste, Victoria. Leave them be before you break them.' He'd always been so particular when it came to these little treasures of his. His mum had once told me his bedroom had been immaculate, even as a child, that he'd never once broken a toy or scribbled on a book, and I could well believe her. I placed them carefully back in their designated spot, then turned away. After a week trapped inside these walls, I had a sudden panicked need to leave the house. To get away from the memories of him that were every-where I looked.

I strode into the hallway, taking my cardigan from the hook and throwing it on, then walked out the door, slamming it closed behind me, and, with a sense of determination, crossed the road to Lisa's house.

FIVE

LISA

I shivered, though the tiny room, which had been chilly on my arrival, was now stiflingly hot, my body tensing at every sound beyond the door, every voice, every footstep. My mouth was dry, my tongue rough against the sticky roof of my mouth; I was desperate for another drink of water, but the thought of calling out and asking for one made me shrink into myself, unwilling to draw unnecessary attention my way.

I shifted on the thin sleeping mat, stretching my legs out over the edge, kicking back and forth to bring life back to them. I'd lost track of time but guessed I must have been waiting here for an hour or so. Time in here dragged, with nothing but my own thoughts to fill the empty minutes, and those thoughts had been colourful and intense, my mind working nineteen to the dozen, taking me back to bizarre conversations I had shared with my teenage son.

Jack wanted to be a psychiatrist in the future, and despite the fact that he was still a complete comedian for the most part, I had no doubt he would achieve his goal. He was doggedly determined when it came to the things he was passionate about, and ever since I could remember, he'd been fascinated with the human mind. He loved to watch documentaries about any number of topics showcasing what he would call 'fascinating case studies'.

There had been those awful ones about attachment theory and the effects of maternal neglect in babies. I'd been horrified at how glassy-eyed the toddlers on the screen were. How at such a young age, they'd already cut themselves off from the world, a self-protective bubble formed iron tight around their hearts. I had squeezed Jack's hand as we watched the programme together, trying not to cry as I thought of *his* baby years, the joy I'd felt feeding and cuddling him. It had been exhausting, but there had never been a day when he hadn't made it all worthwhile with a gummy smile, a dribbly kiss.

Then there were the programmes about mental health. Bipolar disorder. Schizophrenia. Psychopathy. I'd never been keen on those, but Jack watched intently, learning as he went, even taking notes on occasion.

Sitting on the hard, insufficiently padded bench in the confines of my cell, one series we'd watched together kept flashing up in my mind. A programme about the British police force, taking viewers through the arrest and subsequent interviews of suspected criminals. The show had shaken me. There had been so many cases where an individual was clearly guilty. The police knew it. I knew it. *Everyone* knew it. And yet for some reason or other, they didn't have the evidence needed to charge them. They were completely reliant on cherry-picking from the accused's story, hoping to catch them out on a detail, a lie. But this required cooperation.

I'd been staggered by how many cases I had seen dropped because the suspect wouldn't talk. Innocent or guilty, these individuals gave the police nothing, and in the majority of cases, it worked in their favour. Jack found it thrilling, commenting throughout about how ballsy a strategy it was. There were some compelling interviewers too, alluding to evidence they didn't have, bringing up other suspects or people involved in the crime who might be saying more, goading the suspect into their trap, every word an invitation to speak up and defend themselves.

Jack would sit on the edge of the sofa, eyes wide, hands gripped tightly together, glancing back and forth between me and the TV as he compared each suspect with those from cases he'd seen in the past, explaining how two people who had committed the exact same crime could face such different outcomes based solely on their level of cooperation. There was no doubt my son was going to be a brilliant doctor. He understood the way people thought, the little attributes that made them unique, and yet all their similarities too. Right now, he was still, to my relief, a normal teenage boy who loved to have fun, and hadn't lost the balance between work and play, but I could see that with the right training, these skills he was honing would become razor sharp, and he would only grow in his ability to read people.

He was always telling me how we all thought we were so different from other people, that nobody could ever really understand what went on in our minds, and yet fundamentally we were all human – there was only so far you could travel along a spectrum – nobody was truly alone in the way they thought and felt, despite how easy it could be to fall into the trap of believing that. He had the passion to really make a difference, and I was already so proud of him. I couldn't help but think of what he would tell me to do in this situation.

Any minute now, someone would come and take me to the interview room. Ask me questions, twist my answers. I wasn't good at seeing the traps the way Jack would. I might inadvertently let them lead me down a path I'd had no intention of following. I knew exactly what Jack would tell me to do. He would say I should keep my mouth shut. That anything I said to defend myself, any attempt to explain how wrong they'd got it, would be noted, recorded, and that if in the coming days my story changed even a little, they would pounce on my mistake and use it as evidence of my lying to them. They would force me into a corner and make me say things I had never planned on saying.

I wanted to be open, honest, to make them see what kind of a person I was, but it felt like a trap. I would get tired. Muddled. I wasn't good at remembering details – times, dates, names. What if they spun me in circles until I forgot what I'd said, then made out I was guilty because I messed up an answer? I didn't want to be rude – it was against my every instinct to refuse to answer a direct question – and yet the thought of getting it wrong made terror swell inside me. If they got me talking about Russell, I might not be able to hide how I'd really felt about him. And as much as I wanted to be friendly, polite, DS McCormac and the rest of his team were *not* my friends, nor my allies. They were looking to find fault in me. As audacious as it might seem to sit opposite them stoically close-mouthed, right now it felt like it might actually be the only way to stay safe and have a chance of getting back to my family.

Footsteps came along the corridor outside, and I tensed, half hoping they would keep going, half wanting them to stop, just so I could get out of this claustrophobic room for a while, get this ordeal over with. The idea of spending the night here made me want to scream, but I knew if I was strong now, there was a chance it might not happen. They might still have to let me go. I couldn't do it without help though. Maybe Jack would have felt confident enough to go it alone, but I wanted backup. Someone on my side who would see right through any tricks and lead me to safety.

The footsteps stopped outside my door, and I took a deep breath as I heard it being unlocked, stiffening my shoulders in preparation for battle. I forced myself not to panic. It was okay. I could do this. For my family, I could do anything.

The door swung open and I jumped to my feet, my hands

clasped tightly in front of me, my lower lip trembling as I met the eyes of a uniformed policeman – a hard-faced young man who looked barely older than Holly, his brown hair in need of a good wash. I could smell the sweat on his clothes and swallowed as the body odour permeated my cell. I tried not to cough as I took a breath through my mouth.

'I... I want a lawyer. I'm not going to speak to anyone without one.' I heard the tremor in my voice but kept my stance strong, ready to stand up for my rights if I had to.

To my relief, the young PC gave a short nod. 'I'll let them know. You'll have to hang on here a bit longer in that case.'

He didn't wait for me to respond as he turned, slamming the door shut, leaving me to breathe in the stale scent of his body in the airless box.

SIX

VICTORIA

I stood on the doorstep, arms crossed over my body, rubbing my hands nervously back and forth across my shoulders as I waited for someone to answer the door. It didn't take long for Jack's stocky frame to appear behind the frosted glass. He opened the door hurriedly, as if expecting someone else, then quickly composed his features into what I supposed he must have thought counted as a smile.

'Hi, Jack,' I said, trying to mirror his expression. 'Can I come in?'

'Uh...' He looked over his shoulder, clearly uncomfortable.

'It's all right. I've spoken to the police. I know what's happened; I just want a word with your dad.'

Jack shook his head wordlessly, and I could see he was still processing the shock of Lisa's arrest.

'It's okay, sweetheart. I'm not angry. I know it's all a mix-up. Don't worry,' I said, stepping over the threshold and touching his arm lightly. 'This will all work itself out. Trust me.'

He nodded, though he didn't speak, and I wondered if he was trying not to cry. He'd never been the type to show his emotions in front of others, but I knew that his desire for privacy didn't mean he wasn't struggling. He still felt everything, still had to absorb what was happening.

'Thanks, Auntie Vic,' he managed finally. 'I'll go and tell Dad you're here. He's just on the phone at the moment.'

I bent to take off my shoes, knowing Lisa would tell me not to bother, but I had never felt right keeping them on inside someone else's house when I wouldn't do it in my own.

On the hallway wall were a row of framed photos leading towards the kitchen. They dated back years and I paused to look at my favourite, the one taken the summer Russell and I had moved in across the road. Lisa had been six months pregnant with Holly at the time, and on early maternity leave from her TA job at a local primary school because of complications with her blood pressure. She'd been told to rest as much as possible but had been going mad with the boredom of sitting around waiting for her baby to arrive. When our moving van had pulled up opposite her house, Russell's car following behind, she'd been the first neighbour – the only one actually – to come and say hello. She'd brought over a jug of ice-cold lemonade and a plate of savoury pastries that lunchtime, and with Russell busy directing the movers like a drill sergeant, the two of us had really had time to chat and get to know each other.

Sitting on my new front lawn, laughing with me that day, she'd told me that she had no plans to go back to work, that her real passion was cooking and that her dream had always been to be a stay-at-home wife and mother and to cook amazing meals for her family.

'I know it makes me sound like some fifties Stepford wife,' she'd said with a laugh, looking nothing like the stereotype with her cropped elfin hairstyle and oversized bright red knitted cardigan, purple Doc Marten boots and floral summer dress, 'but to me, feminism means being able to choose. And as much as I admire women who can do it all, I don't want that for myself. I want to be a mum more than anything else in the world.' She'd smiled widely, and I'd squashed down a flare of envy as she'd rubbed her hands lovingly over her bump.

We'd bonded over the fact that I didn't work either, and I'd hoped she might think of me as a kindred spirit. We'd sat enjoying the pastries – delicious creations she'd made just for fun the previous day – and all I'd been able to think was how grateful I was to have met her. It had been longer than I could remember since I'd had a friend, and the fact that I'd got lucky enough to meet someone like Lisa had made the move to a new, unfamiliar place so much more bearable.

I'd worried she was just being kind, that it wouldn't last, but the friendship had blossomed, and we'd quickly begun spending more time together. The photo was the first we'd had taken together, the two of us sitting on fold-out chairs in their back garden, her heavily pregnant, holding a burger cooked on the barbecue by Mike. I was laughing, my eyes crinkled and sparkling, Lisa's head thrown back as our hands linked tight together, and every time I looked at the photograph, I was reminded of how these people had turned my life around without ever realising the impact they'd made.

I turned away from the picture, heading to the kitchen, hearing Mike's aggrieved voice before I stepped through the door.

'No, that is *not* okay,' he was saying into the phone, his back turned towards me, his shoulders stiff. His shirtsleeve was rolled up to the elbow, his tanned forearm tensing as he squeezed the phone. 'You can't just keep her there. She's done nothing wrong. What the hell is the police force coming to?'

He paused to listen as the person on the end of the phone replied but was already shaking his head. 'No, I can't accept that. I need to speak to her. She has the right to talk to me, doesn't she?' he demanded.

There was a longer pause, and I waited, feeling tense, watching the way his shirt clung to the tight muscles on his back, a side effect of the rock climbing he and Jack loved to do whenever they could. Russell and I had gone with them a few times, though Russell had stayed on the ground with me and Lisa. Holly had given it a good go, but watching Jack and Mike scramble up that rock face, their sweat-soaked shirts the only evidence of the effort it was costing them, had been mesmerising.

I'd wished Russell would grab life by the horns like Mike did, take up some hobby that took his focus off me for a while, but I knew he never would. His philosophy in life was not to take anything on unless he thought he could be the best at it, and with his librarian's physique and absent muscles, I knew he'd never put himself up for ridicule, unwilling to start at the bottom while someone else passed him by.

I saw Mike's head drop, and he gripped the back of a chair, leaning forward as if in defeat. 'Please,' he said softly, and I felt my stomach tense at the sudden change in tone, the unconcealed need behind that one word. 'Just let me speak to her for a minute. That's all I'm asking. Just one minute.'

I watched, standing stock-still, Jack on the opposite side of the kitchen listening too. Our eyes met briefly, then he looked away, staring out the back window at the garden beyond. I heard Mike sigh, and then he placed the phone down, shaking his head.

'How can they do this?' he muttered to himself as he turned. 'How can they—' His eyes widened as he saw me standing there. 'Oh shit, Vic! I'm so sorry... Did they tell you, the police, I mean? What must you be thinking?'

'Yes,' I replied, stepping forward and taking his hand between mine. 'And I already know it's nonsense.'

'You know she wouldn't have done something like this. It's *Lisa*, for God's sake. She'd be racked with guilt if she'd hit someone; she would have called for an ambulance, stayed with him until the very end. You know she could never have done this.'

'It's not in her nature, I know,' I assured him, still holding his hand. It was warm, shaking slightly, and I ran my thumb over the back of his wedding band soothingly, thinking how different his hands were from Russell's. Stronger, larger. Even in the state he was in right now, they felt more secure somehow. Solid. Reluctantly I let go, and he pressed his palms to his face.

'I just don't know what to do,' he admitted. 'Jack and I weren't even here when it happened – we were wild camping on the South Downs. I didn't even know he'd been in an accident until I saw you on Tuesday, and neither did Lisa. She was as shocked as I was when I came back from seeing you and broke the news. I've tried to get her a lawyer, but I don't know where to begin. Do people just have lawyers?' He shook his head and I shrugged.

'I don't know,' I admitted. 'I think maybe they'll provide her with one.'

'I hope so. It's just crazy to me that they'd point the finger at her. I bet it's because her car was stolen that same weekend. Did I tell you about that when I came to borrow the ladder? Took the bloody thing right off the drive while she slept.'

'You said.' I nodded, hating how agitated he was getting, wondering if I should try to hug him or if it would just make him feel worse.

'It's a bloody big leap for them to make though,' he continued, distracted. 'And if that's all they've got for their so-called evidence, they'll have to let her go.'

'They will,' I agreed.

'I mean, as if she would drive off and leave a man for dead.'

I flinched, and he reached for my shoulder.

'Oh damn, Vic... I didn't mean... I'm so sorry. This must be so hard on you, losing him, dealing with this. You shouldn't have to hear me complain when you're going through so much.' He looked down at me, his face filled with sincerity. 'Russell was my friend. You know that. I just can't believe he's really gone.'

I swallowed, unable to meet his eyes for fear of crying. I hadn't come here for him to comfort me. I didn't want to think about Russell, hear his name.

'I know,' I managed. 'And I don't believe Lisa did this. I know she didn't.'

'Then why did they arrest her?'

The two of us looked up at Jack, who'd spoken the blunt words. He stared at his dad, as if waiting for an answer, and when none came, he picked up his phone from the counter and strode out of the room without another word.

'He's just upset,' I told Mike. 'We all are.'

He nodded, his hand sliding from my shoulder as he sank into a chair. I didn't know what to do.

'I'll... I'll pop the kettle on, shall I?' I said, feeling ridiculously clichéd.

He didn't reply as I walked around the counter, seeing the mess of unwashed dishes, the roast lamb barely touched, congealed gravy glistening on the surface of the wasted lunch. My eye was caught by the sight of Lisa's apron hanging on a hook on the back of the kitchen door – a pretty navy and white design, striped, with a thick blue bow around the centre. She always said she hated housework but that putting this on made it feel less of a chore – that dressing for the occasion and sticking some good music on made it so much more bearable.

I cast a glance at Mike, who was staring despondently at his phone, waiting for a call that refused to come. With a sense of reverence, I quietly padded over to the door, plucked the apron off the hook, slid the strap over my head and tied the bow around my waist. I didn't want to go back to that empty house, with Russell's ghost lurking in every corner. I wanted to be surrounded by people – even in the state they were in right now, they were the people I loved. This family was my family. This house felt warmer than my own, alive in a way mine never could. It felt like a home should. And now, I had a sense of purpose here – the knowledge that I was making a difference. Lisa would want me to take care of her family in her absence. She'd be grateful to see me here.

I smoothed the apron over my hips, then turned towards the mess, feeling more content than I had in a long time.

SEVEN

LISA

News of the climate crisis clearly hadn't made it as far as our local police station, I thought wryly as I scraped a rubbery piece of pasta from inside the disposable plastic bowl with a flimsy single-use fork. I imagined it was hard to find a balance between being environmentally conscious and not providing the inmates with anything that could be used as a weapon, but still, a proper fork would have been nice.

I chewed the dry, tasteless food, feeling guilty for being able to swallow it down under the circumstances. I should have been too afraid to eat, too worried about what my family were going through without me at home, but I had to listen to my body. This was the first meal I'd managed all day – the roast I'd spent the morning preparing gone to waste – and as the hours had passed, I'd become gradually more trembly and nauseous, an unsettled, shaky feeling in the pit of my stomach. I hoped the food, bland as it was, might at least squash that sensation, and raise my blood sugar enough so I wouldn't faint when they called for me.

I chased the final piece of pasta around the bowl with the fork, before giving up and picking it up with my fingertips, popping it in my mouth and chewing hard. There was a carton of blackcurrant squash on the tray, and I scanned the ingredients listed on the back, frowning at the poor quality of the drink. Nonetheless, it didn't stop me from jamming the straw into it – paper this time at least – and drinking it down. The artificial sweet taste filled my mouth, and despite the lack of actual fruit in it, it made me feel marginally more human.

I dropped the empty carton back on the tray and sat back against the wall of my cell, listening to the constant stream of voices out in the corridor.

I felt exhausted, desperate to just lie down and sleep, the adrenaline of the afternoon beginning to fade now that I had some food inside me, replaced with a heavy weariness. I knew that despite the circumstances, if I were to lay my head down on the thin blue mattress now, I'd be out like a light. Maybe that was how prisoners made it through long sentences. Breaking up their days into mealtimes, taking themselves away from their reality by sleeping as deeply and as often as possible. It was the only escape – a chance to be somewhere else for a little while – and no matter how bad things got, nobody could take that from you.

There was a sound outside my door, and I stiffened, hearing it unlock, watching as it swung open. The same young PC as before stood there. This time, I looked closer, past the mask of indifference he wore, and could see that what I had assumed was hardness might actually be a fierce determination to do well at his job. It made me feel motherly and supportive towards him, picturing my own son in his place.

'Have you finished eating?' he asked, nodding towards my tray.

'Yes, thank you.'

'Good. Sorry about the food,' he added, and I caught a hint of a smile on his face, one I couldn't help returning. It was nice to see in this cold, unfriendly place and made me feel just a little more human for a brief moment.

'We're heading down the hall, if you wouldn't mind,' he said, gesturing for me to come with him.

I slid off the sleeping pad and smoothed down my dress, following him wordlessly to the door, where he stepped back to let me go in front. Nobody here seemed to trust that I wouldn't attack them if I were allowed to walk behind, and it made me sad that this young man, barely more than a boy, had to work in an environment where he had to constantly keep his guard up and protect himself.

He indicated for me to continue along the corridor and round a corner, and when we reached the door at the end, he opened it. A woman dressed in a smart grey suit, her short black hair cropped close to her head, was sitting at a table, and she smiled blandly as I entered.

'Let me know when you're done. They're waiting in interview room four,' the young man said, his comment clearly meant for her, not me, making me feel small and voiceless, a pawn in their game. He pointed to a chair, and I sat, waiting for him to close the door and leave us alone.

'I'm Sandy Adamu. Your lawyer,' the woman said, smiling more warmly now that we weren't being watched.

'Thanks for coming,' I said, linking my fingers in my lap, my stomach tensing in anticipation of what she might ask.

She glanced down at the laptop in front of her. 'Do you have anything you want to tell me? Anything that would be helpful for your case?'

I shook my head.

'Any reason you can think of for why they've pointed the finger at you?'

Her expression was carefully blank as she waited for my answer, and I realised she wouldn't care either way. She wasn't here to judge me; just to defend me whether I was guilty or not.

It must be a very strange job. I wondered how she compartmentalised it when she went home at night. How she could sleep after spending her day arguing for the freedom of murderers and rapists. *I* couldn't have. I shook my head in answer to her question.

'You're certainly not chatty,' she remarked. 'And that's a good thing. Let's keep it that way. My professional advice is to answer "no comment" to every question they ask. They'll try to guide you into talking, but stay strong in your position. From what I can see from the limited information I have so far, their case won't stand up. Very flimsy,' she added, tapping her thumbnail against her bottom lip. 'Let's not give them anything more.'

I pressed my lips together, nodding.

'So,' she said, closing the laptop and rising to stand, her palms pressed flat on the tabletop as she fixed me with a challenging stare, 'are you ready to go into the lion's den?'

No, but what choice do I have? I thought, bracing myself. I pushed out of the chair and took a deep breath. 'Okay,' I agreed. 'Let's get it over with.'

Sandy walked ahead of me, an act I noticed and appreciated, that small sign of trust that nobody had shown me as yet in this place. She ignored the waiting police officers as she entered the interview room, first showing me where to sit and asking if I needed a blanket or a drink, before giving a short nod to DS McCormac and taking her own seat. Her focus on making sure I was okay was nurturing somehow, and I was glad of her presence. It gave me strength.

The interview room was only marginally bigger than the cell had been, but at least there was a window, and though the glass was frosted, a small square of natural light was enough to remind me of what I was being kept from. It was amazing how quickly that feeling of being caged had crept over me, making my skin prickle with adrenaline and nerves, my body desperate to run from this place. Instinct was kicking in, demanding I take back my freedom, and yet I couldn't give in to those primal, self-preserving thoughts. I had to stay here. Be calm. Appear on top of the situation. I had to follow the rules if I was ever going to convince the police to let me go.

I cracked open the bottle of water I'd been given, not bothering to pour it into the paper cup, simply gulping it back in huge mouthfuls. It was room temperature and tasted of plastic, like it had been left in direct sunlight for months on end, toxins slowly seeping into the liquid, but it was good enough for now. The second bottle on the table in front of me provided a sense of comfort, and I knew I would finish it too before I left this room.

'Better?' DS McCormac asked, sinking into a seat opposite me as I drained the contents.

I nodded, blotting my lips dry with the back of my hand. I screwed the lid back on the empty bottle and held it tight between my palms, picking at the plastic ring around its neck.

A second officer was in the seat beside DS McCormac. 'This is PC Crawley. He'll be sitting in on your interview today.'

I nodded again, though I didn't reply. I was afraid to break the ice, to let them think I might crack easily. If I was polite now, it would be so much harder to be rude when the questions began. I had no idea what to expect – what they might ask – and I was grateful for Sandy, sitting reassuringly beside me, making me feel far less alone.

DS McCormac nodded to PC Crawley, who recited the date and time, along with my name, and I realised that of course, we were being recorded. I wanted to look up and see if there were cameras on the ceiling but managed to refrain from fidgeting, focusing on the bottle in my hand instead, squeezing the hard plastic lid and finding some relief in the action.

'Would you prefer me to call you Mrs Grey or Lisa?' DS McCormac asked, leaning forward.

I shrugged, fighting the urge not to speak. He had friendly eyes, I noticed. Dark brown and warm, framed by thick black lashes. There were laughter lines in his tanned skin, and a gold wedding band on his left hand. He looked to be in his early fifties, and I wondered if he had grown-up children. If he liked to cook for them on weekends. He looked like the kind of man Mike and I might have been friends with if circumstances were different, and that made it all the more difficult to ignore him when he fixed me with a half-smile and told me not to be scared. That he only wanted to clear a few things up. Get my side of the story.

'You haven't been charged yet, Lisa,' he reminded me, and I glanced up to see him looking at me almost with compassion in his expression. 'I know this is all overwhelming, but it's just the procedure we have to follow. This is your chance to tell us what really happened that night.'

He was good. Jack would have been screaming at the television if he'd been watching us now, telling me not to fall for it. This man wasn't my friend. And as much as he wanted to make out he was on my side, he had come to my home, arrested me in front of my children and taken me prisoner. He wouldn't have done that without reason to believe he had the right person, and as much as I might have liked him in another lifetime, I couldn't let those kind eyes and warm smile cloud my judgement now.

'Russell Fox was your neighbour, wasn't he?' McCormac asked, his voice light, casual.

I could see the expectation on his face as he waited for me to answer.

'N-No comment,' I replied softly.

He frowned, glancing at PC Crawley, then back to me.

'He'd lived opposite you on Dragonfly Close for the past

seventeen years. You would have seen him before. Did you ever speak? Have him and his wife over to the house?'

I squeezed the bottle lid tighter. 'No comment,' I repeated.

'Your husband said he was a friend of the family when we came to your home today.'

I squeezed the bottle lid tighter, my lips pressed closed.

'Lisa, we can't help you if you won't help yourself.'

My mind wandered to the thought of what might happen if this went to court. The idea of standing in a cavernous room with everyone looking at me, a ruddy-faced judge wearing a white wig ready to acquit or condemn, made my stomach clench, the pasta I'd eaten earlier churning heavily inside it. I had no idea if my image of the courtroom was accurate, or if I'd just absorbed so many scenes from movies and TV that it had become reality in my mind, but it frightened me, and I tried to put it from my thoughts. Keeping my mouth shut worked for now, but in front of a jury, my face might give away more than I intended. I had always been an open book, terrible at hiding my true feelings, and the idea of being scrutinised by a group of jurors while trying to conceal my emotions was horrifying to contemplate.

DS McCormac gave a click of his tongue, then leaned in closer. 'Let's talk about something more recent then. Where were you on the nineteenth of June between the hours of midnight and four a.m.?'

I didn't look up this time. There was no point trying to form a connection with the man, no point in my attempting to demonstrate our similarities. I wanted him to see me for who I *really* was. A loving wife and mother. An ordinary woman, trying to get by in this world, no different from him. I so desperately wanted him to understand that I didn't deserve to be here. But nothing I could say now would make that happen. It was his job to prove just the opposite, and hard as it might be to be rude to a man who was simply trying to do his job, answering his questions would only lead me into a tangled, confused web. His only goal was to corner me, trap me. I wouldn't be so stupid.

I clasped my hands in my lap, rubbing my thumb across my wedding band. 'No comment,' I said, my voice clear and steady this time.

'Your car was reported missing on the evening of the nineteenth. Around eighteen or nineteen hours after Mr Fox was estimated to have died. Your husband made the call, discovering it missing on return from a camping trip. Is that correct?'

'No comment.'

'When did you notice the car missing?'

'No comment.'

'Did you see it outside on the night Mr Fox was run down? Go for a drive somewhere perhaps?'

'No comment.'

'I find it hard to believe you wouldn't have noticed it missing come the morning. That you wouldn't have glanced out the front window at the driveway and seen it empty. Was it definitely there when you went to bed the previous night?'

I stared down at my hands. Still as a statue.

'I'm going to need an answer for the record, Lisa.'

'No comment.'

He sat forward, clearly not even close to giving up. 'How long have you been friends with Mr Fox and his wife?'

'No comment.'

'We've spoken to your neighbours. Your own husband described Mr Fox as a friend. There's no need to hide the fact – it's no secret. There are photographs of you with both Russell and Victoria Fox in their home, displayed in plain sight. We know you've had a long-term friendship with them. What we don't know is whether you had a reason to, oh, I don't know, resent Mr Fox perhaps. Some falling-out. Some secret.' He paused, and I could feel him watching me, though I continued to look down at my wedding band.

'No comment,' I said softly. I gritted my teeth, trying not to show how triggering his questions were.

'Listen, Lisa,' he continued, resting back in his chair, the attacking stance he'd held as he'd leaned into my personal space replaced with a casual, far more friendly posture. 'Accidents happen. They happen to the best of us. We make a mistake. We panic. I know that you're a good person, a good mother. Anyone can see that. But a mistake can only be fixed by owning up to it and facing what you've done. Is there a chance you were driving and hit something without realising? Russell was dressed all in black when he was found. He would have been hard to see in the rain that night. His blood alcohol level was well over the limit. You wouldn't have seen him if he'd suddenly lurched in front of your moving vehicle. No doubt it would be a frightening experience for any driver. Who could blame someone for not stopping in the heat of the moment?' he added softly.

I took a deep breath, trying to push the image he'd painted from my mind: Russell weaving along the pavement, his long black trench coat, the one Victoria always joked behind his back made him look like a Sherlock Holmes impersonator, wrapped around him. Drunken, glassy eyes as he looked up into bright headlights. A collision, a crunch, a man lying lifeless on the side of the road. Gone in the blink of an eye.

Beside me, Sandy cleared her throat, and I glanced at her. She gave a tiny nod for me to continue.

'No comment,' I replied.

I looked back at her, and she offered a reassuring smile. I couldn't hold her gaze.

EIGHT

VICTORIA

I wiped the spotless counter for the third time, though the kitchen was now pristine, every cup and plate back in its rightful cupboard, the remainder of the leftover food stored safely in Tupperware in the fridge, ready for when Mike and the kids finally acknowledged their hunger later. I watched Mike pace back and forth on the phone to another lawyer's office, the tension in his broad shoulders making him look like he was carved from stone.

I'd never seen him this way – so full of anger and frustration, so ready to fight for the woman who was the glue that held this family together. He looked nothing like the laid-back cool, calm and collected Mike I knew and recognised. The chilled-out, mountain-climbing, surf-loving guy who'd always exuded an unruffled, down-to-earth energy. But despite his obvious resolve to step up to the plate today, as the hours had passed and he'd called one law firm after another, struggling to get hold of most of them on a Sunday afternoon, I had seen his fight turn to frustration, the determination in his voice become desperation. He was out of his depth – that much was obvious.

Now that I'd finished cleaning up the kitchen, I knew I

should leave the family to their privacy. Jack hadn't come back downstairs, and Holly hadn't shown her face at all, though Mike assured me she was home. The two of them were squirrelled away in their rooms, both as lost and confused as their dad was about how they should act, what they could do to help, and I could empathise with that feeling of utter powerlessness. It was one I was intimately familiar with. I couldn't help with lawyers, and my being here was no doubt uncomfortable for Mike – a reminder of the man who was lying dead in the morgue across town, the reason his wife was gone right now.

I closed my eyes, blinking back the visceral image that made my skin prickle, a shiver working its way down my spine as the memory of Russell's lifeless features, his eyes not quite shut, his mouth slack and silent, forced its way to the front of my thoughts. I had been the one to identify the body, something I'd never guessed they would ask of me. I hadn't wanted to, but the thought of leaving that task to his mother was beyond contemplating. As desperate as I'd been to pass the buck, I had known it was my responsibility.

I had glanced at him for barely more than half a second, but it had been enough for the image to form a deep scar inside my mind, a trauma I knew no amount of time would ever erase. They had been cruel to ask me to do it. I pressed my hands to my eyes, squashing down the memory.

I knew I was outstaying my welcome. I should have left hours ago, but the thought of going home made my stomach churn with dread, so I'd done everything I could to eke out my time here. I'd reorganised the fridge, scrubbed the kitchen sink with a scourer, even mopped the floor, though I'd felt ridiculous doing it. I'd wanted to keep busy, to make myself look useful so I could stay without Mike feeling watched and awkward, but now, I'd run out of tasks to complete, and as much as I wanted to, I knew I couldn't move on to another room.

Mike hung up the phone and slumped down into his chair.

'This is bloody impossible. Twenty minutes on hold just to be told they only deal with divorce and property. You'd think they'd mention that on their website, wouldn't you?'

'They should have. How frustrating,' I agreed, folding the cloth and placing it neatly on the side. I had no doubt the website *did* mention those facts, but I wasn't about to tell Mike he was acting too hastily, not clicking the right tabs. He had never been interested in computers, much preferring to be outside than indoors hunched over a screen, and I wondered why Jack wasn't down here helping him navigate the sites he was working his way through. As a successful landscape gardener, Mike had plenty of skills but none that could be translated into any use in a situation like this.

He rubbed his eyes, looking weary. 'I know the woman I got through to at the police station said she's been allocated a lawyer already, but how am I to know if the person they give her is any good? It could be someone barely qualified who might tell Lisa to say all the wrong things, and before she knows what's happened, she'll find herself in a mess through no fault of her own. I just want her to have the best. Someone who will get her out of there and bring her back to me. I don't want to let her down.'

'I know you don't. And she knows that too. I'm sure she doesn't expect you to figure out all this stuff. How could you? These are brand-new waters you're navigating. And you're doing your best, Mike. Don't be so harsh on yourself.'

He nodded, looking defeated, and I could tell the fight was leaving him. He no longer knew how to keep going to help her. 'I just wish they would let me speak to her. *Comfort* her. She must be so scared.'

I shook my head. 'Lisa is strong. She's always been strong,' I said quietly, thinking of just how true those words were. She had always had a strength of character I'd admired, and even envied at times. When it came to the things that were important to her, she could stand up and fight without shame, without fear. She had been that way for as long as I'd known her. Calm, kind, loving but with a core of steel I had felt from the very start.

I thought back to the moment I'd first realised it, when Holly and Jack had been barely out of nappies.

Jack, always the explorer, had climbed up onto the kitchen counter while Lisa and I were having coffee in the living room. Holly was clingy and fractious – likely coming down with something – and Lisa was just telling me how she had needed settling every twenty minutes through last night, as if she were a baby rather than a child of four, and wouldn't even accept a cuddle from Mike, when we heard the bang. We rushed through to find two-year-old Jack on the floor, a wide gash on his forehead, blood cascading down his pale cheeks, a packet of chocolate biscuits still clutched in his chubby little hand.

Lisa, who'd had no sleep and moments before had looked on the verge of exhausted tears, had gone into autopilot, simultaneously holding a cloth to the dripping head wound, calling for an ambulance with the phone tucked under her chin, and handing me the pack of biscuits to try and distract Holly from the fact that her mummy had needed to put her down for a moment. I'd been flustered and in awe but soon realised I hadn't seen anything yet.

When the ambulance had arrived and Lisa had climbed in the back with both children, the paramedic had told her in a no-nonsense tone that Holly couldn't ride with them. 'Either you follow in the car behind with the little girl, or you leave her here with your friend,' he said matter-of-factly. 'Insurance won't allow siblings to ride along.'

Lisa had strapped herself in, putting the lap belt over both herself and Holly, and I'd seen the look of determination that transformed her features. 'That isn't going to happen. My son needs me. My daughter isn't fit to be left right now.'

'Your friend can bring her behind us then.'

'I don't have a driver's licence,' I'd muttered, feeling embarrassed and useless. 'If she's happy to stay with me, I don't mind looking after her though?' I'd added, looking uncertainly at Holly's red, tear-stained face.

'Thanks, Vic, but no. She needs to stay with me.' Lisa stared at the paramedic. 'We're wasting time. I suggest you get going before my son passes out from blood loss. He needs stitches, and any delay in getting treatment will be a result of your inability to compromise. Let's go.'

I'd watched, open-mouthed, shocked at the absolute nerve, the unbending resolve. I'd never expected it of her. Lisa was so calm, sweet, a bit of a hippy at times. I'd known her to be funny, silly, playful and a wonderful mother, but I'd never seen this side to her. In the years that followed that day, I'd looked out for it, and the more I grew to know her, the more I realised just how strong she really was. Nothing like me, though I wished I could have that unshakeable self-confidence too. Perhaps if I'd had a baby of my own, I could have found those qualities buried deep within me, but somehow, I doubted it. It wasn't in my nature to throw myself head-first into conflict.

Lisa would survive this. Whatever the police had in store for her, she would be strong enough to cope. I wasn't so sure I would fare the same. I didn't share her bravery. Her self-belief. Her courage.

'She'll get through this,' I told Mike, smiling in what I hoped was a reassuring manner. 'And she'll be home soon, I promise,' I added, though I couldn't meet his eyes as I said the words.

I sighed. 'Look, you've had a long day and you're exhausted. And I should leave you to it,' I added reluctantly.

He stood up, shaking his head, and I half hoped he was going to ask me to stay a little longer, save me from going home alone. 'I can't believe I've had you here cleaning my kitchen when you've just lost your husband, Vic. Bloody hell, I'm so sorry – I didn't think. I—'

I stepped forward, placing a hand on his arm, squeezing it gently. 'Don't be silly. I wanted to be here. To help. And it's taken my mind off... Well, it's been a relief. Don't feel bad,' I insisted.

He nodded, though he looked like he didn't believe me.

'Well, thank you,' he said awkwardly. 'Thanks for coming to check on us, despite the unusual circumstances. I appreciate it.'

'Don't mention it. I'll come again soon, and hopefully you'll hear from Lisa in the next few hours.'

'God, I hope so.'

I nodded, knowing I could prolong the visit no longer. Turning reluctantly, I picked up my cardigan from the bar stool and slipped out into the hall.

Holly was sitting halfway up the stairs, and she looked up as I walked past the banister.

'Auntie Vic, you're leaving?'

'Yes. It's time I got back,' I said, though to what, I had no idea.

She stood up, walking down the rest of the stairs and stopping at the bottom, gripping the wooden bulb of the banister, her hand flexing nervously over the smooth polished oak. At first glance, she was so different from both her parents. She didn't have Mike's height, his energy or his bright blue eyes, nor Lisa's petite, elf-like stature and easy laugh. Physically, she was decidedly average, easy to miss, her dark blonde hair usually falling in a curtain over her eyes, her shoulders curved forward into her five-foot-seven frame, as if she was trying to hide from the world. She shared neither of her parents' personality traits either – their confidence, their humour, their witty intelligence. To the casual observer, she was reserved, painfully shy and more interested in books than making friends.

But I knew her better. She had a shell that appeared fragile, weak even, but I knew it was just that. A shell. To a select few who got to break past it, she showed her true colours, and I'd been privileged to see her for who she truly was. Not the cleverest, like Jack, not the most adventurous, like her dad, or the funniest, like her mother, but sweet, loving, kind and creative.

She looked at me now, her pale green eyes wide as they met mine. 'Mum didn't do this, Auntie Vic. You know she didn't.'

I nodded, taking her hand between my own, squeezing tight. 'Of course I know,' I said, swallowing back the smile that always came from hearing her call me 'Auntie'. It made me feel so special. Part of the family. I'd begun referring to myself that way soon after Holly's birth, and neither Mike nor Lisa had objected. Somehow, it had stuck, and as both children had begun to talk, they'd automatically followed my lead, continuing to use the nickname I'd chosen for myself. I'd been thrilled at being brought into the folds of their life so completely. At seventeen, Holly was practically an adult, but the fact that she still used the term so easily – still considered me her family – made my heart swell.

'Will she be home soon, do you think?' she asked, her soft voice barely more than a whisper.

'I'm sure she will. They can't keep her there for long, can they?'

She shrugged, and I saw the tears glistening in her eyes, though I knew she'd never cry in front of me. Like her brother, she was too private a person for that.

I stepped forward, pulling her into a hug, meeting my own reflection in the mirror behind her.

'She'll be back before you know it, darling,' I whispered into her hair. I stared at my hollow brown eyes, then closed them, pushing down the feeling of guilt, knowing I had just lied to a girl I'd loved like a daughter for seventeen years.

NINE

LISA

The monotonous tone of DS McCormac's voice continued relentlessly, making my head ache and my eyes itch with exhaustion. I rubbed my foot back and forth on the worn carpet, wiggling my bottom on the uncomfortable plastic chair and trying not to yawn, afraid to appear rude, though it took all my willpower not to slump back in my seat and close my eyes. It felt like I'd been in this poky little interview room for hours, though I knew it couldn't have been more than one.

Overhead, the fluorescent strip lighting flickered intermittently, the tiny window high above us gradually turning dark – the only indication of the time. I guessed it must be around nine or so, the setting sun giving way to dusk, my favourite moment of a summer's day. I longed to step outside, to fill my lungs with the cool, sweet evening breeze that warm nights always brought. On any other Sunday at this time of year, I'd be sitting out on the patio right about now, squashed up beside Mike on the little swinging bench he'd chained up to the pergola. We'd be chatting about our plans for the coming week, sipping on ice-cold white wine, his strong chest supporting me as I leaned back against him, watching the blue tits dive-bomb the bird feeders in a final frenzy before heading off to roost. But instead, I was here.

My throat was dry and scratchy despite the constant flow of water they provided me with, the continuous repetition of 'no comment' tiring my voice and losing all meaning in my frazzled mind. Was this his tactic? To talk *at* me for so long that I begged for mercy, promised to admit whatever crime he laid at my feet? I could see it working. Despite my refusal to engage, I knew he was wearing me down. And I was fearful that he knew it too. He had to know it.

It all felt too much, the emotion and adrenaline of the day hitting me in one fell swoop, and I suddenly felt as if I might break down, beg him to give me a moment of respite, let me have some peace. I just wanted to go back to my cell, where at least it was quiet and I could take a few minutes to collect my thoughts.

Hot tears of frustration and exhaustion welled up in my dry, itching eyes, and I blinked the moisture away, determined not to let him see, but it was no good. I caught his astute gaze, the way his pupils constricted as if he had his target in his sights. His mouth twitched ever so slightly in the right corner – a smug little smile of victory – and I felt myself tense as he leaned forward. I didn't see what else he could say at this point, what more he could ask. We had to have covered every little detail of the night of Russell's death, though I'd refused to give him anything – to answer a single question.

My lawyer sat quietly beside me, apparently unaware of the change in atmosphere, the charged energy emanating from DS McCormac – a cobra about to strike.

He reached across the desk almost casually, and I felt myself tense, my body leaning forward against my will as he nodded towards a computer screen, pressing a button.

'Recognise this?' he asked softly as the CCTV footage began to play.

I peered up from lowered lashes, trying to keep my face impassive as I saw the grainy image of the corner of Dragonfly Close come into focus.

'Now,' he said, with a smile – a self-satisfied expression that made my stomach flip, 'you refuse to tell me where you were, or if indeed you might have been driving the night of the hit-and-run. However, fortunately for me, I already know that you were. Look.' He gestured towards the screen, and I watched, slack-jawed, as the image of my own dark blue Ford Mondeo rounded the corner. The time on the screen read 01:47.

DS McCormac pressed pause on the footage, freeze-framing the image of the car, number plate and all, though it was too dark to see through the window to who was driving. Without waiting for me to speak, he reached into a drawer beside him, pulling out a clear plastic envelope with a green silk scarf crumpled inside it. A scarf that looked awfully familiar. 'This was found at the scene of the crime. There was a hair on it, and DNA testing has already confirmed it did not belong to Russell Fox. We'll obviously be taking a sample from you to cross-match, but before we do, is there anything you'd like to tell me? Anything at all?'

I glanced to my left, meeting Sandy's dark brown eyes, seeing her alert expression, the way her face had dropped, wiped clean of the easy confidence she'd seemed fit to burst with just moments before. Her eyes were unreadable, and I got the impression she was going through our options faced with this new evidence.

DS McCormac continued, a smug note of victory in his voice. 'We've identified your car driving close to the scene of the crime what must have been moments before Russell Fox was hit. It seems very convenient to me that it was subsequently reported as stolen – by your husband, not yourself – a *significant* number of hours later,' he said, as if that was enough to place suspicion on my shoulders. 'You've given us no alibi, no reason to believe you weren't involved. And' – he held up the plastic wallet, tapping it with his pencil – 'I'm willing to bet this belongs to you, Lisa. It won't be long before we find out for sure. So I'll ask again. Is there anything you want to tell me now?'

Sandy cleared her throat, and I paused, waiting for her to speak, but she seemed lost for words. I chewed the inside of my cheek, trying not to give in to the panic, the harsh reality of the so-called evidence piling up around me. I looked McCormac dead in the eye, unable to think straight, and finally, just as I opened my mouth to speak, Sandy seemed to come to her senses.

'I need to talk to my client. It's time to take a break,' she said firmly, not looking my way.

He nodded as if he'd been expecting this and turned off the tape recorder, standing with an unhurried swagger that annoyed me, then left the room, the second officer trailing behind.

I waited for the door to close, then slumped back in my chair in a combination of shock and relief, my eyes on my knees, wishing I could sink into the ground and make this whole mess disappear.

'You don't seem to realise the severity of the situation, Lisa,' Sandy was saying as she paced back and forth across the worn carpet of the side room we'd been put in so that we could talk privately. A muscle twitched in her cheek, and I stared at it, feeling my own tension grow in parallel with hers. She of all people should be relaxed right now, confident that she could take care of this nonsense and get me home to my family. The fact that she was so clearly rattled annoyed me. After all, what did they really have? A scarf? A car that had already been reported stolen, seen driving down the same road a crime happened to have occurred? They should have been more concerned with finding the car thieves than asking me stupid questions I couldn't possibly answer.

'Lisa, you have to give me something.'

I shrugged. 'I don't know what to tell you. The car has been missing for days. We reported it stolen as soon as I discovered it gone.'

'Right. *After* the hit-and-run. And your husband didn't report it until he got back from his camping trip, some nineteen hours after the crime had taken place.'

'So? It's a coincidence. Admittedly poor timing, but nothing more than that.'

'Not in their eyes, Lisa. To them, it looks like you're hiding something. You could have reported the car missing first thing in the morning, but you didn't. You waited. Bought yourself time, is what they'll argue.'

'Who's to say I even noticed! I stayed in all day. I was busy in the kitchen, and it was pouring with rain. What makes them think I've got time to sit around looking out the window?' I said, hearing the defensive tone and feeling annoyed with myself for it.

Sandy flashed me a dismissive look, continuing her rant as if I hadn't spoken. 'And now we find out it was on the road minutes before Mr Fox was killed. And with your husband having been away that night, you don't have an alibi.' She tapped her foot impatiently. 'Was your daughter home? Did you speak to *her* that night?'

I shot her a warning glance, not wanting to involve either of my children in this mess, sick at the thought of Holly being dragged in here to be questioned by DS McCormac in the same overfriendly, coercive manner. She was only seventeen, but I had little doubt he would let that stop him from wearing her down, harassing her until she felt as broken as I did right now. It would be a terrifying experience for her, and besides, she couldn't tell him anything that would prove my innocence.

'Holly can't help. She—' I broke off, realising that even now, I had to be so careful with what I said. Sandy might be my lawyer, but she was trained to suspect everyone, to look for evidence and prove its validity, true or not. I tapped my fingernail on the table in front of me, feeling frustrated and desperate to leave. 'She was at a friend's house, sleeping over. She came back Sunday evening, around the same time as Mike and Jack.'

Sandy shook her head. 'You're not helping me, Lisa. If you tell me what happened that night, every detail, I can use that to support you. But it's like you're trying to make it harder for yourself. What were you doing? Watching TV? Did you call a friend? Speak to Mike? Did you take the car out to pop to the shops?' She stared at me expectantly, and when I didn't speak, she bent over the table, her hands pressed against the smooth wooden veneer.

'Look, I get that you don't want to say anything to incriminate yourself, but in this situation, I could do with something to work with. An alibi. A shred of evidence that you didn't do it. Because they seem to have plenty to argue otherwise, and I'm pretty sure they'll have more up their sleeve. They like to drip it in bit by bit – you can bet that this is just the beginning. Unless we come up with a counter-argument fast, you're looking at a death by dangerous driving charge at the very least. Your car was seen on the road at the time he was hit, when you should have been tucked up in bed, and just so happens to be conveniently missing at the moment. You've got nobody coming forward to vouch for your whereabouts, and I *saw* the look on your face when McCormac pulled out that scarf. Don't even tell me you aren't expecting a positive DNA test to confirm it's yours.'

I met her eyes, my expression carefully blank, still refusing to utter a word.

'You've got the fact that you've got no record on your side, but even so, we're talking potential jail time. The maximum sentence is life imprisonment. *Life*, Lisa. And the fact that the driver of the car, *whoever they may be*,' she added, theatrically, 'didn't stop to call for help or hand themselves in...' She shook her head. 'It won't go down well,' she finished. 'If you didn't do it, now's the time to speak up and help me help you. Do you understand?'

I took a breath, trying not to let her words frighten me, crushing down the images they conjured, the cold feel of metal, the cell that would become my permanent home. The idea of not seeing my family for days, weeks... or perhaps much longer. It was too much to even fathom. I shook my head, knowing it was impossible to give her any of the answers she wanted.

'Can I call my husband now?' I asked softly. 'He'll be so worried. I've been gone hours and he'll want to know if I'm coming home...'

I left the unspoken question hanging in the air, sure that there was no way I would get out of here tonight. Not unless I started talking, and *that* wasn't going to happen.

Sandy stared at me, the frustration in her expression palpable, then gave an exasperated sigh. 'I'll check,' she said, turning her head away from me in what I was certain was annoyance. She left the room in a flurry of energy.

I leaned back in my chair, feeling shaky and exhausted. *Prison.* Me in prison. It didn't seem possible. I wouldn't belong, I knew that much. I wouldn't cope.

I dug my nails into my palms and sat up straighter as a steely determination washed over me. Of course I would cope. If it came to it, I could do it. I would manage. I always had. I would be strong because my children would need me to be. I wouldn't have their lives ruined over this – let them see me fall apart. Jack's exams were coming up next year, and I'd do anything – put on a brave face and smile through whatever shit came my way – if it meant he didn't have to throw away his dreams out of a misplaced sense of guilt and duty towards me.

And Holly, my sweet girl, who had never let me down, she'd blame herself for not being able to fix this for me. I knew she would and I wouldn't let her.

It wasn't something I had ever considered for myself – a life behind bars – but sitting there in that moment, I let myself give in to the realisation that some things couldn't be fixed, as much as I might wish they could. And no matter what happened over the coming days, I had to remember that. I had to accept my fate.

TEN

I gripped the phone tightly, half afraid that someone might come and snatch it from me before I could utter a word. It rang for barely a millisecond before Mike's voice answered.

'Yes? Hello?' he said, his voice tense, louder than usual.

'It's me,' I replied softly, feeling the tears spring to my eyes, wishing I could fall into his arms and have him hold me, take me away from this nightmare.

'Oh my God, Lisa, I've been out of my mind. I haven't stopped calling, but they said I couldn't speak to you. Are you okay?'

I pressed my fingertips to my eyes, a lump wedging itself in the base of my throat. 'I'm sorry,' I managed to croak. 'I've been asking to speak to you too.'

'Don't cry, Pixie,' he said, his voice softening. 'I can't believe the audacity of these people! Coming into our home like that, taking you away in handcuffs. It's shocking! Completely shocking. They won't get away with it, I promise you. I've been on the phone to lawyers all afternoon. I—'

'You don't have to do that,' I interrupted. 'I have a lawyer here. I'm not alone.' I tried to steady the tremor in my voice. I'd been doing so well at putting on a strong front, but now, hearing his voice made me crumble. Perhaps I should have waited until I knew what to tell him before making the call.

'Does the lawyer know what they're doing? I don't want you lumbered with some idiot who's going to make things worse.'

I thought of my conversation with Sandy – the frustration in her tone as she'd begged me to give her something to work with and been met with my silence. I didn't know if she was going to help – if she even could – but I was firm in my goal to keep silent and let the police chase their own tails. I wasn't sure any other lawyer would give me a better chance.

'She's fine. I don't want to waste money we don't have on hiring someone private. She'll do.'

I paused, swallowing thickly against the ball of emotion lodged in my throat.

'Are the children okay?' I asked, thinking of their shocked, pale faces as I'd been led out of my own kitchen. I doubted Mike had sat down with either of them to ask how they were feeling. He'd never been one for talking about emotions, preferring to take action rather than overthink a difficult situation. During our marriage, in the times that had been most difficult – when his business had nearly gone bankrupt two years after we got married, when Jack had colic and would scream non-stop for hours on end, when we had nightmare neighbours move in next door who'd blasted death metal through open windows at 3 a.m. – he'd never complained, never let it get him down.

Instead, he had disappeared off jogging for an hour, or jumped in the car and gone wild swimming in some off-the-beaten-track river or lake. If he couldn't get out, he would head into the garden and dig, prune, hammer and saw, letting all his worries flow out, exhausting himself physically and yet somehow freeing himself of mental anguish and stress.

He wouldn't know what to say to the kids now. He'd be itching to throw them in the car and head off on a hike somewhere, certain that fresh air and nature would be all that was needed to wipe clean the memory of this afternoon. And to a certain extent, I would usually agree with him. But not with this. Today was going to take more than a brisk walk to fix.

'Have either of them said anything? Were they scared?' I asked, wanting his honesty, yet not sure I could handle the truth.

He sighed. 'They're confused. As am I. We don't understand why this happened, Lis. I mean, why on earth would anyone accuse you of something so terrible? Vic was here earlier, and even she didn't believe a word of it.'

'She was there?' I repeated, my heart stuttering in my chest. I had yet to see her since Russell's accident.

'What did she say?' I asked, hearing the catch in my voice. I was shocked, I realised, that she had come so soon. I'd popped a card and a bunch of lilies on her front doorstep the day after Mike had told me what had happened, not wanting to knock, to disturb her. And if I was honest, not ready to see her. I didn't know how she was taking it. His death. Was she sad? Lost? *Relieved?*

'She said it was ridiculous. I felt awful, Lis. She was here ages while I was phoning round lawyers, and by the time I'd finished, she'd cleaned the whole kitchen.'

'She came in?' I asked, feeling a strange trickle of ice slide down my spine, wondering why the thought of Victoria with my family whilst I was trapped here made me feel suddenly anxious in a way I wasn't at all used to.

'Yeah, not long after you... after they took you. I think she was just desperate to get out of that empty house. I shouldn't have let her do the tidying though. The poor woman's grieving. She looked like she hadn't slept in a week,' he added softly. 'I can understand why.'

I knew he was thinking about the fact that, like Victoria, he would have to go to bed alone tonight. I blinked back tears, thinking of the cell that awaited me. The cold blue sleeping mat, the high, bare walls, the locked door. I closed my eyes, wishing I could teleport through the phone line. I would have given anything to be back in my own home right now, to head up to my own bed, safe and warm, with my children sleeping just down the hall.

Well, almost anything.

'So can I come and get you?' he asked, his voice hopeful.

I shook my head sadly. 'Not tonight,' I said, not adding that it might not be tomorrow or the night after either. 'Will you be okay?'

'Not until I have you safely back here. Where you belong. They can't keep you there much longer,' he said, a note of determination in his words. 'I'm sorry you have to go through this, Pixie; I'd swap places with you if I could.'

The thought of him in my place was almost laughable – and enough to strengthen my resolve. He wouldn't cope. My husband, the man who craved the outdoors more than anything else, would be like a caged animal in a place like this. He wouldn't last a night without tearing down the walls, making things so much worse for himself. It would destroy him. But *I* could manage. I was strong; I could do this.

A loud rap sounded, and I glanced up, seeing Sandy in the doorway, a policewoman just behind her, tapping her wrist in annoyance.

'I... I have to go, Mike. I'll be okay,' I said. 'Try not to worry, and tell the kids the same. And that I love them.'

I ended the call, feeling the instant loneliness that came with severing that line of connection with the one person I most wanted to be with. Every instinct in my body was screaming at me to run home, back to my family, to hide from the world until this all went away. But it was impossible. A childish dream.

Slowly, with as much dignity as I could muster, I rose from my seat, ready to be led back to my cell.

ELEVEN

VICTORIA

I peered through the gap in the bedroom curtains, noting that nothing had changed. Lisa's car was still missing, and Mike's was still in the exact same spot. Their bedroom curtains were half closed in a way Lisa would never have permitted. So she still wasn't back. They had kept her overnight.

I let this thought percolate as I turned from the window, trying to picture her waking up in a cell this morning, and found I couldn't deal with the image, shaking my head as I swatted it away.

Moving to sit at my dresser, I chose a small pair of gold hooped earrings, then checked my teeth for lipstick before sliding a gold bangle over my wrist.

I cast my eyes down, picking at a thread on the frayed knee of my jeans, my skin smooth and tanned beneath the ripped fabric, and wondered absently if I might let go of the high standards Russell had always insisted upon now that he was no longer around to point out my every fault. The weekly waxing and spray tan. The careful lowlights and bonded hair extensions, making my naturally fine mousy brown hair into a more luxurious chocolate and caramel shade. The calorie-counting, weighing and measuring every little morsel that passed my lips. The wardrobe that wouldn't have been out of place in a teenager's room.

There was a part of me that had liked his encouragement to always make an effort – be the best possible version of myself – but there had been pressure there too. I could only imagine how he would react if I did what he would describe as 'letting myself go' now. Stopped the constant stream of appointments at hairdressers, beauty therapists. Ate without worrying about fat content and how far I'd have to run to burn a meal off. Wore those old tracksuit bottoms that he'd always said needed to go in the bin but were so comfy I could never bring myself to let them go.

My stomach rumbled, and recklessly, I considered going to the shops, buying pastries, sausages, eggs, black pudding. I smiled at the thought of coming home to cook it all up – of eating until my sides hurt and my waistband resisted a single bite more.

My feet bare, I padded down to the kitchen and poured myself a bowl of dusty muesli instead, topping it off with a tablespoon of fat-free natural yoghurt. A glass of iced water and a black coffee accompanied my meal. I wasn't ready to break *all* my long-standing habits just yet. But I *could*. There was no one here to stop me now. When I wanted to, I could, and perhaps it wouldn't be too long until I was ready to take that step.

I carried my breakfast on a tray through to the living room, sitting in an armchair by the window facing Lisa and Mike's house as I munched thoughtfully. There had been a message on the answerphone from the funeral parlour when I'd got back from Mike's last night, another oh-so-gentle prompt for me to come in for a chat so we could get started on the arrangements. I wasn't ready. I didn't want to be in that building, look at coffins picturing Russell lying in one of them, to know I was under the same roof as his lifeless body. The hospital worker at the morgue had told me he'd been transferred there, and the funeral home director had made it clear I was welcome to visit at any time, but I didn't want to. It seemed morbid to even consider it.

A part of me knew that the reason I was putting off moving forward with the arrangements had nothing to do with not being able to face up to reality – to him being gone. Instead, it was the fear of being pushed to say goodbye again when we all knew the man who had inhabited that body wasn't there any more. There was just an empty shell left. I didn't need to see that to understand it was over.

A reckless niggling thought in the back of my mind kept asking: what would happen if I never called them? If I didn't organise a funeral, a suit, a coffin... if I just backed slowly away and absolved myself of all responsibility. But I knew, tempting as it might be, I could never do it. It wouldn't look right.

I chewed my breakfast, still watching Mike's driveway for signs of movement. My parents had been due to fly back from Italy this morning – two weeks in a villa near some fancy vineyards I could only dream of visiting. If their flight hadn't been delayed, they would have landed sometime after 5 a.m. and would be home by now. I put my half-finished bowl of muesli on the coffee table, gulping back the scalding coffee. I knew I had to tell them. They would see it on the news, or hear from a friend of a friend or something. It would have to come out sooner or later. But the thought of calling my mother, telling her my husband was dead... I closed my eyes, steeling myself, knowing that it was best to get it over with. Rip the plaster off in one go before I could lose my nerve.

I reached over to the cordless phone and dialled her number. She answered quickly, as I'd known she would, her brisk, clipped voice making my heart sink with trepidation.

'Hello?'

'Hi, Mum. It's me.'

'Oh, you just caught me. We only got back a couple of hours ago, and we're heading out to lunch with Sue and Janice in a little while. It never stops,' she said, sounding pleased with herself.

I opened my mouth to cut in, but she continued with barely time to take a breath.

'We've had the most lovely holiday, Victoria. No thanks to the couple in the villa next door to us, I should add. It's supposed to be a five-star holiday village – you would think they'd be a bit more selective about the type of people they let in. But the weather was just gorgeous, and I was swimming twice a day. Your dad even came in a couple of times, though of course he spent most of his time drinking wine and playing cards. We're both so brown now! And the owner of the vineyard compared me to Katharine Hepburn. Can you imagine? I mean, I *have* lost weight and the dress was flattering, but really!' Her tone gave away her glee at the comparison.

I nodded, feeling like I should jump in and stop her – *tell* her – but unable to interrupt. She'd never liked to be spoken over, and I'd learned to wait my turn.

'And yes,' she continued, 'before you start, I *did* wear suncream on the hottest days. I know you think I'm mad not to smother myself in it, but you don't tan as fast with that stuff plastered all over you, and it's only two weeks after all. I want to get my money's worth, don't I? There's no point going all the way to Italy and then having to pop in for a spray tan on the way back so people can see you've been away!' She giggled girlishly, then took a breath, and there was a brief silence as she no doubt waited for me to launch into exuberant questions about her trip.

Instead, I swallowed, squeezing the phone tighter, the

muesli cold and heavy in my stomach. 'Mum,' I said, feeling light-headed and breathless. 'Something's happened.'

'What? What do you mean?'

I closed my eyes, filling my lungs with air as I felt myself on the precipice of a panic attack.

'While you were on holiday, there was an accident,' I said, my words measured, slow. 'A car accident.' I took a breath. 'It hit Russell and... and he died.'

I realised my voice sounded cold, emotionless, but it was inevitable. I'd never been able to show my feelings with my mother. We had never had the kind of relationship where I could cry. Seek her out for comfort. Ask for her support. I'd spent so much of my childhood squashing down my emotions, conscious of how uncomfortable they made her, that I'd even managed to convince myself I was just fine – for the most part.

I'd recently begun to wonder if that had played a part in my acceptance of the way Russell had been in our marriage. Compliantly submitting to his need to always be the leader, always assume control, because I couldn't face the idea of conflict, couldn't admit I wasn't entirely happy with the way things were between us. I was starting to see that I had lost my voice long before saying my marriage vows.

My mother cleared her throat. 'Dead? Russell is dead?'

'Yes,' I replied, my voice barely a whisper.

She paused, and I held my breath, my heart thumping as if I was a little girl again, awaiting her response having handed her a questionable school report.

Victoria is a daydreamer. She rarely completes the set work to the expected standard. Victoria doesn't join in with group activities. She isn't a team player. Victoria does not make any effort to make friends and prefers to be alone. I could remember it well. Wondering what was so bad about being quieter than my classmates. Why being shy was something to be ashamed of. Nobody seemed to mind if someone was too loud. Too pushy in group activities. Nobody complained that a select few children monopolised the teacher's attention, never leaving room for someone like me to question what I was supposed to be doing, why everyone else seemed to know what was expected. I didn't understand why it was *my* responsibility to battle against the louder voices. Why *I* was in the wrong. But my mother had thought it so.

Now, waiting for her reaction, I felt like I'd failed her again, and despite the ridiculousness of the notion, I was sure she felt it too. She had always liked Russell. Carried an air of surprise that he would choose me to be his wife.

'Have you had the funeral yet?' she asked, an icy edge to her words.

I smiled involuntarily at her predictable response. Of course she would focus on the practicalities. The aspects she could control, grasp hold of, rather than the jumble of messy emotions that came with a situation such as this. Though a part of me deep down wished she would ask how I was coping, how she might help me through this, I'd known she wouldn't. It wasn't in her nature.

'I haven't finalised the details yet. I'll let you know when I do.'

'Right. Good.'

'You'll tell Dad?' I asked.

It was only a formality. I had even less of a relationship with him than I did with my mother. He'd worked away for most of my childhood – a welder on an oil rig far out in the middle of the ocean, where I'd dreamed he was lonely, bored and itchy from the constant spray of salt water whipped up on the wind, an inescapable consequence of life at sea that I felt sure would gradually become more and more unbearable. I could imagine the smell of oil, sweat, metal, the blistering sun, no trees to provide an inch of shade. The feeling of absolute isolation along with the fear of what could happen out there all alone at the mercy of an unforgiving ocean.

Back then, I sometimes wondered if my thoughts were strong enough that he would feel them, all those miles away from home, and that somehow they might bring him comfort, make him think of me too.

He would be gone for up to six months at a time, and my earliest memories were of imagining him coming home – how happy he would be to see me. He would say how grown up I was now, invite me to join him in the things he liked to do, though I never really understood what those things were.

As it turned out, my fantasy couldn't have been further from reality. When he returned in a flurry of pent-up energy, tanned beyond recognition, his booming voice making me shrink back, unable to know how to connect with his larger-than-life character, he would treat me like a stray puppy he didn't want to touch. Curious at times, impatient at others, but, for the most part, happiest when I left him alone, choosing to play in my room while he invited his friends over and spent time with the people who really mattered to him. He had never once spoken to me on the phone in my life, and I doubted now was the time to start.

'Yes,' Mum said. 'I'll let him know.'

I nodded, noting how she could easily have been talking about anything – a lost coat, a storm on the way. Her cool, impassive tone gave nothing away.

'I'd better let you get on then,' she said crisply. 'I... I'm sorry for your loss,' she added, a formal afterthought offered out of politeness rather than any real show of feeling.

I opened my mouth to reply, but the line was already dead.

Dropping the phone on the arm of the chair, I glanced at the wedding photo on the sideboard – Russell dressed in a traditional black suit, me in a sleek white silk dress, both of us smiling. We'd been so hopeful for our future back then. I had really believed I'd hit the jackpot. That I'd finally got everything I always wanted. It felt like a lifetime ago now.

I turned my face away, my mother's stiff condolences ringing in my ears.

'Thanks,' I said out loud to the empty room. 'So am I.'

TWELVE

LISA

'They're what?' I stared in disbelief as Sandy smiled expectantly at me.

'Releasing you on bail. Note, I didn't say releasing you without charge,' she added, her eyes narrowing.

'But… what does that mean precisely?'

'It means you're still a suspect, but they don't have enough evidence to keep you in custody. I've no doubt DS McCormac will have been pushing to extend your time here, wanting to get those DNA results back from the scarf, and the fact that he hasn't been able to secure that permission is very promising for us. After all, a scarf isn't evidence of a crime having been committed, especially given you were friends with both him and his wife. Who's to say she didn't borrow it from you?' She smiled, clearly pleased with herself.

'Or that it was even mine,' I said under my breath.

'Exactly.' She looked my way, her eyes meeting mine. 'Look, Lisa, at the very least, it buys us time. And you get to go home to your family,' she added.

I nodded, though I couldn't allow myself to feel the same elation. I didn't feel like I'd been given a gift. It felt like I was being dropped into purgatory. To have to go home to my children, my husband with all this still unresolved, knowing that at any moment a knock might come at my door, that I might be dragged out of my comfortable life, thrust back into this hell once again, was torture. As grateful as I was to have the opportunity to see Mike and the kids, part of me wished I could just stay here until they had reached a conclusion. Because I knew that it was far from over.

And at home, there would be questions – so many questions I couldn't answer. Things I wasn't ready to face. Victoria, for one. I wondered if she'd been back to the house again in my absence. I could picture her now, in my kitchen, making tea, being there for Mike, a listening ear. Keeping Jack topped up on snacks. Hugging Holly. It made me uneasy.

'So... I can just go?' I repeated. It felt surreal, and I realised I'd already begun to prepare myself for a far longer stay.

'You can.' She nodded. 'Do you want to call your husband?'

I pressed my lips together, trying to rein in the sudden rush of emotion that flooded me. 'Yes,' I whispered. 'I do.'

Mike kept casting furtive glances at me in the passenger seat, his right hand fluttering anxiously on the steering wheel as he drove through the quiet back roads he knew I preferred to the busy high street. With every mile that passed, I felt my chest opening, the crippling fear I hadn't even acknowledged I was feeling lifting from my shoulders.

How easy it had been, I thought, for them to take something from me so vital as my freedom. How quickly I had moved through the stages of my emotions before a numb sort of acceptance had settled over me. It was shocking, I realised now, driving through these familiar tree-lined streets, the sky bright and blue overhead, that it could be done. That we as humans could so readily accept our fate and hand over our freedom as if it meant nothing. As if our liberty weren't just as vital as the air we breathed.

Mike reached for my thigh, squeezing gently, and I forced myself to smile. To place my hand reassuringly over his, a familiar, comforting action that made the strangeness of the situation a little less pronounced. He'd hugged me so tightly when he'd arrived to pick me up, launching into a volley of questions almost immediately, but when I'd told him I was exhausted – hadn't slept – he'd nodded with understanding eyes and to his credit hadn't asked me anything else... yet.

As we turned into our street, I felt my heart rate increase, my palms turning liquid as I remembered in vivid detail the moment I'd been forced to leave, the cold, hard metal of the handcuffs digging into my flesh. The home I'd always considered my sanctuary was no longer safe. It had only ever been an illusion. Just four walls and a door that could be defeated by force, no match for a battering ram and a determined adversary. And I was going back there. A sitting duck, waiting for the next shot to be fired.

What if we left? Just packed our bags, grabbed the kids and drove somewhere we couldn't be found. Where freedom wasn't something we just handed over but something we fought for. Defended. *Owned.*

The idea was so tempting it made my breath catch in my throat, and I realised I was actually seriously considering the possibility.

But then Mike was pulling into the drive, smiling cautiously at me, his eyes uncertain as he unclipped his seat belt and walked round the car to open my door, treating me like a broken child. The front door opened, my children standing there looking so brave, trying to hide their true emotions behind wide, welcoming smiles. But I knew them too well to be fooled. And in that moment, I knew I had to stay.

Leaving now would be seen as an admission of guilt, and

asking my family to walk away from everything they knew and follow me into a life in the shadows was nothing but a ridiculous fantasy. A pipe dream. I wanted to run from the uncertainties I was sure to face over the coming weeks – escape my life, my fears – but the reality could never match the rose-tinted picture I so desperately wanted to step into. There would be far too many questions. Too much hardship for the people I loved. And I would never ask that of them. No. I would stay. I would be the wife and mother they needed and deserved. And I would win back my freedom by standing my ground and staying strong and silent in the face of the police investigation. I wouldn't run away from the life I loved because of this.

THIRTEEN

VICTORIA

Then

'For goodness' sake, don't put the rolls on that plate!' Russell snapped, blocking my path to the back door, his narrow shoulders stiff and tense.

I looked down at the plate, white and unchipped – perfectly inoffensive as far as I could see – but from Russell's tone, I already knew there was no point in arguing. He'd been moody and irritable all morning, and I wished he'd never invited our new neighbours to a barbecue, as much as I liked them. We had only just put away the packing boxes, and I didn't feel ready to start playing host, knowing that the responsibility to make the house show-home presentable would fall squarely on my shoulders, Russell demanding perfection without ever lending a hand. We'd hardly ever had people over at our previous flat, though not for want of trying on Russell's part; his invitations weren't often accepted, and on the rare occasion they were, guests never came back twice.

I couldn't blame them. I was hardly a riveting host – always too conscious of saying the wrong thing or looking stupid to really let go and enjoy myself. And Russell, though I would never tell him so, was always far too intense, talking about himself too much, insisting on going into great detail about every story, making even the most interesting tale a chore to listen to. And he was so caught up in making the right impression that he was always a nightmare before people arrived.

'Which plate would you like me to use?' I asked now, my tone betraying none of my own frustration or nerves. I glanced out of the window, seeing Mike and Lisa sitting on the decking at the far end of the garden, the warm suntrap perfect on a day like today. Lisa was reclining on a cushioned lounger, Mike on a wicker chair beside her. He was laughing at something she'd just said, a glass of beer held casually in one hand, his other resting absently on her swollen belly – a protective, loving gesture, not intended to stake his claim as Russell might have done in the same situation.

The garden was looking as close to perfection as it could get – the rose bushes in full bloom, the lawn mown in contrasting stripes, the chrome barbecue polished and spotlessly clean. It was so quintessentially English, an idyllic summer garden party, and I couldn't help but think of the effort it had taken to make it happen, the long days I had spent out there weeding and pruning, despite my dislike of gardening.

'Here,' Russell said impatiently. He handed me a blue-and-cream patterned plate from a vintage set I'd hoped he might sell for a profit, since it had cost more than he made in a month. But no. Of course he wouldn't miss the opportunity to show it off. Not, I suspected, that Mike and Lisa would care a jot about a bloody plate.

I was still in shock that they'd agreed to come today. We were so different, but this was our third time getting together since we'd moved across the road from them nearly two months earlier – once at theirs, once at the pub and now here – and to my surprise, they hadn't seemed to have grown sick of us yet. I liked them. Lisa's warmth. Mike's easy humour. They made life seem so simple. So easy. I envied them, and yet I couldn't help wanting to be around them. Involved in their lives somehow. Part of me hoped their relaxed, happy-go-lucky attitude might rub off on us too. On Russell in particular.

I took the plate, transferring the burger buns onto it and looking to Russell for his approval.

'Better.' He nodded, taking a bottle of chilled champagne from the fridge. I turned for the door, relieved.

'Oh, and Victoria,' he added.

I paused, turning hesitantly to look over my shoulder.

'Yes?' I asked, trying not to show any tension in my expression.

He smiled tightly. 'Don't embarrass me today, okay?' he said, his piercing blue eyes meeting mine.

A thousand replies went through my mind, but I knew I couldn't say any of them.

'Of course not,' I replied sweetly. I smiled and he nodded, satisfied for the moment.

I stepped outside, my stomach tight, my blood boiling. As I walked down the path towards them, I wondered if Lisa ever felt this way about Mike. It was hard to imagine. They were so strong. So happy. I watched his arm snake around her neck, her wide smile as she looked into his eyes. I didn't think anything could tear them apart.

FOURTEEN

I knew I should wait. Call perhaps, if I absolutely had to, but certainly not turn up on their doorstep twenty minutes after they'd arrived home. I'd watched the sweet reunion on the driveway, the way Mike had held Lisa's arm as if she was returning home from a long stay in hospital, weak and unsteady on her feet. It had been a subdued gathering – warm hugs, cautious smiles – and I'd stared hungrily, wanting to see more, finding myself filled with frustration as their front door closed, shutting them tightly away from the world.

I paced back and forth in the confines of my living room, feeling agitated, *caged*.

As I glanced over at the sideboard, my gaze locked on the framed wedding photograph, the close-up view of Russell's piercing blue eyes, his blonde hair combed down and Bryl-creemed into place, a look that hadn't suited him but was fashionable back then. He always had tried to follow the fashion, though he'd frequently got it monumentally wrong.

I scrutinised the grainy photograph, frowning. Those eyes…

they felt as though they were following me. *Watching* me. Even now, I couldn't escape his presence. It made me want to run, to get as far away from his hard, critical stare as possible.

I strode across the room and flipped the photo face-down, feeling an instant sense of relief, but it wasn't enough.

Slowly, I slid the frame off the sideboard. Opening the drawer, I shoved the photo towards the back and slid it closed. Then I leaned my hands against the smooth wood and took a long, deep breath, closing my eyes as I felt my lungs expand, the panic that had begun to rise ebbing away. When I opened them, I took in the sight of the ugly ornaments displayed proudly along the surface.

Russell had always been so particular about details. Every single piece of furniture in the house, every rug, every lamp and table, had been his choice. He'd prided himself on his good taste, and I'd never had the courage to tell him that expensive didn't necessarily equal stylish.

I particularly disliked the ornaments. Wherever we went, he would always insist on going into musty old shops looking for what he called 'gems'. The brass weighing scales had cost an absolute fortune, and he'd gone on about them for days to anyone who would listen, every visitor having to nod and pretend interest in them, play the guessing game of how much they had cost, which made me cringe uncomfortably. The same was true of his classic car models. He said they would be worth a fortune one day, if we took good care of them, and in the meantime, they were interesting conversation starters. Or, if we were being honest with one another, opportunities for him to brag.

In my mind, they were simply more things to dust, and it wasn't like Russell had ever bothered to pick up a cloth and do the job himself. It was stifling. His things. His treasures. If I stayed in this house one moment longer, I knew I couldn't trust myself not to break something. I felt ready to explode.

I walked back to the window, slipping a finger between the net curtains and edging one aside to peer across the street. I knew Lisa well enough to be sure that right now, all she would want would be a quiet dinner with her family, and an early night with her husband. I had no right to infiltrate her plans, and yet even as I acknowledged those thoughts, I was slipping my feet into my shoes, reaching for my keys.

If we'd had the kind of friendship you see on sitcoms, the kind where you're in and out of each other's homes, an always-welcome open-door policy, it would have been different. But despite our proximity, it had never been that kind of set-up. Russell had been mostly to blame for that, insisting on knowing exactly when social visits would occur and what their purpose was. He'd needed time to prepare, to have the house exactly as he liked it; not that he was happy for either of us to let standards slip in between, mind you. He wanted to be showered and dressed in a fresh shirt, with something impressive cooking in the oven, and the amount of effort that went into him looking casual and relaxed when guests finally arrived was absurd.

In the early days of our friendship, Lisa and Mike had turned up without an 'appointment' once or twice, but I hadn't invited them in, conscious of how badly Russell would take their unexpected appearance. Without ever wanting to, I had laid the groundwork for a more formal kind of friendship – not at all the kind I really craved. I was consumed with fascination for how other people lived, and the idea of being absorbed into their world, a fly on the wall, watching the reality of their daily lives, was something that kept me up at night on a regular basis.

Despite all the boundaries I'd put in place over the years, it hadn't escaped my attention that now, for the second time in a week, I was breaking my own rules and foisting myself on what I knew should be a private family moment. I only hoped they would make allowances – after all, I *had* just lost my husband.

I crossed the road as slowly as I could bear to, walked up the path and, with a shaking fist, knocked on the front door. It was Mike who answered, his jaw tense as if braced for the worst, and I wondered if he'd thought it might be the police back for his wife so soon.

'Oh, Vic,' he said, the words coming in a rush of undisguised relief. 'Everything okay?'

I nodded as Jack and Holly appeared behind him, both wearing the same guarded expression.

'It's okay, Mum,' Jack called over his shoulder. 'It's Auntie Vic.'

'I... I just came to see if...' I trailed off as Lisa, looking pale and small, emerged from the kitchen.

Mike stood back. 'Come on in. We've not long arrived home,' he added, as if I didn't know. 'We were just deciding on dinner.'

'Oh, I don't want to get in the way,' I fumbled, feeling even more awkward.

'You won't,' Lisa said graciously. 'You'll join us, won't you?'

For the first time, our gazes met, and I breathed in deeply, taking in the tired, pink-rimmed eyes, the pinched tension lines around her mouth. She was too polite to send me away – too nice to make me feel unwelcome, as much as she might want me to go.

I should have declined, left them in peace, acknowledged that it was only out of pity that I'd received the invitation, but I couldn't bring myself to turn around now.

I stepped through the open door and nodded. 'Thanks,' I said, offering a tiny smile. 'Dinner would be lovely.'

There was an elephant in the room that only Lisa and I seemed to be aware of. Since that moment at the front door, she had barely glanced at me, busying herself with the task of making dinner, bustling purposefully around her domain as if marking her territory – or at least that was how it felt to me. Holly had barely left her side, wordlessly taking a knife to slice potatoes, never speaking, but showing her support simply by being there. I found myself watching them with a sense of confusion and irritation, wondering why Lisa didn't just speak up, say something. Not one of us had mentioned the obvious – the fact that Lisa had been accused of killing my husband – and desperate as I was to know what had happened at the station, whether she'd been cleared of all charges or just let out on bail, I couldn't seem to bring myself to ask.

Mike seemed oblivious to any tension in the room, so utterly elated was he to have his wife back, watching with serene relief, touching her whenever she came near. His hand would linger on her hip, her back, as if that physical connection could stop her from being taken from him again.

Jack had kept up a constant stream of small talk throughout dinner, something we all seemed to be grateful for, and now, as I raised my last forkful of asparagus to my lips, he leaned across the table, taking Lisa's hand in a gesture that made him seem suddenly very grown up. 'Thanks for dinner, Mum. Nothing beats your home cooking.'

She smiled. 'Thanks, darling. It was my pleasure.'

Jack grimaced, his gaze darting between Lisa and me. 'So, this must be weird for you, huh? You especially, Auntie Vic,' he said.

I met his eyes and was faced with that knowing expression he always seemed to wear, and I realised that he too had picked up on the atmosphere. He was so good at reading people; of course he wouldn't miss a thing. It was a stark reminder to watch myself around him, to be extra careful with what I said and how I acted.

I felt the eyes of everyone in the room move to me. Lisa's cheeks flushed, and she toyed with the stem of her empty wine glass, saying nothing.

'It's been a weird week,' I conceded.

'An especially hard one for you,' Mike added gently.

I nodded. 'You're not wrong. Losing Russell—' I broke off, taking a fortifying sip of wine and shaking my head. I looked up, seeing Jack's sympathetic expression, and wondered if he regretted bringing it up. Holly was silent, her eyes downcast. The atmosphere had turned decidedly uncomfortable in the warm kitchen.

'Whatever happened to him,' I said, 'we all know your mum is not to blame. Lisa, I don't believe for a second you had anything to do with it. I'm sure I don't have to tell you that.'

'How do you know?' Holly looked up at last. 'How can you be so sure?' she asked, almost incredulously. 'The police obviously don't share your view, do they? What makes you think they've got it so wrong?' There was an undertone of panic in her voice, and I felt my heart go out to her, seeing straight through the anger to the fearful child who'd had to watch her mother be taken away in handcuffs.

'Holly!' Mike exclaimed, his concerned gaze falling on Lisa, whose face had gone a deathly shade of white.

'It's okay,' Lisa said, though her voice trembled as she spoke and she looked as if she'd been slapped hard across the face.

'Sorry,' Holly muttered. She flashed an apologetic shrug at Lisa, who shook her head, as if to tell her not to worry, before taking a sip of her drink.

Holly sighed. 'Sorry, Auntie Vic. I just—'

'No.' I cut her off, reaching over to take her hand. 'Don't feel you have to explain yourself, sweetie. I know how hard it must have been on you to have your mum taken away out of the blue, and it's a fair question.' I could feel Jack's eyes on me, analysing, soaking up the energy of the conversation, feeding off the drama. I tried not to let it bother me that he was looking at us like a case study, trying to work it all out in his mind.

'The answer is simply that I know your mum. She's the

kindest person in the world.' I smiled. 'She would never have left Russell in that state, even if she had accidentally hit him,' I said with conviction. 'It wouldn't be the first time the police have got it wrong, would it? And it won't be long before they figure that out for themselves. Honestly, Lisa, I don't believe a word of it,' I insisted, smiling in her direction.

She flashed an assessing look at me before forcing a smile. 'Thanks for saying that, Vic. I appreciate it.'

I nodded, turning back to Holly. 'As if your mum could be to blame. I mean, you do remember Reggie, right?'

Holly's face broke into a reluctant smile, and she nodded as Jack and Mike burst out laughing. 'I do,' she said.

'How could we forget?' Mike groaned. 'Five and a half months – that's how long he was here. Nearly half a year of that cantankerous old man sleeping on our sofa, using my razor, eating us out of house and home and moaning like he was doing *us* a favour.'

I nodded as Jack and Mike began jovially trading stories about Reggie's sudden appearance under their roof. He was a seventy-two-year-old homeless amputee Lisa had struck up a friendship with on a trip into town. It had been a bitingly cold February, ice on the ground, and she'd found him struggling with a pair of rusted crutches, trying to lower himself down onto a pile of cardboard and damp blankets in a shop doorway. She'd helped him to sit, bought him a cup of soup and a crusty roll from the van across the road, and spent the rest of the after-noon listening to his life story.

And what a sob story it had been. His wife had left him the day after his fiftieth birthday, an event, he said, he was entirely to blame for as he had never treated her with the love and respect she deserved. Two years later, he'd lost his left leg from the knee down, along with half a lung – a consequence of poor circulation brought about by forty years of heavy smoking, a habit he held on to with dogged determination, despite what it had cost him.

Losing his leg had subsequently meant the loss of his job as a window fitter, and once he found himself unemployed, divorced and with no hope that life might improve, he'd sunk into a deep depression, too ashamed and exhausted by his ordeal to ask for help or apply for benefits. He'd been on the streets almost seventeen years when Lisa had met him, and as the sky began to grow dark, the air turning bitterly cold, she had made the unlikely decision to bring him home with her, despite the lack of any obvious redeeming qualities on his part.

Her intention, she'd explained, was to get him set up in an old people's home, but as it turned out, it was a long and arduous battle: applying for funding, getting the paperwork sorted, finding a suitable place. What she'd expected to be a short stay – perhaps a week or two – had turned into the best part of half a year. But that was Lisa. Sometimes I envied that about her – that ability to keep giving without any sign of resentment, always finding empathy even when she was inconvenienced by it. *I* wouldn't have been so generous with my home, my personal space. I couldn't imagine many people would be.

I sipped my wine, listening to the animated conversation about good old Reggie, glad to find I was forgotten, the spotlight no longer glaring at me. It was nice to be here.

I'd always suspected that this was what I'd been missing in my quiet home with so many rules to keep to. And now that I'd tasted what life was like for Lisa, I knew I wanted it too. I wanted what she had. And if I got it, I would never give it up.

FIFTEEN

LISA

'I think I'm going to jump in the shower,' Mike said, standing up from the dinner table and stretching his arms over his head. He rubbed the back of his neck, working away at a knot, and I felt guilty knowing he'd barely taken a second for himself since my arrest.

'Yes, go,' I said, nodding. 'You must be exhausted.'

He kissed my cheek, then patted Victoria on the shoulder, and she reached up, giving his hand a squeeze. 'See?' She smiled. 'I told you she'd be back before you knew it. You can relax now.'

He nodded, his eyelids drooping heavily, and smiled at her words as he padded out of the kitchen.

I stood and glanced at the clock, feeling shattered myself. The tumble dryer had finished, and I pulled the heap of hot, static, sweet-smelling clothes from its cavernous interior, dumping them on the counter and organising them into folded piles, realising just how exhausted I really was as I moved robotically through the task. My legs felt heavy and shaky, and there was a dull ache behind my eyes, pulsing in my temples. An early night in my own bed was the only thing I wanted right now.

I glanced at Victoria, hoping she would pick up on the subdued vibe and take it as her cue to leave. Instead, she reached for the bottle of rosé, topping up her glass and reclining against the back of her chair. I tried not to sigh – to show my frustration.

I was a little taken aback at how normal she seemed – still wearing a full face of make-up, nails done, no sign of the grief I'd expected to witness. Her eyes were bright and clear, not the swollen red orbs mine would have been in her situation. But then Victoria had always been private and restrained when it came to showing her emotions. Even when I'd known she was upset – when I'd walked in on the end of a row between her and Russell, when her favourite auntie had moved to Scotland, or when her mother had let her down and failed to come to her fortieth birthday party – she'd never shown a hint of sadness, nor the slightest chink in her armour.

Having met her parents a handful of times over the years, I knew exactly where she got that unflustered, almost cold front from. The stiff-upper-lip attitude that was hard to get past. Her mum and dad both had a showy, insincere air that made them seem a bit fake and self-obsessed, and I found them hard to be around, their lack of empathy impossible to relate to, every conversation leading back to them, *their* stories, *their* achievements. They were openly critical about any number of topics, but that was the only emotion in their arsenal, and despite their loud personalities – both of them far more outspoken than their daughter – they came across as icy, unemotional people, and *that* was something Victoria *had* inherited. It was alien behaviour to me – I was always the first to break down and sob at a sad movie, the most likely to cry in an argument or gush over something sweet Mike had done for me. I wore my feelings right out in the open, and I knew it made some people uncomfortable.

'Do you want a top-up?' Victoria asked now, nodding towards my empty glass on the table beside hers.

'Oh, go on then,' I said, silently admitting defeat. If she wasn't leaving, I might as well relax and enjoy the wait. I managed a smile, though it felt forced and inappropriate given the circumstances, and quickly glanced away, folding Jack's last T-shirt and popping it on his pile.

I left the stacked laundry ready on the counter, walked reluctantly back to the table and sank back down into my seat, taking the full glass Victoria held out towards me.

'Thanks,' I said, taking a tiny sip, not really wanting it.

'So, how are you coping?' I asked gently. I hadn't wanted to bring it up when the kids were still here, not wanting to put her in an uncomfortable position, but now we were alone, it was impossible to ignore the unspoken conversation we'd yet to have. 'It must be...' I broke off, not sure how to finish the sentence, how on earth to articulate what a freshly widowed wife might be feeling.

She shrugged, her eyes on her glass, her long manicured fingers fiddling with the stem of it. 'It still doesn't feel real, if I'm honest,' she admitted, her voice quiet but calm. 'And yet strangely, nothing has ever felt *more* real.' She shook her head, looking up at me with an apologetic half-smile. 'That doesn't make sense, I know. My head is scrambled right now.'

She took a gulp of her wine, her eyes closing briefly. When she opened them, they were bright and clear, staring at me with a sudden intensity. 'I don't know why they came for *you* of all people.'

I held her gaze, unsure if it was a statement or a question, my stomach tightening involuntarily, though I'd known she would want to ask. I had known since the moment of my arrest that this moment would come.

'I mean,' she continued, 'he'd been at the pub all evening. He was almost certainly drunk. Dressed in that awful black trench coat I always hated. You know, the one that made him look like Sherlock Holmes, that he thought was the height of fashion? And of course the council have been turning off the street lights between one and four every night to cut costs. I'd be surprised if whoever hit him even realised what they'd done,' she murmured, her voice analytical, betraying nothing of how she was feeling. 'It would have been a miracle if he'd made it home under the circumstances. I told him to get a taxi. But then Russell always did believe he was untouchable. Superhuman...' She snorted into her glass, and I wondered if she was crying, but when she placed it back down, her eyes were dry, unreadable.

I sensed she'd been holding out for this moment alone with me to unburden herself of these thoughts. She would never have spoken so candidly in front of Mike. It had always been this way. The first few times I met her, I thought she was shy. I could remember being taken aback at how easily she deferred to Russell, how she looked to him almost as if for approval. Mike had made a comment one night after we'd been to a barbecue at theirs about her being a bit of a shrinking violet – sweet and gentle – and it had stuck in my teeth for a few days, because despite outward appearances, I felt sure there was more to this woman that we'd yet to discover. And as time went by, I'd been proven right. Not that Mike would hear a word of it.

I'd been taken aback the first time I'd seen another side to her, though a part of me had been expecting it. We'd been out for lunch and the waitress had got her order wrong. The Victoria I'd seen up until that point would have meekly taken the plate without comment, but she'd shocked me by speaking up. Not in a mean way exactly, but with a confidence that made her almost unrecognisable. Cold and to the point – traits I later realised she'd inherited from her mother. She'd sent the food back, negotiated a reduction on the bill to compensate for our wasted time and taken the waitress to task in a no-nonsense manner that had my jaw hitting the ground.

On another occasion, we'd gone into London to see a show, and at the train station, a teenage girl who looked like she'd been sleeping rough had made a grab for her handbag. Victoria had flung herself backwards, planting her bum on the cold, hard ground, her hands clasped firmly over the strap. The would-be thief had been unbalanced and toppled over beside her. I'd watched, horror-stricken, as Victoria had grabbed the girl by the chin, whispering something that made her eyes grow wide before she scrambled up and ran away. When I'd asked her what she'd said, she'd muttered something about teaching her a few manners. And when I'd told Mike, he'd shaken his head, unable to link either of these out-of-character displays to the woman he thought he knew. To him, and to Russell, it seemed the person I'd caught glimpses of simply didn't exist.

I'd watched her more closely after that, noting the change in her demeanour in the company of men. Even Jack wasn't exempt. As time went on, I started to question if she was even aware she was doing it – the way she held her hands clasped tight between her crossed knees when Russell asked her a question. The way her voice would soften and she would listen far more than she talked when a man joined the conversation. I had been glad to discover she had a bit more about her than I'd initially surmised – to find she was far more likely to speak up when it was just the two of us – but it was disconcerting to see her become this other person whenever we were alone.

I'd asked her about it once or twice, trying to point it out without being rude but needing to understand what was happening. She'd brushed off my tentative questions, making a vague comment about 'girl talk' and men not wanting to hear all the nitty-gritty details of her life, and I'd been left feeling like an over-sharer, wondering if I was reading too much into it. If she was just a little old-fashioned, in essence.

She stared at me now, waiting for a response, and I swallowed, unsure what to say. I didn't know myself why they had come for me, what they thought they had on me, and to agree with her that Russell was indeed an idiot for coming home wasted, dressed from head to toe in black in the wee hours of the morning would surely just be rubbing salt in a fresh wound.

I glanced over my shoulder at the sound of footsteps in the hall, and felt instant relief that we were no longer alone and I was saved from having to say anything.

Mike walked back into the room, his hair damp, wearing flannel PJ bottoms and no shirt. His eyes widened as if he was surprised to find Victoria still seated at the table, and he pulled a clean T-shirt from the pile on the counter, yanking it on and flicking the switch on the kettle. 'Brew, anyone?' he offered, stifling a yawn.

Victoria looked at her now empty wine glass. 'Oh, yes please,' she said, and I flashed Mike a look of irritation that he'd just given her another excuse to prolong her stay.

Sorry, he mouthed, glancing at the back of her head and offering a confused shrug.

I suppressed a yawn, once again wondering when she might leave so I could crawl into bed, then felt instantly guilty about sending her home alone.

I watched as she reached for the mug Mike passed her, taking in her sweet smile and subdued thanks. Her voice was no longer cold and analytical; it was quiet, honeyed in a way that felt insincere somehow. It was that sudden ability to flick the switch and transform into this other person, I realised, that despite all our years of casual friendship gave me a sense of unease around her. It made me feel I couldn't fully trust her, made me want to prove to my husband that the woman he thought he knew wasn't the same woman *I* knew.

But then, I thought, sipping my wine, maybe I was just over-analysing.

SIXTEEN

VICTORIA

'So we're going to go for next Wednesday, ten a.m. at the crematorium, walnut coffin with the cream satin lining. Standard ceremony with no prayers or hymns. And you're sure nobody wants to do a reading?' Mr Harrison, the funeral director, peered at me over the rim of his unframed oval glasses.

'Quite sure.' I nodded, offering no explanation in the hope that he wouldn't push for one.

Professional decorum meant that whatever opinion he might have of the pared-down send-off we'd planned out during our meeting, he kept it to himself. He gave a nod, seemingly unfazed as he jotted a scribbled note in his leather-bound ledger. I wondered if he'd have to transfer his notes onto his computer once I'd left – it seemed far too old-fashioned not to keep a digital record in this day and age, and not at all in keeping with the modern atmosphere in the funeral home.

It was lighter than I would have expected, a big steel-framed window facing a central courtyard where several rose bushes covered in white and blood-red blooms thrived in the afternoon sun. There was something flat and unsaturated about their colours, a hint of morbidity about them somehow, and I wished they'd chosen pink or yellow varieties instead – something with a bit more vitality to them. Even so, the glossy green leaves and velvety petals were a welcome distraction from the intrinsic melancholy of this place.

'So, are we done?' I asked, pressing my hands to my knees as I made to get up.

Mr Harrison tapped his pen thoughtfully on the page open before him on the smooth beech desk. 'Almost. There's just the matter of his clothes.'

'I said I would bring his best suit?' I replied, raising my eyebrow in question, sure that we'd already decided on that.

'Of course. But would you like us to dress him, or would you prefer to do it yourself? Some wives—'

'I'll leave all that to you,' I cut in, my voice coming out sharper than I'd intended. I realised my body had recoiled, pressing hard against the back of my seat as if I could escape the image his seemingly innocuous words had conjured.

Mr Harrison nodded, his face still impassive. 'That's not a problem. We'll see to it that he's well taken care of, Mrs Fox.'

I breathed a shaky sigh of relief, wondering if he thought I was a bad wife. I already knew what Russell would say if he could hear us now. He'd want me to do it. He'd *insist* on it, complain that they would mess it up, comb his hair wrong, not shave him close enough. He'd expect me to see to all the tiny details I knew mattered so much to him.

We had never made a funeral plan – Russell had never been one to consider his own mortality – and now I'd been left to decide what was best. I'd chosen cremation, though I was sure he'd have expected an expensive, ostentatious plot in a swanky churchyard, where I could tend his grave every weekend for the rest of my life. Where I'd be tied to him for ever, buying fresh flowers and cutting the grass to keep it up to his high standards.

I couldn't bring myself to do it, though my choice had weighed heavily on me, and it took all my strength not to break down in the face of Mr Harrison's innocent questioning and do what Russell would have wanted. I'd hurriedly signed the form requesting a simple cremation, and had asked for his ashes to be sprinkled over the memorial garden behind the crematorium at a fraction of the cost of a plot.

A wave of sick guilt washed over me as I considered the low-key ceremony, the mid-range coffin, the lack of pomp and showmanship Russell would have wanted for himself. But then, I reasoned, pushing the guilt aside, Russell wasn't here. He wasn't the one having to make these decisions, having to go through the ordeal of talking to our friends and family, put on a brave face, pretend to be whatever it was they would expect to see as I said a silent goodbye to the man I had once expected to grow old with. No, I would not let myself feel guilty for doing everything in my power to make this funeral as short and as bearable as possible.

I rose from my seat, reaching over the desk to shake Mr Harrison by the hand, resisting the urge to wipe my own on my jeans straight after as I thought of all the dead bodies in the back room he might have been handling. 'Send me the invoice then. And thank you for your help with all of this.'

'Of course.' He nodded again, standing too. 'And once again, let me offer my heartfelt condolences. You are most welcome to visit your husband any time between now and next Wednesday. Our door is always open.'

I nodded silently, my gaze sliding back to those blood-red roses in the stark light of the courtyard so as not to look beyond Mr Harrison to the door that led to the room Russell currently lay in. I suppressed a shudder as I pictured his body splayed on a cold slab close by.

Resisting the urge to run, I turned, walking with as much composure as I could summon out into the fresh air, longing for next week to be over.

SEVENTEEN

LISA

Mike and I were never supposed to meet. That was the thing that had always struck me as so special about our relationship. Had that day been just a little different, nothing in my life would be the same – a fact I hated to even contemplate.

It was July, and I had just finished a year-long apprentice-ship at what was then a brand-new culinary school held in the Morgan Hotel in the town centre. These days, it was almost impossible to get a place there, the competition being so high, but back then, whether through sheer luck or determination, I had managed to get onto the course, and I had loved every minute. At seventeen, I'd been the youngest of the apprentices by several years, but I hadn't let that intimidate me. I'd immersed myself in every aspect of the kitchen, learning to bake, how to choose the right ingredients to balance my own recipes, to cook meat and fish to perfection and make a whole array of rich and delicious sauces, glazes and broths.

I was sad that the course was at an end. Although I'd loved becoming a better cook, I had no ambitions to work in a busy restaurant, nor to open my own. I wanted a slower pace than that life would offer. The freedom to take my time over a recipe.

I didn't want to turn my passion into something I did for a living. I was sure that any pressure, hurriedly throwing together ingredients to satisfy a room full of hungry patrons, would kill the joy, the spark I felt when I was in the kitchen.

So though I'd spent the day cooking a seven-course meal as part of my final evaluation, and was buzzing from the knowledge that it had all come together as I'd hoped, I felt no sense of stress about the results. For me, the course had been about gaining skills, not certificates. I had been in my own head, thinking about the smile on the examiner's face when he'd bitten into the ravioli I'd made, the compliments I'd received for my raspberry sorbet and honeycomb ice cream, so it took me a moment to process what had happened when I found myself lying flat in the road, my ankle throbbing and a tear in the elbow of my long-sleeved top.

'Are you okay, dear?'

I looked up to see an elderly lady standing at the bus stop and felt tears prick in my eyes, a combination of pain and embarrassment.

'You tripped on the kerb, my love. Are you hurt?'

I shook my head, but she was already coming towards me, her beige handbag swinging against her stomach as she moved surprisingly fast. She leaned over me, frowning. 'You didn't bang your head?'

'No. I think I'm okay. It's just my ankle.'

'Not broken?' She made a little hissing sound between her teeth. 'My old man broke *his* last winter and the recovery was horrendous.' Her long, wrinkled fingers wrapped lightly round the circle of my ankle, squeezing gently, and then a little tighter. 'Can you move it, love?'

I tried to turn it in a circle. It hurt, but it wasn't agony.

'I think it's a sprain,' I said. 'If I get up, I'm sure I'll be all right.'

I made to roll onto all fours, needing the position to propel me up, but with a strength she didn't look capable of, she grabbed me under both armpits and heaved me to my feet.

'Thanks,' I said after I'd caught my breath.

'Give it a test then.'

I took a tentative step, limping. 'It's not *too* painful.'

'Maybe you ought to get it checked out. Do you want me to call someone for you? There's a payphone over there.'

I shook my head. Took another step. It wasn't as bad as I'd first thought. 'I'm okay. I think I'll just have a sit-down in the community gardens for a few minutes and then I'll be all right to walk home. I don't live far anyway.'

She looked over my head towards the gate of the park just across the road. 'If you're sure?'

'Yeah, I'll be fine,' I said. I felt shaken, but now that I was back up on my feet, the adrenaline had kicked in, numbing the ache.

'Fine then. You're the expert on your own body, dear. Nobody knows you better than you, do they? All the same, I'll walk you over there,' she said, taking my arm and steering me across the road before I could object. 'My bus won't be here for another ten minutes anyway. I'm always too early. Habit from getting the cane when I was late to school once. Never been able to get over it. Wish I could be the type to rebel and say sod it, I'll show them, and be one of those who turns up an hour after they're supposed to, but it strikes the fear of God into me and I just can't. Anyway, here you are,' she said, coming to the first bench inside the gate. 'You sit yourself down here, love, and take the weight off that ankle.'

'Thanks,' I said, lowering myself down onto the hot metal.

'You sure you'll be okay? Only I really should get back now. I don't want the bus to come early and...' She paused, looking back towards the road, clearly feeling tense at the possibility.

I smiled, wondering where she was heading but not wanting

to delay her any longer. 'I'm sure. Thanks so much for all your help. You've been so kind.'

'Nonsense. Anyone would have done the same. Bye, love.'

She turned, rushing off before I could say anything else, the beige bag slapping against her middle as she moved with small, quick steps, reminding me of a heron running along a riverbank.

I smiled again, then looked down at my ankle, moving my foot from side to side then turning it in a circle. It might be swollen tomorrow, but it would be good enough to get me home. All the same, I decided to wait until the old lady had got on her bus before moving on. I didn't want her to see me walking away after she'd made so much effort to help me.

I leaned into the heat of the bench, my eyes closed, my face tilted up towards the sun, breathing in the scent of the flowers in bloom all around me. It was when I opened them that I saw him. Golden skin, mud smeared across his cheek, and an expression of intense focus and calm on his face. He looked kind, happy. Like a man in love with his life. I watched as he leaned heavily on his spade to dig into the dry earth. He made a hole, then placed a rose bush into it, the buds a soft yellow, promising to flower like butter beneath the summer sun. He watered it well then stood back, assessing his canvas. I was utterly captivated. He caught me staring at him and smiled.

'Isn't it too late in the season to plant that?' I asked, feeling my face flush as he grinned.

'Nope. Not if you give them plenty of water. She'll be fine.'

I nodded, unsure what else to say, and he started to turn back to his tools. I didn't know what gave me the confidence in that moment, but something inside me propelled me up, and before I could question why on earth he would say yes, I was asking if he would help me across to the café, playing up the sore ankle. He agreed without hesitation, calling over to another man, who I later discovered was the assistant gardener at his landscape gardening business.

All the way to the café on the far side of the park, Mike's arm around my waist for support, I asked him questions, wanting to learn everything I could about him, needing to find out who he was. He was five years older than me, had been living in Ashford for the past two, ever since he started his business at just twenty years old, and had dreams of country living – being able to walk out his front door and be at one with nature. He told me he struggled with the hustle and bustle of town, having grown up in the countryside, but that it was necessary if he was ever going to drum up any clients. And that as long as he was outside, he was happy. I believed him. There was a sense of peace within him, and I felt myself smiling wider with every word he said.

When we got to the café, he sat down opposite me and ordered a coffee. Somehow we managed to stay there until closing time, working our way through their selection of cakes and sandwiches, the conversation flowing as we realised there was something special between us. We married just eleven months later and had been together ever since.

And if I hadn't have fallen flat on my face that day, I would never have met him.

EIGHTEEN

VICTORIA

The sky above me turned black, heavy clouds crackling with promise, the air thick with electricity, humid against my bare shoulders. A trickle of syrupy sweat ran between my breasts, my dress sticking to my skin, the soles of my feet slick against my smooth summer sandals. I quickened my pace, desperate to get home before the storm broke. I'd been stupid in leaving it so late, not considering the unpredictability of the English summer weather in my plans. As it was, I'd stayed far too long at the café, chatting with Lisa over ice-cold lattes as she described her holiday in Malta, the adventures Mike had tried to rope her into. I loved listening to her talk, picturing what her life must be like, how different from my own, which felt stifling and empty by comparison.

I'd lost all sense of time and urgency, carried away on the image of black sand beaches and bracing skinny-dips beneath a blood-red moon, and now I'd be lucky if I made it back before Russell got home from work. If I returned with rain-drenched hair and mascara running down my face, I wouldn't have time to rush round and tidy the house before he arrived, and having to make the choice between redoing my make-up to his standards and keeping the house as he expected would mean that one way or another, he'd be annoyed.

I didn't want to admit to him that I'd been out with Lisa. I knew perfectly well his opinion on women who spent their days in cafés, talking and spending their husband's hard-earned money. He would think it frivolous, and on top of that, he'd be put out that I'd arranged a social meet without him. He would want to know why I hadn't invited both Lisa and Mike over for a formal dinner instead. Russell didn't have friends he socialised with without me and could never seem to understand why I might feel the need to have someone other than him to talk to. And a night of him in a black mood, giving me the silent treatment and glaring at me over his whisky, was the last thing I wanted to deal with right now.

I turned the corner into our road, wishing Lisa had been coming straight home so she could have dropped me back, rather than rushing off to pick up Mike from the train station.

The deep rumble of thunder built in the sky above me, and I broke into a run as I felt the first fat raindrop land heavily on my cheek. I yanked my keys from my handbag, rushing up the driveway and diving in through the front door just as the heavens opened and a sheet of rain came crashing down.

Kicking off my sandals and shoving them to the back of the cupboard under the stairs, I glanced in the hallway mirror, wiping the sheen of sweat from my forehead with the back of my hand. I flipped open my handbag, pulling out a tissue and blotting the smudges of make-up beneath my eyes, dragged a brush through my hair and spritzed perfume on my neck to mask the smell of fried food and coffee. Then, without pausing to take a breath, I rushed into the kitchen.

The breakfast things were still on the counter, and I jammed them into the dishwasher, spraying lemon-scented disinfectant on the work surface, sweeping crumbs into a pile and stirring the stew I'd had the foresight to throw in the slow cooker before heading out.

Russell's clean shirt was lying unironed on the table, and I glanced at it, knowing there was no time to do it now – not if I didn't want to have to come up with an excuse for why I'd left it until the end of the day to get on with. Instead, I jogged up the stairs with it, hanging it in the far side of his wardrobe between two thick jumpers, hoping the creases would drop out before he picked it up. If I was lucky, he'd gravitate towards something else tomorrow and I could get it done during the day.

I smoothed out the duvet cover and plumped the pillows, then ran down to the kitchen, grabbing a soft cloth to do the dusting.

Glancing at my watch, I took a shaky breath, finally allowing myself to relax as I moved through the downstairs rooms, wiping ornaments and surfaces. I'd made it without getting soaked, the house looked passable and dinner smelled delicious. I would never have to tell him I'd neglected my post and turned into one of those frivolous 'ladies who lunch' he had so much disdain for.

I pushed open the door to his study, making sure to shine up the brass handle and check for smears. The room was a shrine to his poor taste, I thought, looking at the expensive collection of furniture and art. A huge canvas hung on the wall opposite the window: the splat of brown acrylic paint was slightly off centre, a fact that irritated me daily. I knew he'd only bought it because it made him seem like he understood art. To me, it was clear he'd been swindled. I had no artistic talent whatsoever, yet I knew that given a pot of paint and a brush, I could have done better.

As usual, I tripped over the protruding leg of the ugly brushed-steel desk, a bespoke piece created by some up-and-coming designer in Edinburgh. It had cost close to £500 just to have the damn thing couriered down from Scotland, and I'd spent the whole three-week delay praying it would get lost in transit.

I swore under my breath, bending down to rub my shin, eyes watering. As I glanced under the desk, I caught sight of Russell's prized fountain pen lying on the rug, perhaps knocked off the desk by his wildly gesticulating hands whilst he was taking one of his oh-so-important Zoom calls. I reached across the carpet, closing my hand around the cool weight of it, then rose, moving more carefully around the desk this time, and slid his top drawer open, dropping the pen inside before I fully registered what I was seeing.

The room seemed to pulse around me, a dizzying nausea hitting me in the gut as I stood frozen, my eyes transfixed by the contents of my husband's top drawer.

Slowly, gingerly, I reached down, plucking the offending item up by the tips of my fingers, holding it up to see it fully.

'No,' I whispered, my heart racing as I stared at the pair of women's knickers. They were cream lace with dusky pink roses printed on them, and from a glance, I could tell they had been worn.

I stumbled back from the desk, the pants floating in a whisper to the carpet.

I wanted to stamp my foot over them, pretend I hadn't seen. Brush his mistake under the carpet so it couldn't hurt me, destroy my world.

There had been moments when I'd suspected he might have someone else. When he'd come home late, ignored my calls, been more stand-offish than usual. But then, I reasoned, I had bent over backwards to be the wife he wanted. I had done everything he asked of me, without argument or question.

Lisa often joked that the two of us were more suited to life in the fifties, preferring to stay home and take care of our husbands and homes than go out to work, but while that might have been true for her, the reality for me was that going out to work had never been an option. I had mused early on in our marriage about looking for a job, or even continuing my limited education and signing up to a college course. I hadn't known what I might like to do, but the idea of meeting people and learning something new had been appealing. But Russell had been adamant that it was the wrong path for me. He'd made it clear that he didn't want a wife who was out of the house all the time, not around for him at a moment's notice.

I'd been so in love with him back then that I hadn't questioned his decision, flattered by his convincing words, the picture he painted of coming home to me each night, calling home on his lunch break. He had made it seem like I was too valuable here to take on more responsibility. And I'd quietly let the idea of my own career drift away.

It was only years later, when I'd brought up the topic again, that I began to suspect that it wasn't love but a need for absolute control that made him so against the idea of my working. He hadn't been nearly so smooth during that conversation. He'd pointed out that nobody would hire me with no experience, no qualifications, and that he wasn't going to spend his hard-earned money on unnecessary courses just so he could come home to a distracted wife and a messy house.

It had been the first time in our relationship that I had felt that prickle of understanding, a sense of being trapped, a pet to be trained, not the equal partner I'd always believed myself to be, but I hadn't fought him. I'd agreed, kept the peace, tried to be the wife I'd promised him in the hope he would step up and keep his own promises too. I had been everything he'd asked of me, given him no reason for his head to turn. And somehow, I'd managed to convince myself that it was enough. That for once in my life, *I* was enough. But this... this shattered everything. It made a mockery of our marriage, flawed as it might have been. It didn't matter how much I gave, how much of myself I was willing to suppress in order to please him. With this evidence in front of me, I knew he would never be satisfied. How long had I been blind to what was happening? How dare he disrespect me, our marriage, after all I had done for him?

Clenching my teeth tightly together, I slammed the drawer closed, then scooped up the discarded pants and placed them front and centre on his desk. I wanted him to walk in here, smug and confident, and see them sitting there, taunting him. To be winded by the shock of their presence, just as I had been. Let him scramble for excuses then. Let him be the one having to defend himself for once, because there was no way he could avoid a show of humility now. Not with this evidence leaving no place for him to hide.

I looked up at the sound of his car on the driveway, the tyres turning through the deep puddles, the splash of torrential rain hitting its roof, and before I could back out, I strode into the living room, my heart racing. I wanted to scream, to confront him with the evidence of his betrayal, demand he explain his actions to me, but I took a breath, biding my time.

The door opened and he darted inside holding a newspaper over his head. He tossed it onto the clean tiles, kicked off his shoes and looked up at me. 'Bloody pissing it down out there. Ruined the suede on these,' he added, nodding towards the Versace loafers he'd bought on eBay, the tan now blotched and dark.

'I'm sure they'll be fine once they've dried out,' I said, laying out a sheet of newspaper to put beneath them, scrunching up balls of it to shove inside them.

I stood, and he bent forward, kissing my cheek as he always did, casting his appraising gaze over me, judging, looking for fault. I tried not to stiffen, though anger bubbled inside me as I stared into his eyes, trying to picture his lips on another woman's mouth. Had I even crossed his mind as he touched her? Did I matter to him at all? Despite our issues, there had never been another woman in our marriage, and as I looked at him now, I had to squash down a bubble of hatred I hadn't known I had inside me. I felt as if a locked box deep inside my heart had suddenly been blown wide open, and emotions I hadn't known I was capable of were threatening to spill out of me.

I bit down on my lip, closing my eyes for a brief moment, balling my hands into fists then releasing them with considerable effort.

'Drink?' I asked, heading for the bar before he had time to reply. The answer was always yes.

I poured him a whisky sour, adding fresh lemon juice, a spoonful of sugar and three ice cubes, exactly as he liked it.

'Just what the doctor ordered,' he said, striding towards me and taking the glass, drinking deeply.

'Did you have a good day?' My voice was calm, betraying none of the emotion pulsing through my veins. I looked into his eyes, feigning interest as I always did. He had a rudimentary job working in sales but liked to talk as if he were the CEO of a massive company, exaggerating the stresses and responsibilities he had to deal with as if it was his own business. He tried to make himself sound vital to its success, though the reality was he was utterly replaceable.

'Not bad. Julia from head office came in. There's going to be a big national conference next month. Think she wants me to go and represent our area.'

'Does she?' I asked, sure that he was talking rubbish. I doubted Julia had even spoken two words to him, but I knew I had to play into his story. It wasn't worth the trouble not to.

I tried to picture the women he saw on a daily basis in his office, wondering if it was one of them. Had I kissed her cheek at the last Christmas party? Had there been one who'd stood out? One who'd touched him a little too familiarly? I couldn't recall anything out of the ordinary happening, but maybe I'd had my blinkers on, determined not to see something I couldn't handle.

A sudden unpleasant thought came to mind that perhaps there was no conference – that he was preparing me for his absence so he could go and see *her*. Could he really be so calculating?

'It's a lot of stress for me, and I've already got so much on, but what can you do? I can hardly turn her down, can I?' he said, unable to hide his smug smile.

He turned towards his office door, and all my bravado evaporated. My stomach flipped and I felt panic race down my spine, fear making my palms turn liquid, though Russell didn't seem to notice the change – the way my breath seemed to come in harsh bursts, my heart pounding against my ribs.

'Get dinner served, Victoria,' he said – an order, not a request. 'I'm just going to go over a few numbers.'

'Wait!' My hands trembled as I put the tongs back in the ice bucket, and I leaned against the bar, trying to hide the fact.

He glanced over his shoulder, already gripping the polished brass handle. 'What?'

'I... I think a tile might have come off the roof in the storm. I heard a noise just before you got home. Can you check out the back?' I looked down at the ice, hoping he'd take the bait, knowing the thought of his show home being damaged by a leak would entice him into action.

'Fuck's sake, Victoria, why didn't you say earlier?' He didn't wait for a response as he pulled on his garden boots and a mac and strode outside into the downpour.

I moved without hesitation, rushing into his office, shoving the pants back into the top drawer, removing the evidence before he could find it. It had been a good plan – something I would fantasise about again and again in the midst of our future arguments, imagining the feeling of satisfaction that would have come at seeing his reaction. Having him plead and beg for my forgiveness, admit his faults for once. But I wasn't brave enough to see it through, wasn't ready for my world to fall apart. Not just yet. Not like this. He might not be the husband I'd hoped for; might not have given me the life I'd wanted – the life he'd promised we would share – but he was all I had. I was a childless woman in my forties. No career, no money of my own and no idea who I really was. As much as I longed to escape him, I wouldn't survive without him. He was my everything. And he knew it.

NINETEEN

A knock sounded at the front door for the second time in a row, and I walked ghost-like towards it, pulling it open and blinking against the bright sunlight. Mike stood on the step, a wide smile on his face.

'Vic, hi! I hope I'm not disturbing you?'

I shook my head. 'No, I wasn't busy,' I replied, trying to keep the shrill panic from my voice. The truth was, I'd been going through the photos from Russell's Christmas party on the computer, staring at each of the women's faces, zooming in close, wondering if *she* was the one. It had only been three days since I'd discovered the underwear in his office, and I was still reeling from the shock of it. It was only now, seeing Mike's face, that I realised I hadn't set foot outside since. Hadn't seen another person aside from Russell.

'Great,' Mike continued, glancing over his shoulder as if he was in a hurry. He smiled sheepishly. 'I'm actually after a favour.'

I nodded, distracted. 'Go on?'

'Thing is, I've booked for the whole family to have a weekend in London for Lisa's birthday – shopping and a show

tomorrow, then the museums on Sunday. Not my thing really' –
he grimaced – 'but it's Lisa's cup of tea, and you have to make
compromises, don't you? But as timing would have it, I've
currently got a kitchen full of saplings to take care of.'

'Excuse me?' I frowned, wondering what on earth he was on
about. I was still processing the fact that he was planning to take
Lisa away for the whole weekend, so not only would I miss cele-
brating her birthday with her, but I wouldn't get an opportunity
to confide in her about what I'd found. Not that I'd planned to
tell her outright about my discovery. I didn't want her thinking
my marriage was something to pity – that we were on rocky
ground or anything like that. I didn't want her to look at me like
I was somehow any less when I stayed with Russell despite
what I knew, because even now, I never questioned that I *would*
stay. The thought of walking out on him sent chills down my
spine. I couldn't do it. I didn't have the courage to be alone, start
again. And I wouldn't have Lisa looking at me like I was some
kind of doormat. A woman like her would never understand
where I was coming from. Even so, I had hoped to bring up the
topic of infidelity in a more general manner and gauge how she
might respond in my situation. I had never felt more alone than
I had in the past few days, and it hurt to hear she was going
away.

'Saplings,' Mike repeated. He flashed another grin, running
his hands through his already dishevelled hair.

I knew a weekend in London was far out of his comfort
zone. He was probably feeling stressed at everything that went
into organising it, hence his last-minute appearance at my door.

'All sorts really,' he was saying. 'The greenhouses we
usually rent space in have had a spate of incidents – vandalism,
you know? And these plants are expensive. They're for the
manor house. I don't want to risk them, but the weather's been
blistering this week, and two days without water is far from
ideal. I was hoping you could find it in your heart to pop in and

give them some love? I'd ask one of the lads that work for me, only Jim's wife has just had a baby, and Lewis is right over the other side of the county. Be a long drive for him. But if you're busy, I could ask him, I suppose...' He trailed off, looking dejected.

I shook my head, hoping my smile didn't appear as robotic as it felt on my face. 'Don't be silly. It's no trouble at all, and like I said, I'm not busy.'

'Vic, you're a star. Thank you. I'll pop the keys in before we go and leave the instructions on the side in the kitchen.' He kissed me on the cheek, then dashed back in the direction of his own house.

I watched him go, then slowly turned, closing the door and heading back to the computer to try and figure out what my husband had been doing behind my back.

It was strange being in Lisa's kitchen without the sound of chatter, the clink of glasses, her cooking or throwing together a few salads in the colourful glass bowls she loved to use at barbecues. I had rarely been here without Russell in tow, and it was liberating to be able to look around without worrying about my posture, my hair being out of place, all the little details he would notice and make comment on whenever we went anywhere.

Mike had popped the keys in to me on his way out last night, and I had seen Lisa and the kids already in the back of a taxi, too distracted to even wave to me. It irritated me somehow that they hadn't made the effort to say goodbye, though Mike had been grateful he'd found someone to help at such short notice.

He hadn't been exaggerating when he said the kitchen was full of saplings. Every single surface was covered in plastic seed trays, tiny green shoots poking their heads above the rich brown soil, promising to become something special if only they got the right nurturing in this fragile early stage of their existence. The table, usually strewn with Holly's magazines and Jack's books, looked like it belonged in a garden centre, and I felt suddenly worried I had made a mistake in agreeing to take responsibility for them. There had to be a thousand pounds' worth of plants in here.

Mike had pinned a care sheet to the fridge, and I scanned it, trying to identify which plants needed plain water, which needed the extra feed he'd helpfully left out on the draining board and which I was to leave alone. Thankfully, to my surprise, it seemed that when it came to plants, Mike was perfectly capable of leaving concise and clear instructions. He was good at what he did, and reading through the neat page of information, I felt myself relax, confident that if I worked through the list step by step and double-checked the carefully written labels on each plant, I wouldn't mess up my task.

I moved methodically around the room, tray to tray, enjoying the ritual, the smell of the compost as the water trickled onto it. There was something hugely appealing in knowing I was helping these tiny plants to thrive. And at the very least, it got me out of the house and away from the computer, from the nagging suspicion and anger that had consumed me for the past few days.

The pretence I'd had to keep up for Russell's benefit had been exhausting. To smile and serve him dinner each night. To have him reach across the bed for me and pull me into his arms, his body pressing hard into mine as he rolled me onto my back, knowing he'd betrayed me, and not show the rage and humiliation swirling inside my belly was draining beyond measure. Leaving him in front of the rugby to come here, making sure he had a cold beer and the sports pages open on his lap, had felt like a weight had been lifted. I didn't have to smile and nod and feign interest in his latest piece of insightful advice or laugh at an anecdote he'd told a thousand times before. For a few precious minutes, I could just *be*.

I glanced around the kitchen and realised with a rush of disappointment that I was already finished. It had only taken ten minutes, and I wasn't ready to go back yet. I wondered if I could get away with making myself a coffee. Sit in the chair by the back window and look out over the garden, watch the birds for half an hour without the uneasy awareness that Russell might shout my name at any moment and I'd have to go and play the dutiful wife again. I didn't see what harm it could do; besides, it wasn't like anyone would ever know. And if I dragged it out today, Russell would expect the same when I came here tomorrow.

I smiled to myself, wondering what Lisa did during her long days alone here while Mike was at work and the kids were out. I could picture her pulling the peacock chair into the spot of sunshine by the back door. The way she might curl her legs under her and lean into the cushions, a strong coffee and a home-made biscuit placed on the sideboard within arm's reach. It was nice to imagine her like that.

Making up my mind, I filled the kettle, then pulled open the cupboard I knew Lisa kept the coffee in, and gave a sudden yell as a jar that had been balanced on the edge and relying on the door to stay put lurched forward. I made a grab for it and missed. There was the sound of shattering glass, and then the smell of strawberry jam filled the air.

'Shit,' I muttered, seeing my relaxing cup of coffee in the sun go up in smoke. By the time I'd cleared this mess up, I'd have to get back to Russell.

Sighing, I picked up the bigger pieces of glass, dropping them on the worktop, then took the cloth from the sink, rinsing and reusing it over and over again, wiping up the sticky clumps of jam. When I'd finished, I opened the washing machine to throw the cloth inside, not wanting Lisa to use it by mistake when she returned.

I swung the door closed and straightened up – then froze.

My heart was beating fast, a gasp sticking in my throat, my mind racing to catch up. I felt like I'd been slapped hard across the face without ever seeing my attacker approach.

Slowly, not daring to release the breath that was trapped inside my lungs, I lowered myself to my haunches, opening the washing-machine door once more and reaching a hand inside. It had registered immediately, though it had taken a few seconds to work out why I was so unsettled. That familiar fabric. Cream lace. The dusky pink rose print. It was the matching bra to the pants I had found in Russell's desk drawer. I pulled it out, slumping to the floor, my mind whirling with unanswered questions.

Was it a coincidence? What were the chances of something like that? Of Lisa just happening to own a bra that was the perfect match for the knickers squirrelled away in Russell's drawer? I felt bile rise in my throat at the sudden image that came to my mind. Lisa and Russell. Naked. Laughing. Going behind my back without caring what it would do to me, how it would break me. It had been terrible enough when it was just him, but her? *Lisa?* It couldn't be true, could it?

Was it really possible that she had done this to me?

I could see the attraction from Russell's point of view. Lisa was gorgeous. Funny, clever, the perfect wife – on paper at least. He had always coveted what Mike had, trying to impress him with grandiose stories about his successes. He'd paraded me round like a trophy, but was it possible that while he was choosing my clothes and leading me into conversations about his latest triumphs, he was secretly trying to chip his way between Mike and Lisa, claiming her for himself? I wished I could pretend I didn't think he would do that to me, but I knew he would stop at nothing to get what he wanted. But *Lisa?* Why would she choose Russell when she had a husband as incredible as Mike? Would she really have betrayed him for a man like Russell? Could he have charmed her away from all she was blessed with, to slum it with him? It was hard to imagine, but then, perhaps she didn't realise how lucky she was. How a woman like me would give anything to walk in her shoes.

I jumped to my feet with sudden determination, knowing what I had to do. If I could find a matching pair of pants in the house, then it might all be okay. It could be just a terrible coincidence. I *had* to find them.

Gripping the bra in my fist, I was just about to head up to her bedroom, search her drawers, when I heard the sound of a key in the front door. All at once, it opened, accompanied by Mike's voice as footsteps thundered in, someone running fast up the stairs. Panicked, I threw the bra back into the wash and spun around just in time to see Lisa, Mike and Jack coming into the kitchen.

'Oh, Vic, hi, thanks for doing all this,' Mike said, dropping his bag on the kitchen floor. I looked past him to Lisa, needing to see her face, feeling sure I could read the answer in her eyes now that I knew the question. She looked pale, a sheen of sweat coating her forehead.

'I thought you weren't coming back until tomorrow night?' I said, hearing the tremor in my voice.

'That was the plan,' Mike replied. 'But clever old me decided to buy noodles for everyone at the train station, and we all got food poisoning. Holly hasn't stopped vomiting, and Lisa…' He placed a hand on her shoulder, looking contrite.

She shrugged him off, shaking her head. 'Sorry, Vic. I have to—'

She broke off, her hand pressed to her mouth as she turned, running upstairs. I heard her footsteps in the bedroom above, then the door to her en suite slam shut.

Jack sat down at the table, looking deflated. He was pale but didn't look as ill as Lisa. 'Yep. It's got us all. And let me tell you, a hotel is *not* the place to be when you're throwing your guts up. All you want is your own bed. I don't think it's contagious, but you should probably make your exit before you see something you really don't want to witness,' he added with a grimace as he pressed a hand to his gurgling belly.

Mike shook his head. 'I can't believe after all the planning that went into this weekend, I managed to mess it up before we even made it to the theatre.'

Jack shrugged. 'That's life, right? Can't always go to plan. And we can go back another time. But next time, *I'm* in charge of where we stop to eat.'

'You're on.'

I stood awkwardly beside the washing machine, feeling like an intruder but desperately wanting to stay, to find the answers I needed. I wondered if I could make an excuse to go up and help Lisa, offer to find her some fresh clothes and surreptitiously look through her drawers, but I knew it would never work. I felt lost and confused and completely blindsided by what I had discovered.

'I'll get out of your way then. Let me know if you need anything.'

I handed Mike his keys, then picked up my bag and headed for the front door, my mind spinning, realising that a woman I'd thought I could trust wasn't really my friend at all.

TWENTY

LISA

Now

'I just don't see how we can go, Mike,' I said, turning to make the bed as he stood watching me from the doorway. 'It's not the time to be heading off on holiday – not with everything that's going on. I'm not even sure I'm allowed to. What would the police say about me disappearing when I'm still on bail?'

'Oh, don't be silly, of course you're allowed,' he said, stepping forward, his face animated. 'It's not like you're fleeing the country, Pixie!' He grinned, using the nickname he'd given me on our first date, when he told me my big hazel-green eyes, cropped dark hair and petite frame made him feel like he'd gone out to eat with a woodland sprite. 'It's Norfolk, for Pete's sake. Two nights. We'll be back here before you're even missed!'

I frowned, wondering if he was thinking the same as me. That if they came for me again, this might be our last chance to spend some time together before our lives were snatched from beneath us.

I shook my head, feeling conflicted. I couldn't deny that for

once, the idea of heading into the wilderness with my adventurous husband and teenage children was more appealing than
staying here, surrounded by my home comforts. Mike had
planned the trip weeks ago – two nights of wild camping on the
blustery Norfolk coast, the days spent bouldering, hiking the
Broads, and sea swimming, and the evenings cooking over a tiny
gas stove, drinking wine out of metal mugs beneath a velvety
sky. When he'd first told me the plan, I'd been filled with dread
at the idea of enduring outdoor living with not so much as a
toilet to call my own, wondering if I could convince him to book
us into a hotel instead. But now, the idea of getting away from
everyone and everything was undeniably tempting. To disap-
pear into the wild would offer a sense of freedom I hadn't felt
for quite some time.

'I don't know, Mike. What would it look like to people? And
what about Victoria? She'll be all alone.'

He shook his head as if he couldn't grasp how that was rele-
vant. 'I'm sure she doesn't want us crowding her,' he said. 'She'll
want her family around her at a time like this. Her real friends,
not some nosy neighbours.'

I chewed my lip. 'I don't know. She's been hanging around a
lot lately – even before Russell died. I think she relies on our
friendship more than she lets on.'

'I think you're worrying too much, love. She's going through
a shit time, but that isn't our responsibility to take on. And we've
been through a fairly tough time ourselves this past week,
haven't we? Getting caught up in all that. Bloody incompetent
police. And they haven't even found our car yet. Don't know
what they think they're doing...'

His sentence trailed off, and I noticed the tension in his
shoulders, the ridge between his brows. He turned to the
window, looking outside and I could see how desperate he was
to escape these four walls. My carefree, happy-go-lucky

husband was clearly under a lot of stress, and I was to blame. It had to have been a nightmare for him to watch me be taken away like that.

He turned back to me, forcing a smile to his lips, focusing on the positive as usual. 'Don't you deserve a break?'

I shrugged, though I could feel my resolve weakening.

His eyes sparkled, and I knew he could tell I was on the verge of giving in. 'The kids would be really disappointed if we couldn't go. Holly won't want to camp without you, and Jack wanted to show you this really cool cove we found last time. They need this too, Pixie.'

And there it was. My weak spot. Holly would be turning eighteen next summer. I had been living with Mike, preparing for our wedding, at the same age, though I couldn't imagine Holly following the same path as me. She was young for her age, a fact that I made no attempt to change. I would have kept her – my precious firstborn – as a little girl for ever if I could. I hated the idea that one day, and probably not too far in the future, I would have to let her go. And Jack, at just fifteen, was already so grown up. It made me smile to see how like his dad he was. He had Mike's easy smile, his quick sense of humour, and any attempt I had made to baby *him* had been shrugged off ever since he hit puberty. He was far too cool to want cuddles from Mummy these days, and as much as I pretended I didn't mind, it hurt to see how easy he had found it to cut those apron strings. He might not need me the same way he had a decade ago, but I still needed him. Needed these moments together, quality time that I couldn't take for granted. How many opportunities did I have left before they were too busy for trips with Mum and Dad?

Mike's smile widened, and I felt my own face melt.

'You're a nightmare,' I said, laughing despite myself. 'How can I say no now?'

'You can't!' He grinned, pulling me into a hug. 'Now get packing. I'll dig out the tents. I want to be on the road in an hour.'

TWENTY-ONE
VICTORIA

I stared in disbelief through the gap in my bedroom curtains as Mike loaded tents and bags into the back of his Land Rover. On the driveway, Lisa was attempting to fold a massive blue tarpaulin, struggling to keep it together as the wind caught it. Jack strutted out of the front door, sunglasses perched on his head, his well-worn walking boots tied, looking ready for adventure, a younger version of his father. He grinned and said something that made Lisa lose her grip on the tarp, and she broke into a tinkling laugh I could hear from across the street. My stomach sank as I watched their easy banter, the way Jack dropped his bag and immediately stepped in to help Lisa. How easy life must be for her, with a husband and two children to pick up the slack. To help without her even needing to say a word. She had the perfect family – the life I'd envied so much my skin crawled with sheer wanting – and yet she'd risked it all, and for what?

Jack took the folded blue sheet from his mother's arms, tossing it into the car with a grin. I couldn't believe it. They were going away on a camping holiday now of all times, when my world was falling apart, when I needed them here. How could they even think of leaving with everything that was going on? Did they have no respect? Did Lisa not feel like she needed to be here for me, to support me in the wake of Russell's death?

I watched Mike load the final bags into the monster of a vehicle, sure that Lisa would cross the road and knock on my door to offer her excuses and check I was okay. Ask when the funeral would be, at the very least. She had to be back by then, surely? I would have to smile and pretend it was fine that her life was carrying on whilst mine was frozen, stuck in limbo. I would tell her I didn't mind. That I hoped she had fun. That of course I understood – she'd had a harrowing week after all. I was good at hiding my hurt from the people I cared about.

I wondered if she was crying herself to sleep at night over him. If she spent every waking moment pretending nothing had changed, all the while wishing she could follow him to the grave. I saw her smile at Mike and felt confusion swell in my belly, a desperate need for answers Russell could no longer provide.

She glanced up towards my window, and I stepped back, not wanting her to see me watching. I took a breath, smoothing my skirt over my hips as I checked my reflection in the full-length mirror, waiting for the sound of the doorbell. A moment later, the roar of the Land Rover engine sounded, and I leaped forward, yanking the nets aside, my mouth dropping open in stunned silence as I watched them drive away. She hadn't come. Didn't even care enough to offer an apology for their poorly timed holiday. To pretend she cared about me as much as I always had for her.

Was it guilt that had stopped her from checking on me? Or did I just matter so little to them that I didn't even feature in their plans? I had expected so much more – from all of them. If the tables were turned, I would have been there every moment I could to support Lisa through her grief. I had pictured her coming over with casseroles, stews, comfort food cooked especially for me. When Mike had initially offered on her behalf, I'd done the demure thing and told him not to trouble her, that I was fine, but I hadn't expected that she would take me at my word. I thought she would come anyway. That she would feel she owed me that much. I had imagined her hugging me tight, being the friend I needed her to be. I would have done it for her. But then, I'd never have betrayed her the way she'd betrayed me.

I stared at the empty space where their car had been, anger and hurt chasing through my veins, feeling alone and completely abandoned. I didn't know how long I stood there, blindly staring at the empty house, but slowly, an idea began to simmer in the depths of my mind, and before I could fully grasp it, I could already feel myself moving.

My heart raced and I swallowed against the thick ball of fear in the back of my throat as I walked purposefully down the stairs, slipping my feet into black ballet pumps and walking out of my front door without pausing to question what I was doing.

I dashed across the road and up Lisa's driveway, making my way past the garage to the wooden gate leading to the back garden. It was locked, but I stepped onto the edge of a blue ceramic plant pot, reaching over the top of the gate and sliding the bolt back – something I'd done more than once before.

I slipped through the open gate, pushing it closed behind me, then walked across the lawn to the shed. The door was ajar as usual, and I pulled it wide, eyes searching the gloomy interior for what I needed. The shelves were stacked with old rope, paint tins and jars of batteries waiting to be recycled, while a large petrol lawnmower took up the majority of the floor space. I cast my gaze up high and felt my breath catch. Bingo! There on the top shelf was what I'd hoped to find. An old-fashioned sweet tin, small enough to fit in the palm of a man's hand.

I reached for it, recoiling as my fingers sank into a thick layer of grime, before grabbing it firmly, a cloud of dust making me cough as I pulled it down. I placed it on the lowest shelf, wiping my fingers on my dark blue skirt, not caring about the mess I made. The metal lid was slightly rusted, and I wiggled it back and forth, easing it off, breaking into a smile as I saw what I'd been hoping for. A solitary key. I didn't think Mike had noticed me watching when he'd put it there two summers before, but I'd seen. Heard him in the kitchen as I sat outside beneath the open window, complaining to Lisa about having been locked out after losing his keys on a hike. Listened as she'd told him to keep one in the shed for next time.

I had sipped my white wine, feigning interest as Russell imparted his wisdom to Jack on the best way to barbecue a steak, but my gaze had followed Mike as he'd strode across the garden, dropping something with a metallic chink into the old sweet tin as he walked and shoving it inside the neglected shed, before cracking some joke about an upcoming football match. From the rust and dust that had accumulated on the tin, he'd long since forgotten it was here. But *I* hadn't.

I tipped the key into my palm and squeezed it tightly. Glancing over my shoulder towards the house, I felt my mouth go dry at what I was about to do, but I wouldn't let fear stand in my way now. This was an opportunity I couldn't waste.

I sucked in a deep breath and squared my shoulders. The key was rectangular and short, not at all like the one I'd seen Lisa use for the front door, so I took a chance and tried the back door instead, tensing as I turned it in the lock, half expecting an alarm to sound, though I didn't think they had one installed.

It clicked, quietly and easily, and I gripped the handle, pushing the door open and stepping into the cool silence of the kitchen. It was immaculate, not a dish left in the sink or a thing out of place. Lisa never seemed to stop tidying lately, and I wondered if it was a distraction – to keep her mind off the arrest, that night in a cell she still wouldn't open up about. And to stop her from showing her feelings over the death of *my* husband.

I closed my eyes, a flash of guilt sparking somewhere inside me as I thought of her in that cell. Wondered if it had been my mention of her conveniently missing car that had planted the seed in Detective McCormac's mind when he'd called four days after Russell's death to tell me they had no new information for me just yet. I hadn't meant anything by it, not really, and yet a part of me wondered if anger had made me say it.

When I closed my eyes to picture Russell now, the image was always invaded by *her*. Her smile. Her laugh. The way she moved, her petite frame shimmying across the room, a plate of her home-made canapés balanced on one hand. The way he had looked up and grinned, held out his hand for one, made some inane joke. Every memory I had now was distorted by her. Was it fair that she got to continue her life without facing the consequences of her actions? Did she think that now that Russell was dead, the secrets the two of them had kept would go to the grave with him?

I pictured the way Mike had smiled, a protective, loving expression on his handsome face as he watched her on the driveway just now. Didn't he deserve better than to be deceived by a woman who had lied, who had betrayed their marriage vows in pursuit of her own reckless pleasure? If the tables were turned, wouldn't I want Mike to share what he knew with me?

I slipped my feet out of my shoes, leaving them on the mat by the door, padding barefoot through the house and up the carpeted stairs to Lisa and Mike's room. Their door was open, as if she was a woman with nothing to hide, and I walked into the room, taking in the pale green bedspread, the brass lamps on the bedside tables, the smell of cocoa butter and Mike's deodorant still lingering in the air.

I walked over to Lisa's dressing table, lowering myself onto the cushioned stool and sliding open the top drawer. Now that I was here, I realised there was a complete absence of guilt on my part. Why *shouldn't* I search through her things after what she'd done to me? Why shouldn't I look for the evidence I knew she must have in her possession so that I could present it to her husband, save him from wasting his life with a woman who clearly didn't value him? She didn't deserve him as her husband; it was only fair that he be given the whole picture. I had been lucky to find her underwear when I had. It had given me clarity, made me see Russell for what he really was – a cheat, a man who cared so little for our marriage vows he would choose *her* over me. But Mike would never believe it. Not unless I gave him something irrefutable. Photos. Notes. Videos even.

I couldn't deny, part of what fuelled me now was my own hunger to see these things too. To wallow in the depths of their betrayal, see what they had meant to each other, feel the pain so deeply it justified my actions. They had driven me to this. It was all their fault.

The first drawer in the dresser was full of Mike's balled-up socks, and I pushed it closed, turning to the other side, sliding them open one by one. Lisa's underwear was in the second drawer down, neat stacks of bras one side, a mound of knickers the other. My eyes were drawn immediately to the creamy rose-patterned bra, slotted between a turquoise satin balconette and a purple cotton T-shirt bra. I felt my chest tighten at the sight of it, a thousand awful emotions boiling up to the surface.

I slammed the drawer closed, opening another, looking for a diary, a hidden phone, *something*, but as I sifted through each one, I felt my breath growing unsteady in my frustration, my efforts to move meticulously, leave no trace of my meddling, fast becoming more erratic as I rifled fruitlessly. I stood, going to her wardrobe, flinging back the door with such force I froze, worried the hinge would break. When it didn't, I fell to my knees, pulling out shoeboxes, old handbags, emptying their contents onto the carpet, letting out a cry of disbelief when still I came up empty-handed. There had to be something here. Something solid, irrefutable, that would give me the evidence I needed to prove to Mike what kind of a woman he was married to. A memento of Russell's, some trinket he'd gifted her, sealed in a love note.

I moved to her bedside table, sliding open the drawer. My hands shook as I searched through the contents, finding dog-eared novels, a pile of drawings Holly had given her of horses and other cutesy animals.

I flipped up the lid of her jewellery box, my fingers moving through stacks of bracelets, a little pot overflowing with earrings, all jumbled in together. A ring box, which, when I pushed it open, had an old-fashioned gold band with a missing stone nestled inside it. My fingers ran along the velvet edges of the jewellery box, hoping to find some secret compartment that might lead me to the truth, but it was frustratingly simple and I slammed the lid closed, letting out a scream of frustration. There was nothing here. Nothing!

I sucked in a breath, feeling the room sway and distort around me.

The house seemed to pulse, the silence heavy and unsettling, and I spun in a slow circle, looking around at the walls, lifting the pillows, sliding my hand beneath the mattress, my fingers searching fruitlessly. It made no sense. None at all. I *knew* she had done this to me. I had *seen* the two of them with my own eyes.

Finding that bra had brought a whole host of unwelcome questions to mind, but for those first days that followed, I had held on to a shred of hope that I was somehow mistaken. That it could all be explained away. And I had wanted that so badly. I *wanted* to be wrong, though my gut had screamed at me that of course he would want her. Of course I should have expected this of him. I would have done anything to make it not true, but

I couldn't force myself to believe the lie. I had too much self-respect for that, despite how little the two of them clearly thought of me.

Now I wanted Lisa to feel the pain I felt.

I shook my head, staring at the marital bed she'd betrayed, the memory of a bright pink sundress, a scene witnessed in broad daylight as I hid like a criminal, forcing its way to the forefront of my mind, the moment I had known my suspicions were true. It had always been her. She had risked my marriage, our friendship, the bond our families shared, to go behind my back with him, and it was unforgivable.

Hurt and anger formed an acrid potion in the very depths of my heart. I didn't know how to release it, how to cope with the pain of losing them both.

I lowered myself down to sit on the side of the bed, my fingers roaming over Mike's pillowcase, my mind racing. There was a photograph of him and Lisa on his bedside cabinet, both dressed in raincoats and walking boots, a view of damp green fields blurring in the background.

I ran my thumb over the glass frame, then pressed it over Lisa's face, blocking her from view, my eyes seeking out Mike's. I hadn't got what I'd come for today, but perhaps the time had come to share what I knew with DS McCormac. One way or another, Lisa deserved retribution for her choices. Actions *always* had consequences. Karma would seek you out in the end. Russell had found that out for himself. And now, it was time for Lisa to pay too.

I ignored the twinge of guilt, the knowledge that she might not have been at the wheel that night, that I had no proof to say she had killed my husband. There was more than one way to destroy a life, and she had taken mine. She would have to live with whatever came next.

TWENTY-TWO

LISA

The howling wind was biting against my cheeks, and I pulled my raincoat tighter around myself, wondering where summer had gone. We seemed to have left it back down south. Amongst the scrubby grass behind me, Mike and Jack were wrestling with the tents, yelling jovially above the shrill whistle of the gale. The second we'd arrived, Holly had volunteered to walk back to the shop we'd passed in the village to buy something for dinner, quietly declining my offer to go with her. I hadn't argued.

She'd returned forty minutes later and immediately taken herself off to a chunk of driftwood halfway up the beach, sitting silently absorbed in her book, though when I glanced at her now and then and saw her glassy expression and tense shoulders, I felt sure she wasn't actually reading it.

I cracked open a bottle of beer from the cool box I'd packed in haste, and wandered down the sand to sit and watch the waves crash in. The beach was deserted, save for a family a few hundred yards in the distance, their pair of kites tangling and crashing to the ground. The shouts of the little children sounded jarring somehow – too happy for such a bleak outlook.

A half-eaten ice-cream cone lay abandoned on the sand ahead of me, and I watched as a seagull circled it then landed, giving a cry that alerted several others to come and investigate. I watched, frowning as the cone was surrounded, the original gull chased off and attacked, though he'd yet to take his share. He screeched and dived at the intruders, trying to defend his territory, but it was clear that he was outnumbered, his lunch forfeited to the stronger birds.

Why do they do that? I wondered. Why call in the others, tell them what you've found when you know they'll take it for themselves? Why not keep it secret? There's value in silence.

The birds continued to caw and screech, and I longed for them to leave. I looked over at my daughter, still staring blindly at the pages of her book, and sighed.

TWENTY-THREE

The dread I'd managed to suppress during our short stay in Norfolk grew stronger and stronger as Mike drove through familiar roads, heading back home. The nights spent in a wind-blown tent, shivering on a thin ground sheet with a lumpy sleeping bag for warmth, had been far from my idea of a decent holiday, but there had been no fear of police knocking on the tent flap demanding I explain myself. Just having Mike and the kids close by, that sense of being off grid, had made the back-ache and the one-pot meals cooked over the camping stove worth it. But now, that escape was coming to an end. I was heading back to reality, and I had no idea what that might mean.

Mike had talked non-stop on the first few hours of the drive home, but when we'd seen the first signs for Kent, his anxious chatter had faded away and we'd all grown silent, lost in our own thoughts.

I cast a glance across to him, noting his firm grip on the wheel, the set of his jaw, and realised that he too had no idea what we were returning to. Had it been reckless to just disap-pear without informing the police of our plans? Would they re-arrest me for breaking some rule I hadn't been aware of? Or maybe they'd have produced some more evidence of my supposed involvement in Russell's death. The thought of going back to that police station, of sitting in the artificial light of the interview room to be grilled again and again, of having to maintain that same strength I'd managed to find that first awful time, was beyond thinking about. There was only so far I could be pushed before I would break.

Mike turned the Land Rover into our road, and I caught Holly's eye in the mirror in my sun visor. She looked pale, her cheeks pinched, her small frame thinner than ever, and I decided to make paella, her favourite dinner, to entice her into finishing a plate for once. If we weren't careful, we would lose control of the situation. I knew how easy it would be for my sweet, sensitive girl to fall prey to the clutches of an eating disorder, and I would not let it happen. I wouldn't allow her to endure that.

My stomach turned cold as Mike pulled into the driveway and I saw Victoria leaning into the boot of Russell's silver Audi coupé on her drive. I watched in the mirror as she straightened up, willing her to go back inside, but instead she waved, then crossed the road. I sighed internally and pasted on a smile that made my cheeks feel tight and unnatural as I clambered out of the passenger seat.

'Hi, Lisa,' she said, stopping in front of me with a pinched smile. She looked tired, dark circles only partially hidden beneath her make-up, her collarbone jutting out above her spotless white fitted shirt. 'Been away?' she asked, and I nodded, feeling like I'd been caught breaking the rules.

'Just a couple of nights camping. Mike organised it. Needed the fresh air,' I added.

She nodded, her eyes narrowing as if she wanted to say something, but I was saved by Mike and Jack coming round the car. Holly, I noticed, was still in the back, her head bent low over her book, in no rush to get out.

'Vic, hi,' Mike said, leaning in to kiss her cheek. He stood back, and I watched Victoria's expression soften.

'I hear you've been off on another adventure,' she said, smiling more warmly now.

'Just a short one. How are you?' Mike asked, reaching forward to squeeze her shoulder.

'Bearing up. You know.' She shrugged, and Jack opened the boot, clearly uncomfortable with the direction the conversation was taking. Ordinarily he was the person you would want around in this situation, offering the perfect combination of a listening ear and insightful advice. But in these circumstances, I knew he felt torn between comforting Victoria and potentially upsetting me by bringing up the topic of Russell. He wouldn't want to remind me of my ordeal – not that it was ever far from my mind.

'Had a nice time away, Jack?' Victoria asked. She waited, smiling, for him to stop what he was doing and look her way, but I noticed a coolness in his expression that confused me. It wasn't like him to be rude, or to miss an opportunity to talk about his latest adventures, and as far as I had seen, he'd enjoyed the trip.

'Yeah, it was all right,' he replied, not quite meeting her eye. 'You going to give me a hand with the bags then, Dad?' he said over his shoulder, lugging a tent into his arms and staggering towards the house.

'Bloody cheeky bugger,' Mike muttered with a grin. 'Carries one tent and thinks he's a hero. Coming, son!' he called jovially, nodding politely at Victoria. He heaved a bag and the cool box from the boot and followed Jack.

Victoria watched them head into the garage, then turned and rapped on the back window, startling Holly. 'Not getting out, Hols?'

I bit my lower lip, wanting to tell Holly she didn't have to but not wanting to be rude to Victoria. Holly closed her book and stepped out onto the driveway. She made an effort to smile, though I noticed it didn't reach her eyes. I felt a sudden intense urge to wrap her in a hug and take care of her. I hated that she seemed to be slipping away from me, and longed for the simplicity of her childhood years when I'd been able to protect her from all the world had to throw at her. I remembered only too well how hard it was being her age.

'Hi, Auntie Vic,' she said, her eyes darting back and forth from Victoria's face to the paved driveway beneath her feet. 'You all right?'

Victoria raised an eyebrow without replying, then addressed us both. 'I just wanted to let you know about Russell's funeral. It's all sorted for Wednesday morning. Nothing too formal, but we'll stick to traditional black – it's what he would have wanted. I have a few dresses that might suit you if you need to borrow something?' she offered, looking at me expectantly.

'Oh, I—' I broke off, looking behind me, hoping Mike would come back and save me from having to respond. There was no sign of him, and I bit my lip, feeling uncomfortable. 'I'm so sorry, Vic, but I don't think it's a good idea that I come, given the circumstances. What would people think, me turning up after all that business with the police?'

'What do you mean?' She frowned, folding her arms tightly across her narrow chest. 'Of course you'll be there. Nobody thinks for a second that you had anything to do with it. Besides, nobody needs to know what went on, do they?' She formed her mouth into a smile that didn't meet her eyes, making her look like a strange ventriloquist's dummy, cold and unnerving.

I shook my head. 'These things have a habit of finding their way into public knowledge. I would hate to think I'd made a spectacle and taken the attention off Russell. People are there to say their goodbyes – my coming would just cause drama. And the police might have more they want to ask me. I told you, I'm just on bail. They haven't said it's over yet. I don't know what they're going to do next,' I admitted.

I couldn't help but wonder why she was so confident I'd been caught up in a misunderstanding. If it had been *my* husband who'd died, my friend who'd been accused, I wasn't sure I would be so understanding, but Victoria had given no indication that she'd had even a moment of doubt. I was grateful that she wasn't on the attack, but still, something about her apparent blind faith when it came to my innocence was unsettling.

I shook my head. 'It's not right for me to be there at the moment, Vic. I'm sorry.'

She stared at me as if considering her words carefully, and I braced myself for an argument, but instead she turned to Holly. 'You'll be there though – to support me.' She let her words hang in the air, and I saw Holly's discomfort at having been put on the spot.

'Where's that?' Jack said, catching the tail end of the conversation as he and Mike emerged to collect the next load of baggage.

'Russell's funeral,' Victoria replied, bowing her head demurely. 'I was just telling Holly I hoped she would make it.'

'Course she will. We'll all be there to give him a decent send-off, won't we, Hols?' Mike said, slinging his arm round Holly's shoulders.

I flashed him a warning glare, and he paused, as if realising I might object. His brow puckered and I shook my head ever so slightly, willing him to shut up.

Seeming to realise he'd put his foot in it somehow, he changed tack awkwardly. 'I still can't believe he's gone.'

'Neither can I,' Victoria said softly. 'I keep expecting him to come through the front door.' She stared at Holly, her eyes clear and intense as she stepped forward to pat her arm. 'I'm glad you'll be there, Holly. I'm sure Russell would have wanted that.'

Holly swallowed and gave a nod. 'Of... of course,' she muttered, stepping back and breaking contact.

I wanted to dive between them, shield my baby girl from the horrible situation, but instead, I stood uselessly by and did nothing.

Victoria turned to me with a shy, sad expression on her face that I couldn't help thinking was for the benefit of Mike and Jack, who had returned to their task of unloading the car.

'See,' she said softly. 'Everyone will be there. I hope you'll change your mind and come too, Lisa. I need you there.'

She turned without waiting for a reply, crossed the road and disappeared back inside her house. It was only then I realised I was shaking.

TWENTY-FOUR

I sat on the side of the bed, still wearing my pyjamas, casting glances in the dressing-table mirror as, behind me, Mike dressed hastily for the funeral. He'd left the house at 5 a.m., and I had lain stiff and silent, pretending to be asleep as he'd crept out of the door. I hadn't dared to breathe until I heard the roar of his car engine starting, the sound fading as he drove off down the road.

Climbing out of bed, I had wandered barefoot downstairs, smiling when I saw the open door to the cupboard beneath the stairs where he kept his fishing gear. When he'd told me last night that Tony, one of the new gardeners he'd employed, had invited him out this morning, I'd nodded, murmured my agreement, neglected to remind him of the date. I'd hoped he would lose all sense of time out on the riverbank. That the lure of a good bite and beautiful scenery would steal his attention so completely he would forget all about the funeral taking place this morning.

It would have made everything so much simpler, but to my frustration, I'd heard him pull onto the driveway with twenty minutes to spare, jogging up the stairs and banging on Holly and Jack's bedroom doors with a shout to suit up, all the while stripping off his own clothes and leaving them in a heap at the top of the stairs. He'd plucked a suit from the back of his wardrobe, thrown it on, spritzing some aftershave on his tanned neck, and somehow managed to look like a younger, more rugged version of Brad Pitt on the red carpet at the Oscars – and with time to spare. Despite the tension I'd been feeling all week, I couldn't ignore how bloody gorgeous my husband was, nor fail to be just a little bit put out at how easy it was for him. He hadn't even bothered to shave.

His eyes met mine in the mirror. 'Come on, Pixie,' he said, raising his eyebrows hopefully. 'I know we'll be late, but we can wait a few minutes for you to throw on a dress and some shoes. Victoria doesn't care about all this nonsense with the police. She wants you there.'

He leaned over the bed to pick up the tie he'd laid over the pillow, frowning in concentration as he knotted it like a noose around his throat. 'Jack's missing a morning of school so he can be there. Can't you just—'

'No.' I shook my head. 'I'm sorry, but I can't face it. It would be a spectacle, and that's the last thing Victoria needs right now.'

I glanced at the alarm clock on the dressing table. 'You're going to be late.'

He groaned. 'Damn...' He slipped his wallet into his pocket and pursed his lips thoughtfully. 'You're absolutely sure you won't come?'

'Sure.'

'I'll send your best wishes then.'

He darted around the bed, kissing me full on the mouth, his body buzzing with energy as per usual. 'I need to make a quick snack before I go though. I'm bloody starving. Tony ate all the rolls before I got there. Hols, hurry up, will ya?' he called as he dashed out of the bedroom.

I let myself smile, noting that he'd spoken without a trace of resentment. He had always been like that. Never angry with me, always respectful of my decisions. It almost made me want to change my mind, just to support him. I was sure he hadn't envisioned going it alone today, and funerals made him tense and fidgety, so completely out of his depth in the formal setting. He would be worse than the kids when it came to sitting still and listening to whatever the celebrant had to say about Russell.

I sighed and stood up from the bed, going to find Holly.

Her bedroom door was closed, and I stood outside on the landing for a few seconds, collecting myself, before pushing open the door.

'Hey, baby,' I said.

She was wearing a navy smock dress and flat black shoes, and her long blonde hair was scraped into a French twist at the base of her neck. She looked somehow simultaneously like a young child and a sophisticated woman, and in that moment, I really felt how close I was to the precipice of losing my little girl. If I hadn't already.

In the loose-fitting dress, she looked tinier than ever, her pale cheeks hollow, her lips unsmiling.

'Hi, Mum,' she said. 'Dad said I had to get ready for...' She paused, swallowing as if the words were stuck in her throat. 'For the funeral.'

I walked over to where she sat at her small pale pink wooden dressing table. 'Budge up,' I said, sliding onto the stool and wrapping my arms around her bird-like frame. I pressed my lips to the top of her head, a gesture I'd done every day since she was born.

'Are you okay, Mum?'

I looked up, finding her watching me in the oval mirror. 'Of course.'

'But you're not coming.'

'No.'

She nodded, and I could tell she wanted to say something else. When I didn't speak, she coughed, her gaze falling to her folded hands in her lap. 'I... I could stay with you. If you wanted me to? If you don't want to be alone?'

'You mean, miss the funeral?' I asked, my shoulders tensing. I would never have been the one to suggest it, but to have her here with me was exactly what I wanted right now.

She nodded. 'If you need me?'

I smiled, hugging her tighter, my chin resting on top of her head. 'I do. You know I do. Thank you, baby,' I whispered.

She smiled back, and I felt the tension in the room dissipate. 'What about Dad?' she asked. 'Won't he be annoyed that it's only him and Jack going? I know how much he hates funerals.'

I shook my head, still smiling. 'No, darling. I'll talk to your dad. He'll be fine – don't worry about it. I never want you to have to worry about a thing.'

I felt her relax into my arms, and my chest loosened, letting me take a full breath again for the first time in a long while.

'How about you and I do some baking for when they get back? Cookies? Or a cake?'

'Always cake,' she said, squeezing my arm.

'Cake it is then,' I whispered into her hair.

TWENTY-FIVE

VICTORIA

I didn't want to get out of the car. Mr Harrison, the funeral director, had kindly offered to provide me with a black car and a driver when he'd found out I didn't have a licence, and although I had hated the idea initially, worried we would have to follow the hearse and make up some kind of horrendous procession, he'd convinced me that I could choose to arrive discreetly instead if I preferred. Now, obscured behind the dark tinted windows of the BMW, watching the small group of friends and family mill about outside the crematorium, I was glad I'd taken him up on the offer rather than approaching someone to ask for a lift. I felt shielded here, protected from having to face them, hearing their condolences and feeling compelled to offer up my own.

Predictably, I'd received a text message from my mother just as I'd been heading out the door, sending apologies, condolences, excuses for why she couldn't make it. I hadn't even been surprised, numb as yet another of her bullets wounded me. I was too used to her standing behind the smoking gun, oblivious to the damage caused by her disinterest in her own daughter, to let myself acknowledge how much it hurt. Morag, Russell's mum, was standing hunched over, surrounded by distant relatives I hardly recognised, already blotting her creased eyes with a cotton handkerchief, her ankle-length black dress loose against her bony frame. She looked so much older than when I'd last seen her. I didn't think I could bear to look her in the eye, to see the grief she was living through. The thought of going over to join them all, shaking hands and receiving well-meant hugs, made me recoil even further into my seat.

These people would want me to perform – to act the grief-stricken widow and share all the details of how it had happened, how I was coping. It made my stomach churn to think of it, playing out the scenes I'd been dreading all week and cringing away from them. I didn't want to talk about him, hear his name on their lips as they offered their sad little nods, as if they could possibly understand what I had been through. That false empathy, their loss diluted by distance. Some of them hadn't so much as called in the past decade. Why were they even here? They would go home tonight and forget all about Russell. About *me*. Perhaps they might raise a glass to a life cut short, but then they would move on to whatever came next, whilst I remained living under his roof, smelling his aftershave every time I opened the wardrobe doors, seeing him everywhere. Unable to escape even now.

I watched as a smartly dressed woman with cropped blonde hair and soft, smiling eyes emerged from the main entrance, holding a clipboard that singled her out as the celebrant. She glanced around, presumably looking for me, and I chewed my lip, guilty at not playing the part so much better. Russell would have been seething at the idea that I wasn't there to greet her, drumming up conversation and chatter on his behalf, reminding everyone of who he was, what he'd achieved.

I ran my hands nervously over my dress and heard the snag of the sheer black fabric as a jagged fingernail caught, leaving a nasty pull front and centre. I winced, almost hearing his voice in my ear, berating me for making him look bad, for not getting my nails done – for not being the beautiful wife he wanted to show off.

If he'd been here, he would have tossed his jacket at me and stormed off, already coming up with a story about how I couldn't handle the cold. His eyes would have been on me from the second we left the car until the moment we got home, and I wouldn't have dared to take off the coat and show him up. I would have smiled and sweated through it all, pretending to shiver just to keep him sweet.

I looped my finger through the stray thread and pulled with vindictive satisfaction at the obvious imperfection, the dress ruined beyond saving.

Morag broke free from the crowd, heading over to the celebrant and holding out a bony hand – lapping up the attention, I thought, before chiding myself for my spite. She was mourning her son, her only child, just months after losing her husband. She had every right to seek comfort in any way she chose.

My driver cleared his throat then glanced over his shoulder. 'It, ah, looks as if they're about to head in.'

I followed the direction of his gaze, seeing the hearse coming up the long driveway, the suited men standing by, ready to lift the coffin. I didn't let myself think about what was inside.

'Do you want me to walk you over there?' he offered.

I ignored him, my eyes fixed on the drive, watching the familiar Land Rover that was following slowly behind the hearse. I stared hungrily at it, waiting for Mike to pull into a space, looking to see if they had all come after all.

She would come. What woman wouldn't want to be at the funeral of the man she loved? I had to assume she'd loved him. Or had it just been something to do? A way to escape the drudgery of being a stay-at-home wife? A homemaker. I knew just how hard it was to survive day after day of crushing monotony. But then Lisa had her children. A husband who treated her like a queen. Her days were full of laughter, purpose. *My biggest responsibility was making sure the house plants didn't get dusty.* So it had to have been love. Somehow, in my mind, that was easier to take than the idea of the two of them throwing away Mike and me for the sake of a sordid fling, though I still couldn't picture them having a connection. Lisa was too good for Russell. And to discard Mike for him, well, the idea was ridiculous.

I drove myself mad with this circular thinking, trying to work out what had gone on behind my back. I needed to know the truth. I had to know. It was the only way I'd ever be able to escape the sham that had been my marriage and finally leave Russell firmly in my past.

The Land Rover parked and Mike got out, Jack hopping out of the passenger seat. They slammed their doors and strode up to the entrance, handsome and out of place, looking too rugged for their smart black suits. Mike seemed uncomfortable in his, pulling discreetly at the stiff white collar, far more at home in an old pair of shorts and well-worn trainers. So very different from Russell.

I shook my head, looking back to the car for signs of Lisa and Holly, but it was clearly empty. They hadn't come.

'They're going inside now,' the driver repeated, a note of urgency cutting through his polite tone.

I nodded and tucked my hair behind my ears, swallowing against the ball of nerves lodged in my throat.

With obvious relief, he jumped out of the car and opened my door, standing back to let me out. I stepped into the sunshine and walked, head held high, to watch my husband be reduced to ash. I felt nothing.

TWENTY-SIX

LISA

'What was it like?'

I glanced up as Holly spoke, her head bent as she used her long fingers to fish a shard of eggshell from a pale green mug. She was barefoot, still dressed in the navy shift, but her chignon had come loose, leaving her hair trailing down over her narrow shoulders.

'Hmm?' I replied, distracted as I weighed out the flour, tapping the edge of the sieve gently, the fine white powder raining down into the glass mixing bowl.

'Being locked up... What was it like?'

I felt my grip tighten on the handle of the sieve, my heartbeat stuttering in my chest. 'Oh.'

I paused, taken aback by the innocent question. Since coming home, we hadn't spoken of it, hadn't even acknowledged the horrible thing that had happened, how terrifying it had been for all of us. I had wanted to. I knew it was my responsibility to bring it up and make sure she and Jack were okay, that they were coping. I had so much I wanted to say to reassure her, but somehow I hadn't been able to get it out, and as the days passed, it had become increasingly difficult to find the right words.

'It was fine,' I said, my tone too chirpy, too brittle. 'It was over so quickly, I hardly had a chance to think. Besides,' I added, giving the sieve one last shake, 'I knew I wouldn't be there long.'

Holly didn't reply. Carefully, she placed the mug on the counter, her eyes trained downwards. I stood frozen, waiting for her to respond, suddenly wishing I hadn't lied. She wasn't a child anymore. She couldn't be fooled with a bright smile and a few flippant remarks. I felt her disappointment in me, held in her silence, heavy in the air around us, and wished I could take back the pretty little story and tell her what I really felt. That being locked in that cell had been one of the most terrifying experiences of my life. That I'd felt like an animal in a zoo, the claustrophobia crushing, my world ripped out from under me. That I'd wanted to say or do anything to get out of there – get back to her, Mike, Jack.

There was so much I'd kept locked inside, but I wouldn't put that on her shoulders. It wasn't fair on her. She didn't need to know that I wasn't sleeping. That I lay beside Mike every night, staring up at the dark ceiling, sick to my stomach with blind terror at the memories that flashed in full colour on a loop in my head. It would do her no good to know any of that.

I took in her jutting collarbone and pale, pinched cheeks and felt the familiar overpowering urge to protect her from the harshness of the world. It was only right to lie. I had no choice. There were things that were best left unsaid, and as her mother, I was happy to accept the burden of those unspoken words. I pretended not to see the sadness in her downcast eyes as I turned, rifling through the larder.

'So!' I announced brightly. 'Chocolate? Or lemon? Or we could make both? We have everything we need here.' I didn't wait for an answer as I began grabbing ingredients, lining them up on the worktop in front of me.

Finally, I turned back to face her and found I was alone, the sea green mug abandoned, her stool at the counter empty. For a second, I was filled with doubt, wondering if I should go after her, talk honestly about everything we both needed to say. Would it make any difference, or would I just make it all so much worse?

I stared at the kitchen doorway, chewing my lower lip, wishing I knew what to do, how to be the mother she needed. Then I sucked in a breath, squared my shoulders and picked up the mug, tipping its sticky contents into the mixing bowl, focusing on a task I knew I couldn't mess up.

TWENTY-SEVEN

VICTORIA

I felt the bony hand grab my arm seconds before I made it out the crematorium door and tensed, turning to see Morag, a deep frown creasing her already wrinkled brow, her thick dark eyebrows knitted in a familiar mask of disapproval. 'Victoria,' she said, her fingertips digging into my skin as she stepped back from the doorway, forcing me to accompany her. 'I'd expected to see you before the service. Everyone wants to know what's happening with the investigation. Have they got any closer to finding out who did this to my son?'

I shook my head, looking towards the door for an escape and realising I was trapped. 'No, Morag. I don't think so. I don't know.' I shrugged, wishing I'd had the foresight to slip out a few minutes early but knowing it would have been impossible. The celebrant had met me as the coffin was carried through the cool, air-conditioned hall, shaking my hand warmly before leading me to the very front row. A mark of respect, I knew, but all I'd wanted was to sit at the back, where I wouldn't be watched by every single person who'd come to act the spectator to my grief.

Morag folded her arms across her narrow chest. 'I would have thought you of all people would be doing everything you could to spur them on. You need to be calling the police station daily – twice a day even! – to remind them of their duty. Tell them we're waiting for answers and we won't rest until we get justice for Russell... for my boy...'

Her voice cracked, her eyes glistening with tears, and I nodded, hoping she wouldn't fall apart now.

'It's okay, Morag,' I said, patting her arm awkwardly. We'd never been touchy-feely, and it felt wrong to offer a hug, even now. Thankfully, I saw her sister approaching from behind her, a hard-faced woman in her seventies who I'd never once seen smile.

Taking in the scene, she wrapped her arm around Morag's waist and nodded towards the door. 'Let's get you a drink. I think you need one. We'll see you at the wake, Victoria?' she asked, her tone leaving no room for argument.

'Oh... of course. I'll catch you up,' I said, picturing the function room at the local pub, the room-temperature vol-au-vents and stale scones at the buffet I'd felt obliged to arrange. An afternoon of being trapped, listening to everyone sing Russell's praises, harassing me for information on the police case. I couldn't face it.

'Lovely service,' said a man I didn't recognise as he passed me to get to the door.

'Thanks... thank you.'

Mike and Jack stood by awkwardly, looking as if they couldn't wait to leave yet wanting to be respectful. 'Thanks for coming,' I said to Mike.

'Don't be silly. We weren't going to miss sending him off, were we?' he replied. 'Uh, shall we see you at the pub then?'

I nodded, already sure that I wouldn't go but unable to come up with any excuse that wouldn't make me look callous.

Taking my silence for sadness, Mike smiled sympatheti-cally, then kissed me on the cheek. Jack gave a quick, polite nod and the two of them headed outside into the heat of the summer's day. I waited a few moments, until the rest of the mourners had left, then followed them, wanting to get back to the safety of the blacked-out windows of the BMW.

Stepping out into the sunshine, I squinted, then paused, a flash of cropped brown hair catching my eye at the far end of the car park. I shielded my gaze from the sun and was just able to see the back of a petite woman, a silver earring glinting, as she climbed into the back of a taxi and it drove away. There was something about the way she moved, the hourglass curve of her hips, that made me instantly think of Lisa.

Could it have been her? Had she come and I'd missed her somehow? It would have been easy for her to slip in the back unseen, then wait at the far end of the car park to be picked up. So many secrets, so many lies.

I set my jaw, a wave of determination washing over me, then turned, walking back to my car, making up my mind that the time had come to confront Lisa. I had to know the truth.

The unfamiliar car was proving a very valuable asset today, first shielding me from the mourners at the crematorium, and now, pulling up a few houses down from mine, allowing me the opportunity to stare unseen across the road.

Lisa was standing on her front path, her feet bare against the grey stone, her maxi dress a bright green floral design. I wondered if she'd run in and changed the moment she arrived home, or if I really *had* imagined her at the crematorium. Seen what I had wanted to see. She had a parcel clasped against her chest and was deep in conversation with the postman, a kind-hearted man who must have been pushing seventy, with a wife going through lung-cancer treatment and a daughter living in Dubai who he missed terribly. Whenever he knocked, you were guaranteed an update on his life – a habit that meant that the post was almost always late, because he stopped every ten houses for a natter.

Lisa, smiling empathetically in a way that looked entirely genuine, was completely focused on him. I watched as she reached out, gave his shoulder a squeeze, subtly moving from one foot to the other, the concrete clearly cold. From here, she looked so sweet. So caring. It was what had made me fall in love with her when we moved here. Her open-hearted approach to the world. Her caring eyes and warm smile.

Had all of that been a lie? I couldn't put the two conflicting sides together. The way she could make you feel as if you were the most important person in the world and yet could go behind my back, not to mention Mike's, and sleep with my husband without a thought of what it would do to me. How it would destroy me. She had been like a sister to me, her kids as good as family – I loved them as if they were my own, and now, nothing made sense. Despite knowing what she had done, there was still a confusing mixture of love, a need to be in her life, and despite my desperate desire to hate her, I couldn't make it so black and white in my mind. It was far too complicated for that.

Russell, too, gone so suddenly from my life, could not so easily be erased from my thoughts. He had been far from the perfect husband, our life together often a lesson in endurance and submission on my part, but I had been surprised over this past week to realise that a part of me missed him more than I would ever have imagined possible. I should have felt grateful for my freedom, but I wasn't yet ready to accept it was real. Without him, I was no longer sure who I was, how to behave, and what should have felt liberating was in reality completely terrifying. Grief – for Lisa, for Russell, for the life I'd longed to have that had never materialised – lay heavily on my heart, and despite the deep-rooted belief that I should hate the both of them, my conviction wavered time and again.

'Thanks for today,' I said, my eyes briefly meeting the driver's in the rear-view mirror.

I got out of the car on the pavement side so as to be obscured by the vehicle, not wanting Lisa to catch sight of me right away. I straightened my dress, ran my fingers through my hair and flicked it over my shoulder as the BMW pulled away from the kerb. Lisa, her attention caught by the sound of the engine revving, glanced my way, her face freezing, a deer in headlights.

'Lis,' I called, dashing across the road as the postman moved on with his rounds. I saw her urge to run back indoors, to pretend I wasn't there, but her sensible side won out and she remained where she stood, clutching the parcel against her chest, her cheeks pale and pinched.

'Hi, Vic. Shouldn't you be at the wake? Mike and Jack aren't back yet.'

I ignored her probing comment, not willing to explain myself to her. 'I thought I saw you at the crematorium just now. Getting into a taxi.' I watched her face closely for any sign of guilt, but her expression remained frustratingly blank.

She shook her head slowly, her eyes sinking down to her bare feet. 'No... it wasn't me. I'm sorry we didn't make it, but Holly wasn't feeling well and I didn't want to leave her here alone.'

Her cheeks flushed as she spoke, and I wondered if she was lying to me. She glanced over her shoulder to the house, clearly desperate to head back inside.

I pursed my lips. 'So you weren't there?' I pushed.

She raised her wide hazel eyes to meet mine. 'No.' She looked so innocent, so incapable of lying, but I knew that impression was deceptive.

'I'm sorry,' she added, her words barely a whisper, her face the picture of sincerity. I held her stare, sure that she was trying to find a way to tell me more. If only she would admit what she had done, maybe we could find a way to bring back that closeness between us.

Despite everything, I wasn't ready to give up on her. Russell had been a hard man to refuse when he had his mind set on something. I could only imagine how easily seduced Lisa might have been if he'd made it his mission to win her over, just as *I* had been in the early days of our relationship. He knew exactly what to say, how to blow hot and cold in just the right amounts until I had fallen so hard for him I hadn't seen through the mirage until I was in too deep.

Lisa, despite her love for Mike, would have been blown away by his charm when he'd turned it on for her. I couldn't blame her entirely. It was *him* I was most angry with. Even today, watching his coffin being carried in, knowing he was really gone, I hadn't been able to shake it – the betrayal too deep to forget, even for a moment. It stung that the opportunity to confront him with his lies was lost to me for ever. That I'd never get to see the expression on his face when I stood up to him, showed him the evidence that he wasn't the man he wanted everyone to see him as. He would have been humiliated if his secret had got out, the facade of the perfect marriage he wanted to showcase to the world shattered in an instant, his ego beaten and bruised.

I couldn't imagine it would have made him a more humble man – humility wasn't something he had ever been capable of – but still, I would have liked to show him I wasn't the doormat he believed me to be. That I was more than just a trophy wife to be seen and not heard.

I waited, willing her to say more, to save me from having to make a call I didn't want to make. Since deciding to contact the police with the tip-off I held in my arsenal, I had picked up the phone countless times, but every time, I chickened out, unable to do it. I didn't want to be forced to make her pay. What I wanted was an apology from her. An admission of guilt. An explanation for *why* she had done it, why she had hurt me so deeply. I clamped my tongue between my front teeth, my heart pounding, willing her to say the words, but when she didn't continue, I felt the frustration bubble over.

'Sorry for what?' I snapped, my tone thin and hard. I didn't want to have to drag the truth from her. I wanted her to have enough respect for me to tell me straight.

She chewed her lip, making it red and sore, the pause long and agonising as I forced myself to wait.

'For your loss,' she finally replied. 'For everything you've been through. I really am sorry.'

She turned and walked back inside, leaving me standing on the path, blood pulsing in my ears, wondering if that was the only apology I would get from her. I deserved so much more.

TWENTY-EIGHT

I felt absurd – awkward and conspicuous, which would have entirely defeated the point of today, had I not caught my reflection in a shop window and seen the vastly different silhouette staring back at me. The cropped plum-coloured wig made my scalp itchy and hot, my hair squashed into a tight bun beneath it. I'd bought it for a fancy dress party a decade ago, though in the end I had gone with another costume, and had found it this morning right at the back of my wardrobe, still wrapped in cellophane. I'd spent the past few days in and out of charity shops, looking for things I could buy for a couple of pounds so Russell wouldn't ask about the charges on my bank card.

My usual skinny jeans had been swapped for baggy brown cargo pants a couple of sizes too big for me. I'd pulled the canvas belt as tight as it would go, and the result was a balloon of fabric that made an unpleasant swooshing sound with every step I took. I'd bought a thick, frumpy grey-and-black patterned jumper to hide my figure and paired it with a cheap-looking nylon jacket that dwarfed my frame. My shoes were off-white

Nikes, and as I crossed the road feeling utterly ridiculous, I bowed my head low, obscuring my face beneath the polyester fringe, casting covert glances in front of me every few steps, making sure I hadn't lost sight of my target.

This was what Russell had driven me to. Disguising myself in these awful clothes that smelled of old people and cats because I'd been too afraid of washing them in case he came home early and caught me. Following him through the town like a private detective in a cheesy black-and-white movie. I hated him for making me stoop so low, for making me succumb to this kind of behaviour, but I had to know what he was doing behind my back.

It had been eight days since I had found the knickers in his desk. Four days since I had found the matching bra in Lisa's laundry. The idea that *she*, of all people, had gone behind my back, shared something special and secret with my husband, was tearing me apart. I hadn't slept. Had barely eaten. Had taken to sitting all day on a chair beneath my bedroom window, my eyes trained on their front door, watching the family coming and going, waiting for some clue, some evidence of her betrayal. And it was all his fault. He'd forced me to become this neurotic, paranoid excuse for a human being, and right now, I hated myself almost as much as I hated them.

I'd been through all his belongings, looking for more clues. I'd watched him sleep. Even sneaked out to the car in the middle of the night to search through the glove compartment and check how many miles he'd travelled each day, mentally calculating the distance between our house and his office. And all the while, I had put on a smile. Done my hair. Concealed the dark circles beneath my eyes. Made his fucking drinks and cooked his dinner, let him berate me for my faults, comment on the way I kept the house, the outfit I was wearing, apologising to him for my inadequacies and inwardly seething at the injustice of it all.

I was drained, exhausted to my core and desperate to know the truth.

When he'd taken this afternoon off work, claiming the computer system at the office was down and they'd all been sent home, I'd nodded, though something had told me he was lying. But then, when he'd made a seemingly spontaneous decision to head into town under the guise of picking up a table lamp he'd ordered for the living room, instructing me to wait in in case we missed a delivery, my hackles had risen and I had known the moment had come. He clearly didn't want me with him, which could only mean one thing. He was going to meet her.

I saw the flash of his blonde hair crossing the road up ahead, and then, just as I was about to cross too, I realised he had stopped in front of a coffee shop. I stood, half concealed by a postbox, as a bus trundled past. When the road was clear, I realised he was still in the same spot. If I crossed over now, he would see me. Instead, I ducked into a card shop, making my way over to the window, pretending to look at the rack of condolence cards, which seemed oddly fitting, given my situation.

I searched for his blonde head, a surge of panic passing through me as I realised he'd moved from the spot on the pavement, hoping I hadn't lost him in the crowd. But then I saw him. And there she was. That bright pink sundress. The big dark sunglasses propped on top of her head. She looked beautiful. Envy poured through my veins as I stared at her, sitting there at one of the outdoor tables without an ounce of shame, saw the wide smile on my husband's face, sure that this was why he had left me home alone today. To come here. See her. *Be* with her.

I gripped the metal frame of the card rack, anger making blood roar in my ears. And then I watched as Lisa stood. They were having some argument, some disagreement, I realised, and I cursed myself for not choosing a better spot to watch from, needing to know what was being said. Was she angry at him for not having left me yet? Was *that* what she wanted? To see me discarded like a worn-out pair of shoes, left without support, without his name? I wouldn't allow it. Wouldn't stand for the disrespect – it was too much. I had put up with a lot over the course of our marriage, but I would not accept this.

I saw an expression cross his features that I realised I had never seen before – not in one single moment of nearly twenty years together. An expression I hadn't known he was capable of. Some strange combination of apology, regret, *fear* even.

I pressed my hand to the glass, my mouth dry as tears filled my eyes. He was in love with her, afraid of losing her. And she was walking away. I could see the panic in his eyes, his whole body desperate, needy, unrecognisable from the man I knew. What did *she* have that could make him show such vulnerability? Why hadn't I got to see this side of him?

I felt the tears stream down my cheeks as I watched Lisa grab her bag and stride away from him, powerful, righteous, and as Russell stared after her, I knew that I had lost him. And that for the first time in his life, he wasn't in control.

I felt a hand on my wrist and spun round, my heart catching in my throat as I looked down to find the elderly shopkeeper staring up at me, her soft steel-grey hair freshly permed, her mouth painted in a rosy pink that made her look warm and homely.

'Here,' she said, handing me a box of tissues.

I took one gratefully, wiping roughly at my damp cheeks, ashamed of the show of emotion, which felt so alien to me.

She patted my arm. 'That's better. I can help you choose, if you need me to?' she offered, her voice kind and nurturing as she gestured towards the rack. 'I know it's hard. Was it someone very close to you that you lost?'

She reached forward, plucking a white card with the image of a blue glass vase, a single sprig of forget-me-nots nestled inside it, the words *Sorry for your loss* printed in swirling italics.

I took it from her, staring down, sniffing, then glanced back towards the café, noting that Russell had gone. I should get home before he did, get out of these awful clothes.

I took a breath, looking back to the card clasped between my fingers.

'Yes,' I answered finally. 'Yes, it was.'

TWENTY-NINE

LISA

The shopping threatened to burst free from the bag for life, the cheap canvas strap cutting into my shoulder, far too heavy for the long walk home. I had only intended to pick up a few things, deciding that the walk to the local supermarket would clear my head and at the very least, give me something to think about other than the relentless worries that had been driving me to distraction. We only needed milk, eggs, maybe some fresh bread for sandwiches, but when I'd begun my slow, meandering route through the aisles, I'd found myself grabbing an expensive bottle of wine. I'd stopped at the deli counter, picking up spicy olives and all manner of yummy things I knew Mike would salivate over. I'd added garlic bread, fresh pasta, prawns, double cream, tarragon, the ingredients for tiramisu, piling my basket high until I could barely lift it to unload it at the till.

I had an overwhelming urge to treat my family. To have them smiling and relaxed and happy, their bellies full of the rich food I had made for them, my love for them undeniable, the effort I had made translated onto their plates, showing them exactly what they meant to me. It was a need almost bordering on compulsive – to nurture, to take care of my family – and once the idea had come to me, even the thought of having to carry the heavy bag of groceries home wasn't enough to deter me from my plan.

Now, though, with my neck and shoulders throbbing from swapping the weighty bag back and forth from one arm to the other, I was wishing I'd had the foresight to borrow Mike's car. The insurance company, when Mike had phoned them to report mine missing, had found a convenient loophole in our policy and told him without apology that they were under no obligation to provide a temporary vehicle for me while they processed our claim. I was sure they were trying to pull a fast one, but knowing that they were wrong and having the energy to actually fight their decision were two very different things. I was exhausted. And what with all the drama around the bloody car, it was the last thing I wanted to think about.

Every time Mike mentioned it, my blood ran cold, a pervading sense of claustrophobia engulfing me, suffocating, terrifying. I could smell the interior of the police car, the pine air freshener that hung from the rear-view mirror, DS McCormac's musky aftershave. I could almost hear the crackling radio and quiet click of the indicator. I didn't want to think about where *my* car was now, or what would happen if it was found. The uncertainty of my future – of what they might try to pin on me next – was enough to make me sick to my stomach. And the only cure for the nausea was to eat. To fill the emptiness inside me until I'd squashed those feelings with the weight of a good meal.

As I made it to my driveway, I heaved the bag higher up my aching shoulder, hearing the clink of bottles, picturing the smile on Mike's face as I served him all his favourite foods.

Pulling the house key from my pocket, I unlocked the front door and stepped inside, freezing as I heard a familiar voice. My eyes closed involuntarily, as if I could make her go away.

Victoria. What was she doing here again? It was getting too much, too invasive. I felt awful for her – of course I did – but didn't she realise how much we needed our privacy too? How her constant presence made it impossible to forget the whole horrible situation? It felt like she'd crossed a line since losing Russell and made herself far too comfortable in my home. I had to find a way to re-establish the boundaries we'd always had, but doing that without offending her seemed impossible.

I rubbed my eyes with my free hand, hoping she was just popping in and would be on her way soon so I could get on with making my special family dinner, then took a deep calming breath and walked into the kitchen.

Mike was leaning casually against the counter, a mug of coffee in front of him, talking animatedly about a local kayaking trip he'd taken three years previously – a story I had heard a dozen times before, about him capsizing and being caught in a rip tide. He had swum three miles along the Kent coast to escape being drowned and thought he might end up in France. He'd eventually been picked up by a fishing boat and spent the rest of the afternoon drinking whisky with the oilcloth-clad men, who'd been out at sea for a week, arriving home stinking of brine and barley, smiling from ear to ear about the story he'd collected and the memories he'd made. I was certain Victoria must have heard the chronicle before too, but she was smiling and laughing, her eyes fixed on Mike as he spoke, giving no indication that she might be bored by the tale, which grew more and more outrageous with each telling.

'Hi,' I said, heaving the heavy shopping bag onto the kitchen table and rubbing my shoulders.

'Hey, gorgeous. What have you got there?' Mike asked,

coming over to kiss me. He poked his fingers into the bag and I batted him away.

'Just a few bits for dinner. I thought I'd cook something special. Where are the kids?'

'Holly went out to a hockey match and Jack's at the cinema with some friends.'

'Oh...' I felt the disappointment hit me like a steam train, my plans for a lovely family dinner shattered in an instant. 'I wish they'd said they were going out. Some of this won't keep, and I really wanted some family time.' I hoped I was managing to hint just enough to get Victoria to take notice without being rude, but I feared I was treading on thin ice.

'Never mind, love. I'm sure we'll manage it between us.'

I nodded. Maybe a date night with just the two of us was just what I needed.

'I'm happy to help you cook,' Victoria said, standing up with a smile. 'It looks like you've got enough to keep you tied to the kitchen for hours. Let me give you a hand.'

'Oh, no, that's kind of you, but I really don't mind. And I'm sure you need to get on.'

'Don't be silly. It's no trouble at all. I love cooking.'

She walked over to the hook on the back of the kitchen door and took my favourite blue-and-white apron from it. She seemed to pause for just a second, then her smile widened and she stepped towards me, slipping it over my head, her eyes meeting mine, unreadable, unsettling.

'Did I ever make my chicken vindaloo and chapattis for you two?' she asked, turning from me and rummaging in the shopping bag. 'I know how much you like a bit of spice, Mike. You'll have to come to me and try it one of these days. Oh, look at these ingredients! We're going to have quite the feast.'

I glanced at Mike, trying to catch his eye, but he was typing something on his phone and didn't seem in the least bit fazed that our rare chance for a romantic night together was going up in smoke.

I opened my mouth, trying to find words that were firm yet polite but couldn't think of how to even begin. Her husband was dead. She was alone. And I was the worst kind of person for not welcoming her into my home. She was just a lonely, sad woman needing a friend.

I tied the apron belt around my waist, watching her unpack the shopping bag, one item after another, her long, slender hands laying claim to my plans, and wondered, if that was true, why I felt so uneasy?

I seethed inwardly as Victoria poured more wine into Mike's glass before sinking her spoon into the dessert I'd made for my husband, licking the cream from her lips in a way that looked innocent but I felt sure was for his benefit. She'd sat right beside him, and as the meal had gone on, it had been impossible to miss her chair moving closer to his, her shoulder bumping against his arm every time she leaned across the table. I was sure I wasn't imagining the way she looked at him – enraptured, attentive... possessive, almost.

To my annoyance, Mike was doing nothing to discourage her. It wasn't his fault. He was far too accustomed to women fawning over him to place any significance on their attentions, and I knew he probably hadn't even noticed the way Victoria was touching him, laughing too often at his jokes, blushing like a schoolgirl. But *I* had. She'd always been submissive around him, but this behaviour was something else. It felt like she was taking it too far. Like it had intent.

I glanced at her glass, wondering if she'd had too much to drink, if I could make an excuse for her inappropriate behaviour, but she'd barely had half a glass, though I'd drunk almost three just to keep the bubbling stress suppressed in my gut. I wanted to get up and show her the door. To push her away from my husband and stake my claim, a realisation that took me by surprise.

I'd never been a jealous wife. Mike, despite his magnetic energy and friendly personality, which could be mistaken for flirtatious by opportunistic single women, had never given me reason to feel insecure in our relationship. It had never bothered me when he'd laughed with other women, hugged them when they were down, been a supportive friend when they needed an ear to bend. He was often employed by women to do their gardens, and even if one or two of them might have flirted a bit too much on occasion, called him up for specialist advice on their rhododendrons after hours, I had always just laughed it off, secure in the knowledge that Mike was mine and no amount of eyelash-fluttering would do anything to change that. So why then did I feel sick watching him laugh with Victoria? Why this visceral desire to get her out of my house and protect my family from something I couldn't put my finger on?

It was a new and unsettling feeling, and I realised that part of it stemmed from never having spent much time alone with her. We'd been out for coffee, just the two of us, and in the first few years of knowing her, we'd occasionally gone shopping or to see a show, but for the most part, we had socialised with our husbands there too. I'd preferred it that way, often struggling to find common ground when it was just the two of us. And now that I thought about it, I actually couldn't recall a time when she'd been around Mike without Russell in tow. She was different without her husband here beside her. He had always dominated the conversation, dictated when they left, a stickler for manners, and I'd never felt that they were outstaying their welcome. He'd been a bit of a show-off, always bragging about his latest purchase, critical of people he knew from work – people we had never met – but he had been entertaining company. I realised now how sidelined Victoria had been on the occasions we'd shared together. Now, without him looming over her, his confidence suppressing her personality, for the first time I was seeing her for herself, and I realised I had never truly known her.

'It's getting late.' I stood up, clearing away the dessert bowls, not even caring that my tone was too cool, rude even.

'Let me help you with those, Lisa,' she said. She stood, her body pressing briefly against Mike's side as she slid out of her space, carrying her own half-empty bowl to the counter.

'There's no need. I'm just going to throw them in the dishwasher. Everything else is done,' I said pointedly.

'Holly and Jack are due back in the next half-hour,' Mike said, looking at his watch. 'I hope they've eaten – they'll be so jealous when they hear they've missed your garlic prawns.' He rubbed his flat belly, his T-shirt rising up to display a sliver of tanned skin.

'Yes, it was delicious, Lisa. You'll have to give me lessons; you're so much more adventurous than I am in the kitchen. Russell always wanted the same few dishes, so I never had an opportunity to experiment...'

She let her words hang uncomfortably in the air, a reminder of how alone she was, what she was going through, then picked up her glass and drained the dregs of her wine. I willed myself to stay silent, to give her no choice but to take the hint and leave.

Mike, though, couldn't seem to handle the awkward break in conversation. He jumped up, coming to join us by the work surface. 'Coffee?' he offered. 'I'll pop the machine on and we can try those new pods.'

'That would be lovely. Thanks, Mike.' She squeezed his arm and smiled at him sweetly. *Too* sweetly.

I gritted my teeth, resolving to have a word with him about reading the mood and not encouraging her. It wasn't healthy for her to latch on like this. She needed to branch out and start figuring out where life would take her from here, not weave herself into the fabric of *my* family. I couldn't cope with having her here much longer.

Mike switched on the coffee machine, he and Victoria talking back and forth about the best coffee places they'd tried, and the worst. I turned to scrape the pudding bowls into the bin and realised it was full. With more force than was necessary, I yanked the black bag from it, tying it in a clumsy knot and heaving it down the hall, irritated that Mike was more interested in playing host to Victoria than in stepping in to take the rubbish out for me. I didn't like leaving the two of them alone together.

The night was clear and inky black, and I threw the bag into the wheelie bin, then inhaled deeply, staring up at the bright pinpricks of stars scattered across the velvety sky.

It took me a moment to realise that the darkness had been tarnished by a pulsing light. I felt my whole body tense, the urge to run instantaneous as I turned my head, knowing what I would see before I even laid eyes on it. The flashing blue light, the silent police car speeding down the road. It pulled up at the end of the driveway and stopped, just as I had known it would. I turned away, walking briskly back inside, even as DS McCormac called my name. I didn't bother to shut the door. There was no point.

'Pixie, I was just telling Vic about that time my credit card got cloned at that café. And the worst part was the coffee tasted like pond water.' Mike grimaced, his eyes still twinkling. 'Was it Margate? Or Brighton maybe? It has to be fifteen years ago,' he added, not waiting for my reply. 'I wouldn't be so casual with my card nowadays.'

Victoria's eyes met mine and her smile fell. 'What's wrong?' she asked, somehow more intuitive than my own husband.

I was shaking, my palms soaked with sweat, unable to speak, to think straight.

A deep voice came from behind me. 'Mrs Grey?'

For half a second, Mike's face was creased with confusion as he took in what was happening. Then his eyes widened, his cheeks flushing with anger.

'Oh, you've got to be kidding me!' he said, slamming his coffee cup down hard on the counter and rushing over to stand between me and DS McCormac, his chest heaving.

A female officer with thick ginger hair poking out from beneath her hat stood silently behind McCormac, her face blank as she waited. I could see Mike shaking, his whole body reacting to the trauma we'd both been silently dreading since I got back home. I wanted to wrap my arms around him, comfort him, but I couldn't move – I was glued to the spot, frozen with terror.

He clenched his jaw, shook his head. 'I hope you don't think for a second that you're taking her again. I won't let you! No fucking way.'

'I'm afraid I am. Lisa Grey, you are under arrest for the murder of Russell Fox. You do not have to say anything, but anything you do say may be used against you later in court. Please come with me.'

'No! Not again. Don't you dare take her!' Mike yelled, grabbing my wrist and holding me so tight it hurt.

I wanted to speak, to tell him it would be okay, but I couldn't find my voice. All I could think was, *Thank God the kids are out. Don't let them have to see this. Not again.*

'Sir,' the ginger-haired officer said, stepping forward now. 'If you don't let go, you'll be arrested too, for obstructing an arrest. Do you want your children to have to deal with the consequences of that?'

I could see the despair in Mike's eyes, the panic at facing losing me again, not knowing what was happening, why they were taking his wife from him. I swallowed, blinking back tears, trying to find the courage to tell him that he had to let me go, but before the words would come and we could have our good-bye, Victoria was there.

She slid her soft, pretty hands around his strong forearm, shaking her head. 'Let her go now, Mike. We'll figure this out. You can't help her if they take you too, can you?'

Her words were reasonable, sensible even, and yet they sent a bolt of terror through me.

'No,' I whispered, wanting to warn him, to tell him to send her home, away from our family. But her voice was like honey, seeping into his ear, his grip loosening on my wrist as he gave in – gave up on me.

'Good decision,' DS McCormac said, guiding me roughly by the elbow through the house, out to the waiting car. I was pushed inside, a callused hand protecting my head from the door frame, and then, before I had a chance to register what was happening, he was turning the car in the road to head back the way he'd come, with me a prisoner inside once again.

Mike stood bewildered on the driveway, tears streaming down his face as he watched them take me.

I caught Victoria's eye, and there was a glint there that made me suck in a breath, a tiny twist of her mouth that almost made it look as if she were trying to suppress a smile. The tension I had been feeling all night, that awful sense of dread at having her in my home, so intensely entwined in the folds of my family suddenly made sense, the pieces of the puzzle slotting into place. Had *she* done this? Had she told the police something, planted some seed of evidence that had made them come back here again? And if she had... if she wanted me out of the way, it could only mean one thing. She knew the secret I'd been so careful to hide. She *knew*, and she wanted me out of the way so that nobody else would ever discover the truth. So that her marriage could remain a protected relic, perfect on paper, because who would ever question the memories of a grieving widow?

I wanted to scream out of the window and tell Mike she couldn't be trusted, that this was all her doing, but I was incapable of anything. The last thing I saw before we drove away was Victoria stepping up behind my husband and pulling him into a hug.

THIRTY

VICTORIA

'What the hell is taking you so long?' Russell called up the stairs, making me grit my teeth and close my eyes, reminding myself to keep my cool. He'd been in a terrible mood from the moment we'd woken up, and I wished we could just stay home rather than heading to what was sure to be a long and exceptionally dull party at his office, where I would have to watch him don the mask of chivalry, cracking jokes I had to pretend were funny – often at my expense. I didn't know why his colleagues seemed to throw so many parties in the middle of the day anyway. To me, it just seemed like an excuse to slack off work, and it meant that the quiet Friday afternoon I had hoped to enjoy without Russell looming over me, criticising my every move, was now forfeit to his plans.

'I'm just coming!' I called back, careful to keep any hint of irritation from seeping into my tone. 'Wait in the car if you want – I'll be right there.'

I heard him say something that sounded far from complimentary, then the jangle of keys. Seconds later, I heard the car start up and knew that if I didn't get out there within the next sixty seconds, he would start pressing hard on the horn, alerting all the neighbours to the fact that he was having to wait for me. I didn't see why it always had to be so stressful whenever we went anywhere together. He would get ready far too early and then comment on every aspect of my appearance until my confidence was in tatters and I was ready to crawl back under the duvet and forget the whole thing.

I stood now, looking into the full-length mirror at my basic black dress – an outfit Russell had deemed 'classic' but I thought was the height of boring. My hair was straight down my back and my make-up perfect, presentable, unremarkable. I was under no illusion that I wasn't a good-looking woman. Russell would never have married me if I hadn't lived up to his beauty standards.

Back then, I'd been infatuated with every single thing about him, from his thick dirty-blonde hair to his bright blue eyes, though after the fog of those early years had lifted, I'd realised he wasn't actually a very good-looking man, at least not on paper. His frame was narrow, pale and soft, his hair wiry, and his features, once I'd spent enough time watching him talk down to me, resembled a rodent's – ratty and hard. It was difficult to believe now that I'd once thought he was the most beautiful man on the planet, but that was the spell he managed to cast. His unshakeable confidence and self-assured attitude made him attractive, and even now, with the curtain lifted, knowing that he was all bravado and very little substance, I still found it impossible to stand up to him. The infatuation was over, but I was still in awe of him, cowed by his strength, his unwavering belief that his way was the right way.

I lived in terror of him tossing me out, of having to find the courage to hold my head up and tell my family that my marriage was a failure. I'd achieved so little in my life, but whatever opportunities I might have missed, I had the title of 'wife' at the very least. I wasn't going to risk that for anything. I knew it was an old-fashioned way of thinking, but being married, at least in *my* family, meant something. It made me respectable. Worthy, somehow. I could still remember my mother's face when I'd walked down the aisle on my wedding day – that look had been the closest she'd ever come to telling me she was proud of me, and I treasured it like a nugget of gold, clasped tight in my palm, unwilling to ever let it go.

I had seen women forced to start again in their forties, moving into tiny studio apartments in grotty neighbourhoods. Taking menial jobs – long hours in exchange for pennies, being treated like shit by employers who lorded it over them. Downloading apps to parade themselves on, degrading themselves for the chance of a date, dreaming of a Prince Charming who, in reality, would never turn up to save them. Divorce wouldn't solve my problems. It would only transport me into a whole new plethora of challenges I wasn't strong enough to overcome. And I could just imagine what my mother would say if I had to follow in the footsteps of those poor women. As much as I longed to be the type who could say fuck it, not care what the world thought, to have the confidence to start again, I would never be that person. I wouldn't even know where to begin.

So I kept myself tied to Russell's beauty standards religiously. My forehead was smooth, thanks to the Botox he had 'suggested' I start getting, gifting me my first session on my thirtieth birthday, along with fillers to freshen me up, in his words. My hair was glossy and thick, and I knew how to do my make-up to make myself appear slimmer, younger. But I wished I had my own style. Something that was mine, that made me feel more like my own person, rather than the cardboard cut-out I'd become.

Not that I was sure what that style would be if I had the freedom to choose. I had no sense of what I actually liked, probably because I'd never explored my options.

Before I met Russell, I had stolen style tips from everyone around me. Copied the girls at school who seemed to have it all figured out. Imitated women who looked like they could walk into any room, their confidence and self-worth stamped on their foreheads, leaving me with a sense of envy and longing. I felt like if I wore the same clothes, did my hair the same, I would somehow become like them too, but it never worked out that way. These days, I was guided by Russell's taste, inspired by influencers in tight jeans and low-cut tops, and the women he met through his work, hence his choice of outfit for me today. No doubt there would be plenty of them wearing basic black mini dresses the same as mine when we arrived at the event.

I slipped open my dresser drawer and pulled out a brown padded envelope. With a glance over my shoulder at the window, I tipped the contents onto the bed. The turquoise silk scarf and pretty matching earrings. Usually, I would have wound the scarf round my neck, but today, I flipped my head upside down, slipping it under my hair and tying a floppy knot on top of my head. I ran my fingers through my hair, giving it a bit more volume, then flipped back up and put the dangly earrings on. My reflection was immediately transformed from dull and predictable to something far more interesting. An artistic, carefree vibe, this time appropriated from Lisa. I'd long admired the way she dressed, the sensual individualism she managed to make appear so easy. I longed to have a slice of that unshakeable confidence she seemed to emanate. Not loud or showy, but an essence I couldn't quite pin down that was uniquely her.

The car horn sounded and I glanced once more in the mirror, feeling terrified about walking outside looking like this and yet determined that for once, I *would* have my own way. It might be Russell's work thing we were heading to, but it wasn't like they would take one look at me and sack him because I'd worn a bit of colour. It was only my husband who would have an issue with it, thinking people were judging me. Judging *him*. I just hoped he wouldn't be too angry. That for once I might not be made to feel like I'd let him down.

I picked up my bag and ran down the stairs.

The second I stepped out the front door, I could feel his eyes on me – angry, penetrating little rocks, set deep in his hard, reddening face. I looked down at my feet but kept walking forward, hoping I could distract him enough to get away with it.

He was out of the car, heading towards me before I knew what was happening, his hand clamping tight around the top of my arm, swinging me round as if he were going to march me back inside like a naughty child.

'Russell, mate!' a voice called from behind us.

We both turned and saw Mike heading across the road, waving in our direction.

'All right, you two? You off to that work do then?' he said, his smile wide, clearly unaware of what he'd interrupted.

Russell, ever the chameleon, transformed in an instant. 'That's right, mate. You know how it is. Got to keep up appearances and show willing if I want to be noticed. There are a few promotions on the horizon, and I want to make sure I'm in line for one of them.'

'I'm sure you'll wow them.' Mike grinned, looking at me with warm eyes. 'That a new scarf, Vic? Lisa has one just like it.'

I felt suddenly self-conscious and had to grab my wrist to stop myself from pulling it off my head. But then he spoke again.

'Suits you. Brings out your eyes.' He flashed me a wink.

'I... uh, thanks.' I could feel myself blushing and looked back down at my feet.

'Well, have fun, you two. I best be off. Got a new contract to do the gardens at this huge manor house out in the country, and I'm itching to get my hands in the soil. It's going to be beautiful.'

'With you on the job, no doubt,' Russell said, and I knew he was imagining the pay cheque Mike would be getting with a contract like that.

I stayed where I was as Mike crossed back over the road, waiting for Russell to speak. He looked slowly in my direction, his eyes travelling from my head to my feet, making me feel exposed and humiliated. Then he walked back to the car and climbed in.

'Get in then,' he called, shoving his keys in the ignition. 'We're going to be late as it is.'

I felt a tiny sense of victory and knew I had Mike to thank for Russell's sudden change of mood. If it was good enough for Mike, Russell was sure to want it too. It had always been that way.

As I climbed into the car, I reflected on how, as much as he was loud and outspoken about his opinions when it came to how I should dress, act, *speak* even, he was no more confident than I was when it came to knowing what image he wanted to present to the world. He was influenced by the people he envied and admired – a copycat just like me.

THIRTY-ONE

LISA

Now

It was happening all over again. The scrape of DS McCormac's chair on the hard floor as he eased his bulky frame into it, dragging it closer to the table. The smell of cheap coffee, Sandy's vanilla-scented perfume, her smile, intended to be reassuring no doubt as she met my eyes, before leaning forward to hear what the detective had to say.

The last time had been surreal, as if I were playing out a movie scene, the strong, unbreakable lead who couldn't be goaded into talking. As scared as I had been then, deep down I'd felt sure they couldn't keep me here. Not for long anyway. This time though, the smug look on McCormac's face, the new swagger in his posture had me filled with doubt.

'So, Mrs Grey... Lisa,' he said, having concluded the preamble about how we were being filmed. 'Tell me again what went down the night your car went missing.'

I frowned, seeing the trick immediately, knowing I'd told him nothing about that night, though Mike had informed him it had been stolen and Sandy had backed this up, pointing out that a report had been filed. He had a knowing smile on his face, just waiting for me to slip up and give him something he could use against me.

'No comment,' I said quietly, watching the flicker of irritation play at the corner of his mouth.

Sandy cleared her throat, placing her hands on the table. 'As you're aware,' she said, her tone chiding, confident, 'my client's car was reported stolen on the evening of the nineteenth of June, when Mr Grey returned from his camping trip and noticed it missing.'

'I'm aware,' McCormac replied gruffly, not bothering to look at her, his eyes trained on my face.

I held his stare, unwilling to break first.

'What I'm not aware of, however, is how your car came to be parked in a field in the middle of Essex. Any ideas, Lisa?'

I looked down at my lap, my tongue dry against the roof of my mouth as I tried to hide my shock. I had known they would find it eventually, but for it to be discovered so far from home wasn't what I had expected to hear. I had so many questions myself, and yet I knew I might never get answers for any of them. My hands shook as I pictured the car pulling into a dark field. That stormy, moonless night, that driving rain... A wave of nausea washed over me, and I swallowed a mouthful of saliva, trying to train my expression into a mask of indifference.

'Mrs Grey,' DS McCormac pushed. 'Answer the question please. Can you tell me why your car was abandoned so far from home?'

I shook my head. 'No... I mean, no comment.'

He continued as if I hadn't responded. 'And do you know what else I've been wondering, Lisa?' His voice was smooth, conversational now. 'Why, and indeed *how*, did your car come to have traces of blood on it? Not just any blood, I should add. DNA analysis has confirmed that the blood on your bonnet was that of Mr Fox. I must say, I found those results very interesting.

Oh, and perhaps now would be a good time for me to tell you that those other results we were waiting on came back. The hair found on that scarf was indeed yours. Now it's not looking so good for you, is it, Lisa?'

I shrugged, trying not to let the fear I was feeling show in my expression. Beside me, I felt Sandy lean forward, heard the scratch of her pen as she scribbled something in her notepad.

DS McCormac, with an air of total relaxation, stretched his legs out in front of him, nodding to the second officer in the little interview room, who stood and began to set something up on the small TV screen across from me. I didn't know what to expect, but I knew it wasn't going to be good. He wouldn't have been looking so pleased with himself otherwise. So damn confident.

'You know,' he continued, 'I couldn't piece it together. Why you would hit Mr Fox – someone your own husband described as a family friend – and just keep driving. Why wouldn't you call for help? And then I wondered if perhaps this wasn't simply a case of reckless driving, because I don't care who you are – if you hit a friend with your car, you're going to stop and make sure they get the help they need. Anyone would. But you didn't do that, did you, Lisa? You didn't wait with him. Didn't call an ambulance. And the only explanation for that – and please tell me if I'm wrong,' he said, scratching his stubbled chin with the end of his pen – 'was that you *meant* to hurt him. To kill him,' he added, the words cold, hard.

I wanted to press my hands to my ears, stop him from talking, but I couldn't. I simply sat there, frozen, terrified, trapped.

'So then I started thinking of all the reasons a woman might want to kill the man she lived opposite, and boy, did my imagination run wild. Anything to say about that, Lisa?' He barely waited half a second before he smiled. 'No? Didn't think so. Let's have a look at this then, shall we?'

His colleague pressed play on what was clearly CCTV footage.

As the image filled the screen, I recognised the coffee shop I liked to go to sometimes when I had a day to myself. I would order a pot of tea, a jacket potato and maybe a cake, and spend the afternoon sitting with a book, watching the world go by. As a stay-at-home mum, I sometimes found I needed to get out and break the routine to refresh myself, and the owners of the Green Flamingo were fun to talk to and made the best cakes in town.

I recognised the bright pink sundress first. The woman smiling up at the waitress from her seat at the table on the terrace as she thanked her for the wedge of fudge cake. It was me. Unmistakably me. I had never noticed the camera before, but it had clearly been pointing right at my table. And then the penny dropped as I recalled the last time I'd worn that dress. Knew what I would see next.

I wanted to look away, but I forced myself to keep staring at the screen, to hold my face rigid, expressionless. Russell, dressed in a navy-and-white vertical-striped cotton shirt, paired with cream denim shorts, looking like he was trying to get a job as a Topman model, stopped by the low hedge separating the tables from the pavement and, clearly recognising me, called across to me. I felt my face grow hot as I watched the scene. He waved, and when I didn't look up from my book, he walked around the hedge, coming to stand by my table. There was no sound on the video and I didn't know whether to be grateful for that or not, but one minute I was sitting in the sunshine, book in hand, cake in front of me, the next I was on my feet, the look on my face filled with all the emotion I couldn't show now.

Russell said something to me, reaching forward to touch my arm, and I may as well have been grabbed by a Rottweiler the way I reacted, lurching away, the backs of my thighs pressing up against the hedge. He stepped closer, arms thrown wide as if he might hug me, and I held up a hand, demanding he stop. In silence, I watched the clip of us standing inches from one another, his expression hurt, mine furious. For a moment, we just stared at one another. Then, coming to my senses, I picked up my book and my bag, and, without another word, pushed past him, leaving him standing alone, running his hands through his blonde hair, looking shaken and confused.

'We spoke to the owners of the café,' McCormac said as the screen turned black. 'They said you left without paying your bill that day – something they thought was very out of character for you. Now, I don't know about you, Lisa, but I don't tend to get into heated rows in public with any of my neighbours. Would you like to tell me what you were discussing with Mr Fox that day?'

I swallowed. Picked up my water bottle and took a sip, feeling sick, dizzy. 'No comment.' I sat back, gripping the bottle tight to stop my hands from shaking.

'Looked like a lovers' tiff to me. Were you having an affair with Russell Fox, Lisa?'

I felt the rage shoot through me at the accusation and had to squeeze the bottle tighter to keep from reacting. The urge to deny it, to defend my marriage, explain myself, burned inside me, and it took every last drop of my self-control not to speak, to yell.

'No comment,' I bit out through clenched teeth.

'Were you trying to cut off a romantic relationship before your respective partners found out? Was he threatening to tell your secret?'

'No. Comment.' My chest was rising and falling rapidly, the sweat pooling at the base of my spine, behind my knees. I pressed my lips together, fury and fear combining in a potent cocktail inside me. I could feel my bowels churning, my insides turning liquid. I wanted to get up and run, every instinct in my body screaming danger, my stomach cramping rhythmically. I pressed my hands hard into my belly, trying to suppress the pain.

There was only one other time in my life I could remember feeling this afraid – the knock on the front door from Lucy, the wife of Henric, one of Mike's climbing friends. The two of them had driven to Snowdon for the weekend, and I hadn't even batted an eyelid at their plans to summit. I'd heard so many people talking about it, I'd naïvely assumed it was no more than a beginner's trek. When Lucy had told me that a storm had blown in, Mike and Henric getting separated, I still hadn't grasped the severity of the situation. Why couldn't they just meet back in the car park? Why had she come to tell me in person?

It wasn't until Henric had called from Wales, his voice whipped in the wind as he yelled over speakerphone about a rescue team, dogs, helicopters, *casualties* that I began to understand what was happening. Realise that I could lose Mike. That fear had descended on me like an iron bar to the chest, leaving me gasping for breath, unable to fathom a life without him. I had known with perfect clarity in that moment that if he didn't make it back, I wouldn't – *couldn't* – survive it. I loved him too much to go on without him.

The thirty-eight hours that followed had been agony, not just mentally but physically. My digestive system had been paralysed by the white-hot terror that flowed through my veins, my bowels in constant spasm, my throat too tight to breathe, let alone consider food. I hadn't slept, adrenaline and what-ifs keeping me on red alert, pacing, staring at the children as they slept, wondering what would happen to us if Mike didn't survive.

The call, when he'd finally got down from that mountain, that moment I'd heard his voice, had been enough to make me collapse in a heap on the kitchen floor, sobbing without restraint in sheer relief. It had been the most terrifying experience of my life, waiting, wondering what my fate would be. And now, trapped here with my freedom at stake, another separation from my family threatening to fall upon me, I felt that same blinding fear.

DS McCormac was watching me with an intense stare, like he'd cornered me and wasn't about to let me escape again. 'Still no comment,' he mused. 'Interesting. Because before, we might have been talking about causing death by dangerous driving. But now we have the scarf. We have evidence of your car on the road at the time of the hit-and-run. We have the victim's blood on your bonnet and – the cherry on top – we have what looks like an argument, *four days* before Mr Fox was killed. Or what I personally like to call *motive*,' he said, the satisfaction dripping like poison through his words.

He leaned back in his seat, a wide smile on his face. 'I'd say now's a good time to start talking, Mrs Grey. Wouldn't you agree?'

THIRTY-TWO

VICTORIA

Mike's body trembled against my own, his breath uneven in my ear as he tried to regain control of his emotions. I stood, holding him as tight as I dared, determined to be strong despite the situation as I watched the police car disappear around the bend with Lisa secured inside. The night was cool and clear, the road silent now that the sound of the car had faded away, and I felt oddly exposed, surrounded by dark windows, my own empty home an eerie witness to this moment.

So, they had come for her. The detective had said murder. Was it possible she wouldn't come home this time?

I stroked my hand over Mike's hair, smoothing it down as I waited for the shock to pass. I had made the call anonymously in the end, just a casual remark that they might want to look at the CCTV from the café that day.

'Why are they doing this to us?' His voice was muffled, his face pressed into my shoulder, and I closed my eyes, breathing in deep in an attempt to steady myself. He raised his face to meet mine, and I saw the despair in his eyes before he stepped back, pressing the heels of his hands into the sockets.

'Why, Vic? You said yourself it was an accident. A hit-and-run because he was drunk and dressed in black, walking along the road in the middle of the night. Why the hell are they acting like Lisa had anything to do with it? She wasn't even driving that night – she was at home!'

He looked down the road in the direction the car had gone and shook his head. 'They're treating her like a cold-blooded killer. You and I both know she didn't do this, so why do they keep targeting her?'

I shook my head. 'I don't know,' I replied, my voice soft, soothing, reminding me of the thousands of times I'd had to talk Russell down in the past, keep the situation calm, play the peacekeeper. 'They haven't told me anything,' I added truthfully. I didn't want to admit that I hadn't asked.

I took his elbow, guiding him back to the open front door, not wanting to stand out on the pavement any longer. I hated feeling so exposed, so watched, though I knew I was being silly. Mike, pliable and still pale with shock, came easily, clearly at a loss at what to do next.

I closed the door behind me then headed to the kitchen. Lisa's apron was back on the hook, the mug of coffee Mike had made for her turning tepid on the counter. I picked it up, emptying it into the sink.

A moment later, there was the metallic jangle and click of a key in the front door, and his eyes met mine.

'How am I going to tell them?' he said, his voice cracking.

The sound of laughter, Holly and Jack kicking off shoes, arriving back together, filled the house, and my heart swelled, the horrible circumstances of the evening momentarily forgotten, replaced by joy to be in the home of a family who so clearly loved one another.

Holly walked in first, Jack hot on her heels, making straight for the fridge and pouring a large glass of orange juice.

'Mum's in my bad books,' she announced, though she was still smiling. 'Where is she?' She looked around, then continued without waiting for an answer. 'Got to the changing rooms and realised my sports bra was missing from my bag. I bet she borrowed it again, didn't she?' Her eyes were accusing as she looked to her dad.

He nodded soberly, though Holly didn't seem to pick up on the mood. 'She went for a run early this morning,' he said, answering in a monotone.

'Well tell her to buy her own and stop pinching my underwear. It's annoying.'

'Here,' Jack called across the kitchen, rifling through the basket of clean laundry on the sideboard. He fished out something that made my stomach flip as I recognised it – the creamy lace bra with the dusky pink roses emblazoned across it, the matching piece of the set still squirrelled away at the back of Russell's desk drawer.

I hadn't known what to do with the pants, hadn't even set foot in his office since his death. Bile rose up in my throat at the colourful images that came automatically to mind at the sight of the bra, and I made up my mind to sneak it out of the house, burn it as soon as I got the chance. I never again wanted to be confronted with it, with the image of Lisa and my husband in bed together.

Jack tossed it at Holly, who caught it, surprised. 'Why don't you steal hers and then you'll be even?' he teased.

Holly glanced down at the bra clasped in her long, pale fingers, and I watched her smile slide away. She dropped it onto the counter as if it had scorched her, stepping back with a shake of her head. I watched in confusion as she struggled to put on an expression of nonchalant amusement, but not before I saw something else there, something that made an iron fist clamp hard around my heart.

'That's *mine* anyway, idiot!' she said. 'And I don't even like it. I haven't seen it in—'

She broke off, and I held my breath as she looked across the room at me, her eyes meeting mine for the briefest of moments. Just enough.

'In weeks,' she finished softly. She glanced back down at the bra, then without another word, opened the kitchen bin with the foot pedal and swiped it off the counter, letting the lid slam closed. She looked like she was about to vomit, her guilt and embarrassment impossible to disguise.

What the hell *was* this? I stared at her, putting all the pieces of the puzzle together, trying to rewrite what I'd thought I knew. Was it *her*? *Holly* and Russell. Not Lisa. I had loved her like a daughter, like she was my own blood. Russell and I had known her all her life, watched as she morphed from a chubby toddler picking daisies in her front garden to a long-limbed pre-teen learning to ride her bike up and down the pavement outside our house. I'd helped her make a Mother's Day card for Lisa the year her teacher had forgotten to do them at school. I'd talked her through a falling-out she'd had with a friend. I'd put plasters on her scraped knees and cuddled her on my lap through countless barbecues, while the sky faded to black and the grown-ups stayed up talking, her soft golden hair twined around my fingers, her warm body curled against mine as she drifted in and out of sleep. Was it possible that despite everything I had done for her, all the love I had showered her with, she had betrayed me? Taken the one thing that was mine?

Where Lisa and Russell had never made sense in my mind, this was different. Holly was young. Mouldable. Her body was slim and unmarked by age. She was naïve, still treated like a little girl by Lisa and, as far as I knew, had never brought a boy home. Would he have seen her as the perfect project? The new and shiny thing to replace me with?

For him to look at her in that way was more than a betrayal of our marriage vows. It was incestuous somehow. Had he watched her transform into a woman and begun to see her in a new light? The thought of him turning on the charm I knew he was capable of, seducing her with just the right words, convincing her he was everything she wanted was sickening, and yet, I knew just how easy it would have been for him to make her fall in love with him. She would have been wooed, infatuated, unable to resist all he offered her, the sweet promises and seductive words. He was a master when it came to getting his own way. I knew that all too well, because it was exactly what had happened to me.

I leaned heavily against the counter, my legs turning to jelly as I opened a door to this new and far more unsettling conclusion.

Holly turned away from me, her narrow shoulders hunched as she poured a glass of juice from the jug on the counter, drinking it down. Her fingers were shaking, I noted. She didn't look my way, didn't even glance up.

Mike stood looking nervous, oblivious to the torment I was experiencing. 'Guys,' he said, rubbing a hand up and down his arm, an unconscious self-soothing gesture. 'Come and sit down. I need to talk to you.'

Jack put his glass on the table. 'Where's Mum?' he asked, his voice suddenly small, scared – a lost little boy searching for his mother.

'Just come with me.'

Mike walked out of the kitchen, heading for the living room. Holly and Jack followed without a word of protest. I stayed by the sink, my head swimming as I tried to rewrite history in my mind, picturing not Lisa but Holly going behind my back, allowing herself to be seduced by my husband, and my blood ran cold. I would never have imagined she had it in her. There was a time when I'd believed that what she and I had – the closeness we shared – was stronger than anything she'd ever experienced with her mother. Lisa was always so busy, too distracted by life, by her perfect husband, to see Holly for who she really was, the changes in her as she'd blossomed into a woman. Holly had always sought me out whenever she wanted to discuss the challenges of growing up, arguments with friends, troubles at school. These little chats had been our special little secret, and I had missed her over the past month or so.

Now that I thought about it, I realised that recently she seemed to have pulled back from me. Was *this* the reason? Had I been too busy looking at Lisa to see the truth in front of my eyes?

I turned on the tap, running my wrists under the cold stream of water, taking in big gulping breaths as I tried to calm myself, locking my emotions up tight inside my chest. Then, serene and composed, I followed the others into the living room, ready to stand by Mike's side as he broke the news to Holly and Jack that their mother had been taken from them again. Whatever I discovered next, there was one thing I was sure of – I couldn't let them shut me out now. I had to be a part of this, included, *trusted*. Whatever happened, I *had* to keep them on my side.

THIRTY-THREE

'Goodnight, you two. Try and get some sleep. It's late and you both look exhausted,' I said, trying to picture what Lisa would advise Jack and Holly to do right now and make sure I did the same. I hadn't been able to tear my gaze from Holly during Mike's harrowing revelation that Lisa had been arrested again, watching her eyes fill with tears, the way she pulled her knees up beneath her chin, holding them tight, still so much like the little girl I had fallen in love with. How many times had I wished she were my child? That *I* could be the one who got to tuck her into bed at night, read her a story, soothe her when she woke from a nightmare? How many times had I envied Lisa the simple pleasures and responsibilities she seemed to take for granted?

Picturing Holly with Russell made my skin crawl. When she absently rubbed her hand up and down her calf, I couldn't help but imagine *his* hands roaming over her skin. Touching her. His mouth on her pretty rosebud lips. His voice saying her name, laughing at some joke she'd made, making her feel special, the way he once had with me. When those images had seeped into my imagination, it was all I could do to stop myself from screaming out loud, envy and disgust mingling inside me. But it couldn't be true. She would never have done that to me, and Russell, for all his faults, would never have seen her that way. She was barely out of childhood.

I shoved the awful thoughts down, focusing on the deep timbre of Mike's voice as he explained the events of the evening, studying the details of Holly's expression, the little gestures that were uniquely her. It was so much easier to ignore the nagging questions that demanded answers; instead, sinking into Lisa's role, giving instructions and sending Holly and Jack off to bed like the children I had always considered them to be.

They had nodded without offering a reply, too tired to even speak, though I got the feeling that sleep wouldn't come easy for either of them tonight.

Mike looked like a broken man as he watched them trail out of the living room. They'd taken the news of Lisa's second arrest in vastly different ways. Jack had raged in disbelief, reminding me so much of his father, then quickly gone into fix-it mode, voicing every idea he could think of to remedy the situation, though no solution seemed to exist. Holly, however, hadn't said more than a few words.

Glancing at the photo of Jack and Holly above the fireplace, taken on the beach when they were little, I felt grief hit me harder than anything I had felt for Russell. She wasn't just another woman. She was the little girl I had wanted for my own. *My* Holly. Russell had to have known the pain he would be causing me in choosing her over anyone else. He knew just how I felt about that girl. I shook my head. I was mad to even contemplate it. There was no way it was Holly. It must be Lisa.

I had to protect Holly now – to be a mother figure while Lisa wasn't here to do it.

Mike had been calm throughout the conversation, though his voice had trembled as he told them everything they had missed. I should have felt like an intruder sitting by his side as he broke the news, but they had all been so wrapped up in their sadness that I wasn't even sure they'd noticed me there. It was as if I belonged. As though I were meant to be there with them, a part of the family, accepted without question, and *that* made my heart sing. To think that they were discussing the killer of my husband was too surreal to contemplate, so I found that I just didn't. I compartmentalised it, made it feel far away, disconnected myself to the point that I could hear his name and pretend it meant nothing. It was just easier that way.

Mike and Jack had talked until just gone one in the morning, and then, seeing the exhaustion in the slump of Jack's shoulders, the dark circles beneath Holly's eyes as she clutched a cushion to her chest, curled in a tight little ball in the armchair, I'd suggested quietly that they go up to bed. That we would try and find a solution in the morning. When they'd both nodded, taking my advice, I'd understood what it must be like for Lisa, what it would be like to be a mother to these children, to be able to give advice or instructions and have them heard and followed. It made me feel special – important somehow.

As I listened to their heavy footfall on the stairs, I remained perched on the arm of the sofa, half an arm's length between myself and Mike. He made no attempt to move away, and again I felt how much I was needed here, even if the three of them didn't yet realise what I had to offer.

'Mike,' I began, reaching to touch his shoulder. 'You should get some sleep too.'

He sighed but made no attempt to get up.

'Do you want a drink?' I offered. 'Tea? I could put the kettle—'

'Why would they come back, Vic? Why take her again? It doesn't make sense.'

I shrugged, looking down at my feet, unable to meet his eyes as I spoke. 'Do you think... I mean... is there a chance she *was* involved? We've always said there was no way, but the police aren't going to waste their time if they don't feel they have something solid to work with. I just…' I shook my head, pursing my lips, unable to hold back the thoughts I'd tried to suppress all evening.

I knew I was treading on dangerous ground, and a part of me willed myself to shut up, *stop* before I said something I couldn't take back. But I couldn't seem to prevent the words from coming, couldn't ignore the image of me being needed, valuable, something more than the trophy wife to a man who hadn't deserved me.

'What if she knows something, Mike?' I heard myself ask. 'I think we need to consider the possibility that she isn't telling the whole truth.'

'You think after everything she's been through this week, she wouldn't say something to me?'

There was an unmistakeable edge to his voice, and I slipped off the armrest to sit beside him, my hand finding his, squeezing it tight.

'Sometimes it's not that easy. I'm not saying she was involved, that she was the driver…' I paused, letting the words linger, watching his face change as the idea seeped into his thoughts. I kept my hand on his, unwilling to break contact. 'I'm not saying she made a choice to do anything. But everyone is capable of making a mistake. Keeping quiet when they should speak up. Even Lisa,' I continued, my words soft. I didn't want to come across as too harsh, too keen to jump to conclusions, but he had to see that there was a possibility he'd been wrong.

'She would have told me,' he said. He shifted on the sofa to face me, moving further away as he did, his hand slipping from my grasp.

I tried not to let my disappointment show on my face, wishing he would let me comfort him when he needed it most.

'We've never had secrets between us. Not ever. If she knew

anything, she would have said.' He ran his fingers through his hair, his eyes pink with exhaustion.

'What if she was afraid? Can you imagine how she would feel if she *had* been driving? I know *I* would have gone into shock. What if it was an accident? If she was too scared to tell anyone? What if she meant to get help but lost her nerve? I... I don't know what really happened that night, Mike, but what I *do* know is that my husband is dead.'

I was surprised to find that my eyes had filled with tears as I said the words aloud, and I blinked them back, feeling flushed and embarrassed at the display of vulnerability. I shook my head, my voice barely a whisper as I tried to regain control of myself.

'He's dead, Mike. Someone hit him and drove away. The thought that Lisa might have had anything to do with that breaks my heart in two, but what if...' I shook my head, sniffing as I felt a fat tear roll down my cheek, despite my best efforts to stop it.

Mike was horror-struck as he realised I was crying. I saw the panic on his face, coupled with discomfort.

'Oh, God, I'm so sorry, Vic. You've dealt with everything so well, it's been too easy to forget what you're going through. You're so composed, but it's my fault for not being more sensitive.'

He moved closer again, pulling me into a hug, his arms strong around my shoulders, and I let myself lean into him, breathing in the woody scent of his skin, his hair pressed against my cheek.

I gripped him tight, burying my words in his neck. 'It's not your fault. It's easier for me to keep going, to keep busy. And I want to be here for you.'

I felt him nod against me. 'But I *am* sorry. I know you've lost the most important person in your life. You've lost your soulmate. But now... now I'm losing mine, and I'm so scared she won't come back this time.'

'She *will*,' I said, though I wasn't sure any more.

He shook his head. 'I can't lose her. This family needs her. *I* need her.'

'I know,' I said, pulling back to look him in the eye, though I didn't release my hold around his neck. The closeness was intoxicating. When was the last time I had been held like this? When had I felt so protected?

I sighed. 'I'll help you through this, Mike. No matter what happens, you'll always be able to rely on me.'

He gave a watery smile, and I wondered if Lisa knew just how lucky she was. I would have given the world for a man who valued me the way Mike did her. Russell had never been a proper husband to me, never made me feel he truly cared, or that he even knew the real me.

'You're so good, Vic. You've lost your husband, and still you're the first person to offer comfort. You're here in the trenches with us when you have every right to be wallowing at home in your own grief. You didn't deserve what happened to you – to lose him like that.'

He shook his head, his brow creasing as he glanced towards the window, as if he was expecting to see a car pull up on the drive, Lisa to walk back in and make it all okay, though we both knew she wouldn't be coming home tonight.

He gave a sigh and looked back at me. 'I don't know how you're so strong when I'm falling apart.'

I smiled, trying to reassure him. 'I've learned to accept that there are things you can change and things you can't. Once I got my head around that, life became a lot simpler. That's not to say it doesn't hurt sometimes. That my mind doesn't drag me down dark alleys to memories I'd rather forget. But I can feel it and let it pass. I don't allow myself to drown in it.'

He smiled, though it didn't reach his bloodshot eyes. 'You're strong. Stronger than I will ever be.' He gave a wry laugh. 'I can climb a mountain no problem. But take my wife from me and I'm nothing. I break.'

'Oh, I don't know about that,' I said, pulling him back into a hug as I spoke the soothing words into his ear. 'You might find you surprise yourself. You never know what you're capable of until you're challenged.'

He grunted in response but didn't pull away. My lips curled into a soft smile as I held him tighter, not wanting to let him go.

THIRTY-FOUR

LISA

'Hello?'

I leaned forward, as close as I could get to the payphone on the wall, aware of people walking back and forth along the hall behind me. There had been no offer of a side room to make a call this time. Even that illusion of privacy had been stripped from me. I glanced over my shoulder at the young PC who'd been charged with babysitting me, my legs shaking with exhaustion as I turned my back on him, trying to pretend my every move wasn't being catalogued. 'Holly?' I said, hearing the female voice on the other end of the line.

'Lisa! Thank God you called. How are you? What's going on?'

My head snapped up, the exhaustion instantly dissolving as a burst of adrenaline shot through my limbs, making me tremble. 'Victoria? What are you doing there? Where's Mike?' I asked, half wondering if I'd dialled the wrong number in my delirium. The white plastic clock on the wall told me it was gone 2 a.m. Why was she still there? Goose pimples broke out over my flesh at the realisation that she was with my husband, comforting him, stepping into my shoes without my permission.

'He fell asleep on the sofa. He was pretty upset after you... Well, you know. We had to tell the kids of course, and they took it pretty badly, so I thought I'd stick around and...'

Her voice muffled and I heard her talking to someone in the background, though I couldn't make out what she was saying. After a moment, she was back on the line. 'Mike's just stirring in the other room. He's coming now, I think.'

I blinked, wondering what on earth was happening, why she'd slotted herself into my world so fully, taken it upon herself to be my husband's support system when I couldn't be there. The thought of her talking to my children about me, telling them what I'd never wanted to have to burden them with in the first place, rankled no end. I had never felt so impotent, unable to be the mother they needed, the wife Mike deserved.

I tried to moderate my tone, wondering why it was taking Mike so long to come to the phone, why he seemed in no rush to wake up and speak to me.

'I... I suppose it must be hard, going back to that empty house?' I asked, hoping she would say yes, admit a weakness, give me a reason that might explain why she was there that I could at least empathise with.

'Not really.' She lowered her voice, and I had the impression she was speaking only to me, ensuring that Mike was unable to hear her. 'To begin with, it was strange. But if I'm being honest, I got used to being alone in that marriage a long time ago. Rolling over and finding his place in my bed empty. Seeing him look past me to someone else...'

'Really?' I was shocked by her candour, her admission that Russell was anything but perfect. I'd never heard her say anything like that before, never realised she felt he wasn't present in their marriage.

I shivered, wrapping my free arm around my body, wondering why she would say such a thing now of all times. I wanted to ask so much more, dig deeper and find out what she really thought of the man she'd been married to all those years. I wanted to tell her to leave my husband alone, that we didn't want her hanging around, reminding us of what had happened, bringing Russell's ghost everywhere she went, clinging to her like smoke, a memory we couldn't move on from. I had to get home, back to my family, and yet, I couldn't do it. I didn't know how best to protect them.

My mind spun in circles as I tried to process what was happening, think what to do next, how to keep the people I loved safe.

I glanced over my shoulder again, seeing the watchful eyes of the uniformed officer on me, his face neutral. I held my stance, remained calm on the outside, though inside I was screaming. It reminded me of the meeting I'd had with Holly's teacher when she was twelve and being relentlessly bullied by a couple of girls in her class. I'd wanted to yell, to demand the bullies be expelled. I'd wanted to roam the halls of the school, find those awful girls and grab them by the collar, tell them that if they continued to make my daughter's life difficult, I would make theirs hell, but I'd swallowed those thoughts and pasted on a serene smile. I'd been polite, empathetic to the teacher's struggle, knowing that the only way to win the war was to keep the upper hand.

Now was no different. I had to be steady. Patient. It had worked then. The girls had ended up being suspended, a new no-tolerance bullying policy introduced, all because I'd managed to hold in my raw fury and hone it into something productive, valuable. For Holly's sake, I'd had to learn to suppress and hide my true feelings for the bigger picture. I'd got very good at it since becoming a mother.

'Oh,' Victoria replied. 'What does it matter? After all, it's not like me and Russell can fix our issues now, can we? Water under the bridge, hey?' she said, as if I wasn't currently under investigation for his death. 'Anyway, here's Mike for you. Good luck, Lisa.'

I opened my mouth to reply, to tell her it was time she left, went back to her own home, but she was already gone.

THIRTY-FIVE

VICTORIA

The smell of the expensive perfume Russell had bought for me last Christmas brought back a flicker of a memory as I sprayed it on my neck and wrists, batting the image of his face away, though I couldn't help but think of that morning. The coffee I'd brewed, the rare treat of pastries for breakfast as we sat beside the realistic-looking gas fire in the living room exchanging presents, the smell of blue spruce needles permeating the air. With thick frost blanketing the driveway and windowsills, and the Trans-Siberian Orchestra playing Christmas music through the speakers, the house had felt cosy rather than oppressive. Russell had always been good with gifts, though his motivation was more about me telling everyone how generous he'd been than an actual desire to please me. Usually, he spent far too much, and my tastes didn't feature in his decision-making process, but I had wanted this perfume for a while and was pleasantly surprised when I opened the gift-wrapped box.

I had hugged him, and when his parents had arrived for lunch, he'd come into the kitchen to get them a drink and walked up behind me, kissing the side of my neck in a way that made me wonder if he'd made too early a start on the wine.

Even so, it had been a nice moment, a memory I'd wanted to hold on to, especially as it had turned out to be the last Christmas his dad would share with us before his sudden heart attack.

Russell had made jokes under his breath to me about the way his mum nagged his dad incessantly: *Use a coaster, Bruce. Don't tell that story!* Even when his dad got up with a laboured sigh to use the bathroom after lunch, she couldn't help blurting out, 'Wash your hands properly, Bruce!' as if he were a toddler rather than a man in his seventies with all his faculties intact. Russell usually couldn't help but snap at her when she harassed his dad like this, but for some reason, his mood was light that day, and he'd winked at me as he topped up her glass. But now, I was in no mood to replay the expression he'd worn on his face, the little smiles we'd shared between us as he'd relaxed in a way he rarely allowed himself to.

I placed the pretty glass perfume dispenser down on my dressing table, checking my lipstick in the mirror and glancing at my watch. It was almost ten, and I was sure, despite his late night, Mike would be up already, fretting about Lisa. As I grabbed my bag, slipped on my shoes and made my way over the road, I wasn't worried about disturbing them. They needed me – that much was obvious.

I hesitated at the front door, wondering if I should knock or just try the handle and walk in like a member of the family would have done, but I lost my nerve, rapping on the glass instead, not wanting to make anyone jump. Jack answered, still dressed in an old white T-shirt and pyjama bottoms, his hair scruffy from sleep. I had a motherly urge to brush it for him, something I'd done once or twice in the past when I'd had the chance to babysit them, but that was years ago, and I doubted at fifteen he would appreciate the offer.

'Hi, Vic,' he said, his usually jovial voice muted, his eyes sad.

I frowned, noting that he hadn't called me 'Auntie'. It was the first time I could remember that he hadn't used the endearment, and I suddenly wondered if he was angry with me – if he might know more than he was letting on. I had been so careful to moderate my behaviour these past few days, not to show any animosity towards Lisa, knowing how astute Jack was and how he would pick up on even the merest hint of resentment on my part. I knew he would be watching, taking it all in, wondering how I was feeling with his mother under arrest for my husband's murder. But now I wondered if I had been *too* subdued, too quiet when it came to my feelings on the subject. If perhaps my lack of reaction had set off alarm bells for him and made him watch me all the more closely. Not for the first time, I wished he was a little less observant.

He made no attempt to move aside, and I felt a wave of irritation at his show of poor manners. 'Can I come in?' I asked, my tone as sweet as ever, though it cost me not to snap the words out.

He shrugged, his eyes locking on mine, and I felt myself blush, automatically looking down at my feet. Without a word, he swung the door open and stepped back, allowing me to enter.

I stepped past him, pretending not to notice the frosty reception. 'Dad around?'

He nodded towards the back of the house. 'In the garden. He just got off the phone. They won't let him speak to her.' His voice cracked, and I reached for his arm, squeezing it, determined to win him over.

'It'll be okay, sweetheart. We'll figure this out. Come on, let's go and find him, yeah?'

Jack didn't reply as he followed me through the kitchen and out to the garden, where Mike was sitting on the edge of a sunlounger, a mug of coffee clutched in his hands. His eyes were bloodshot and rimmed with red, but that was the only colour his face held. Beneath his tan there was an ashy grey pallor that told me just how terrified he was. Fear radiated from him, a palpable cloud of adrenaline that seemed to pour from his very being. I felt my heart lurch in sympathy. For a second, I questioned myself – whether I should have come, whether I was intruding on a private moment – but then he looked up and managed a half-smile.

'Hey, Vic,' he said, his voice an octave higher than usual, a skittish, panicked tone at odds with his usually laid-back demeanour. 'What can I do for you?'

I smiled. 'As if I'd come for a favour now. I've come to do you one actually.'

I sat down beside him on the lounger, and Jack plonked himself on the decking, rubbing the sleep from his eyes.

'Any news?' I asked Mike.

'Nothing. It's unbearable.' He shook his head. 'I'm going to have to go down there and see what I can find out. Talk to her lawyer or something. It's not fair that they're targeting her like this. It's really not okay.'

'I'll come with you, Dad.' Jack's face was earnest, and I could see in him the same overwhelming need to be doing something, to fix this somehow and make it all go away. He was such a sweet boy.

Mike shook his head. 'No, mate. I appreciate the offer, but Mum wouldn't want you being mixed up in all this.'

'But I want to come. What else am I going to do? Sit around and wait? I have to do something!'

I cleared my throat, feeling oddly nervous. 'I might be able to help with that.' I fixed Mike with what I hoped was a reassuring smile. 'Why don't I take Holly and Jack out for the day? Take their minds off everything?' I offered.

Jack shook his head. 'I want to help Mum.'

I nodded. 'I get that, sweetie. But right now, there's nothing you can do. And if I know Lisa, she'll be worrying herself sick about how this is impacting you and Holly. Think how relieved she'll be to hear that you've been able to take a break from the stress of the situation and do something fun.'

He frowned, looking at his dad, and I saw from Mike's expression that he was considering my point of view. He would do anything for Lisa. If I was ever going to get them to agree, this was the right argument.

'I'm not talking about anything too elaborate; I know you won't want to go far, and besides, I don't drive,' I said.

As usual, I was embarrassed to remind them of that fact. I wished I'd learned when I was younger, but Russell hadn't wanted me to get lessons, arguing that he didn't want me denting his fancy car and that we couldn't afford another decent one. He would never have allowed me to have a cheap runaround, seeing it as a poor reflection on his ability to provide for me. I would have been happy with a second-hand Mini or a cute little Smart car, but he wouldn't hear of it, preferring to tell anyone who asked that I was too scared to learn, and being financially dependent on him had pretty much ruled out my chances of getting my licence.

'I thought we could get the open-top bus downtown, maybe do a bit of shopping, lunch, a movie? On me of course.'

Jack's eyes lit up, and I realised I had swayed his fickle teenage heart with the thought of a shopping trip on my cash. I swallowed a smile at how well I knew him.

'What's this?'

I looked up to see Holly, dressed in jeans and a T-shirt, her face bare and pale, standing at the back door. 'I heard talking and thought it was Mum.' The disappointment was thick in her voice and I tried not to take it to heart.

'Sorry,' I said, offering an apologetic smile. 'I was just saying, I think it might be a good idea if I take the two of you out for the day. It's not good for you to be cooped up in here waiting for news.'

She was shaking her head before I'd even finished my

sentence, and I felt a wave of irritation. As much as I wanted to help Mike, a larger part of me wanted to get some time alone with Holly. Ask her the questions that had been swirling in my mind ever since last night. See her face when I mentioned Russell's name and watch her reaction. This was a girl I had known for ever. Surely I would be able to tell if she was lying to me?

'I don't really feel like going out. I'll just stay here with Dad. I want to be at home in case Mum calls.'

Mike frowned, rubbing his hands over his face, and I was sure he was wishing Lisa was here to tell him what to do. Dealing with the kids' emotional meltdowns seemed to be something he left to her, at least from what I had witnessed, although admittedly, I had to assume they were on their best behaviour when I'd been invited over. I hadn't had the privilege of seeing what went on day to day behind closed doors, at least not before these past few weeks. I was glad that was all starting to change.

He looked at me, and I nodded reassuringly, giving him the push he needed.

He pursed his lips then set his jaw. 'I think Vic's right, Hols. I'm not going to be here anyway. I'm going down the station in a minute, and I'm sure you don't want to be here alone all day,' he added, and I saw by her expression that he was right.

'Your dad will call me if he hears anything, won't you, Mike?' I added, trying to persuade her. 'We'll turn around and come right back if we hear anything, but you know how long these things can take. Waiting around here will just make you worry,' I said, making it sound like Lisa's release was just a matter of bureaucracy, though I wasn't so sure about that.

Holly folded her arms, but Jack stood, moving to her side.

'Auntie Vic's right, Hols,' he said, and I felt a swell of joy that he was back to calling me by my proper title. Aside from my father, I had always been good at winning over members of the opposite sex. I knew how to placate them, knew how to make myself small so they could feel strong, in control. It was that dynamic that had made a success of my marriage for so many years.

'And we can look for a present for Mum while we're at the shops. It'll give us something to focus on.' He hugged her, and I smiled at how close they still were, despite all the teenage teasing between the two of them.

'Okay, okay,' she relented. 'I'll just get ready.' She turned with sad resignation, and I silently made it my mission to make her smile at some point today.

Jack looked at me. 'I'll go and get dressed. Give me ten minutes, 'kay?' He didn't wait for an answer as he sprinted into the house.

Mike patted my knee, and I pressed my shoulder against his. 'Thanks, Vic. It's probably just what they need. I hope Holly won't spoil it for you – she's been hard work lately.'

'We'll be fine – I'm happy to take them. You sure you don't want to come too? I hate to think of you alone trying to deal with the gatekeepers at the station. I'm not sure how far you'll get today.'

He sighed. 'I know it's a long shot, but I need to be there. To be close to her, even if I can't do anything to help. I have to talk to that lawyer and see what else I can do for her. There must be something. And if there isn't, it keeps me sane to at least try.'

I nodded. 'We'll bring back something for dinner.'

The kids appeared at the open doorway, ready to go, and I stood up, looking at them with a deep sense of pleasure and pride, determined to give them the best day out possible.

THIRTY-SIX

LISA

I gripped the phone between my palms, listening to it ring, imagining it on the table in the living room, the pictures of Holly and Jack on the walls, the comfy threadbare sofa where Mike and I spent our evenings cuddled up under the throw I'd laboriously crocheted the first winter of our marriage. It felt like a thousand years had passed since last night, when I'd stood in this same spot in this noisy hallway, waiting and hoping for Mike's voice to say hello.

After our brief chat last night, I'd been taken back to the cell, where I'd drifted in and out of sleep, one nightmare following another, until I'd been too afraid to let my eyes close for fear of what I might see. What I might yell in the depths of a dream. I'd curled my knees up under my chin, my back against the hard wall, listening to the echoing sounds of people coming and going outside the door. I'd heard a drunk man threaten to punch someone before being locked up, the shrill scream of a woman's voice – *That bitch started it! She needed a good slap!* – all the while wondering if it was still dark. If Holly and Jack were sleeping. If Mike would cope if I never got out of here.

I'd tried to focus on the positives, forcing myself to

remember happy memories of holidays we'd taken, my laughter-filled kitchen as I prepared Sunday lunch. The way Holly had spoken with a little lisp until she was six and she lost her front baby teeth. I'd forgotten about that until now. The memory had made me smile but only briefly. Try as I might, I couldn't seem to stop darker thoughts pushing their way to the forefront of my mind.

The CCTV footage from the Green Flamingo, reminding me of memories I would rather have put to bed. Russell's voice, the last time I'd heard it before his sudden death. The smell of his aftershave, something I'd never paid much attention to before but now couldn't seem to erase from my mind. Victoria, practically spending the night just after my arrest. The way she'd looked at Mike throughout dinner, those little 'accidental' touches.

It had been easy to convince myself at the time that it was all in my imagination, but sitting in a cell with nothing else to focus on, overtired and scared, it was impossible to push those thoughts aside. What was she doing? Why did she keep coming over, now of all times? As far as I could see, we'd given no indication that we wanted to form closer bonds with her – it was all coming from her side, and with Russell barely in the ground, it felt like her priorities were skewed.

I tried to imagine what *I* would be doing if it were Mike who had died, and the thought made a jolt of pain hit me in the gut. I would be barely functioning. Not sleeping. Not getting showered and dressed. Certainly not turning up at the neighbours' at every opportunity to flirt with someone else's husband.

I'd dwelled on her intentions and new strange behaviour the remainder of the night, until a kind member of staff had brought me a breakfast tray. After that, exhausted, tearful and feeling not nearly so strong as I had in my first interview, I had endured hours of interrogation, the same questions being thrown at me over and over in ever more creative ways. I felt like DS

McCormac was trying to trip me up, catch me out, but despite my resolve being tested to its limits, I hadn't broken. My throat was scratchy and sore from repeating 'no comment' over and over again, and I had watched the steadily increasing frustration build on the detective's face as the day dragged on. They had my car. The scarf. The video footage, which admittedly looked pretty damning. In his mind, it was a done deal. I could sense his dislike of me. I knew he believed he'd caught the killer. He was just waiting for a confession, and his tactic was to wear me down until I was so emotionally fraught, I was liable to confess to just about anything.

It had been a day that had taken all my strength to get through, but despite keeping my silence, I still hadn't been released and had just been told that I wasn't going anywhere tonight. Now, with a microwave meal of greasy meatballs and pasta sitting heavily in my stomach, all I wanted was to hear my husband's voice.

The phone, pressed hard to my ear, rang once more, and then I smiled, my eyes filling with tears, as I heard Jack answer. I swallowed, not wanting to upset him by hearing me cry, determined not to let my voice crack. 'Hi, darling, it's me.'

'Mum! It's Mum!' I heard the muffled shout and pictured him yelling over his shoulder. 'Are you okay?' he asked urgently. 'What's going on? Are you coming home now?'

I opened my mouth to speak and choked on my words, my throat thick with tears. I couldn't burden him with the details, couldn't let myself fall apart, and that was exactly what would happen if I talked about what today had been like.

'Not tonight, sweetie,' I said, trying to keep my tone breezy. 'Not much to report here. The food is terrible and the coffee is lukewarm. But enough about that – what's been going on there? Have you kept your room tidy? Watered my tomato plants?' My words came in a hurry as I tried to lead him on to more comfortable topics.

'I'll water them in a sec – I forgot. We've just got back in – well, Holly and me. Dad's in the shower. He went down to the station first thing, but they wouldn't let him talk to you. He was there most of the day, but they made him leave a little while ago. He's really angry – they wouldn't even speak to him.'

My heart thudded at this news. My husband had been under the same roof as me for hours and I hadn't even known. The realisation made me want to scream. Couldn't they have just let me see him for a minute or two? It would have given me the strength to keep going when I was so close to breaking point. But then, that was exactly why McCormac *wouldn't* want me to see Mike. He *wanted* me alone and scared. I tried to push away the hurt I felt as I imagined Mike here at the police station, begging to see me, being sent away distraught and alone.

'Where have you and Holly been?' I asked, needing Jack to keep talking, to hear his sweet boyish voice as I breathed through the wave of tears that threatened to start falling.

'Auntie Vic took us into town. We had lunch at that Thai place Holly likes and then went round the shops and to the cinema,' he admitted. 'She said you'd be worrying about us and that we needed to get out, and to be honest, Mum, it was a good idea. We needed a distraction.'

I opened my mouth to respond but couldn't find the words, so shocked was I to hear that Victoria had taken it upon herself to surprise my kids with a fun day out while I was rotting in a cell. Was I being oversensitive to be so upset? It didn't seem like normal behaviour to me – not with so much going on.

There was an uncomfortable silence as I tried to process what I'd heard, picturing the three of them laughing together – Jack cracking sarcastic jokes to lighten the mood; Holly, my sweet girl, trying to smile and join in so she wouldn't seem rude or ungrateful. I couldn't bear it.

Jack broke the silence first. 'We just don't know what to do, Mum... We're going crazy here. And, well, Auntie Vic—'

'She's not your auntie!' I snapped, instantly upset with myself for being so petty. I sighed. 'Sorry, sweetheart. I'm grumpy and tired. I didn't mean to bite your head off. I just...'

'It's fine. I know it can't be easy.'

I blinked away tears, proud of how mature and insightful he was. Beneath his devil-may-care exterior, he had always had a depth to him that only a special few got to see. I wanted to reach through the phone and hold him tight, as I had when he was a little boy.

'I am sorry though,' I replied softly. 'And I'm glad you got to get out and have some fun. It was a good idea. Maybe you and Holly can go to the pool tomorrow?' I suggested, wanting to offer alternatives that would get them out of the house before Vic turned up and tried to take over again. I felt like she was trying to step into my shoes while they were still warm.

'Yeah, maybe. Holly's here now – she wants to speak to you. I'll pass you over and go and hurry Dad along. I'm not sure he heard me call him.'

'I love you,' I said, but he was already gone. I heard the breathy voice of my daughter as she took his place.

'Mum?'

'Hi, darling. I don't have long. They only give you a few minutes. How are you?'

'I'm scared. I hate this. Are you coming home soon?'

'I... I'm not sure,' I admitted, unable to lie to her. 'I hope so. Have you eaten dinner?'

'Mm,' she replied in a non-committal way that made me sure that she hadn't. I hadn't wanted to make a fuss to Mike and Jack about keeping an eye on her. They both had the subtlety of a rhino in a bikini and would only make her feel so much worse, shining a spotlight on her every move. She needed gentle pushes, regular but firm reminders to eat, but I knew that when she was worried, she found it almost impossible. She'd always been that way. It was as if her body just couldn't cope with the anxiety, her appetite vanishing at the first sign of stress. When she'd started infant school, she'd gone two full days without taking a bite, and I'd been so worried I had almost taken her into hospital, until, on the third day, she'd made a few friends and had come home ravenous, wolfing down a man-sized dinner followed by crumble and custard.

It wasn't intentional on her part, and from what I'd read, it wasn't a typical eating disorder. It was a reaction to stress rather than a need to control her world – her stomach hurt too much to even contemplate food, and the GP had said she should focus on meditation, deep breathing, anxiety management – but knowing that made it no less frightening, especially since right now, *I* was the cause of that stress. I decided that I had to change the subject. Highlighting her need to eat when I couldn't be there to support her would only make it worse.

'How was today?' I asked instead. 'Jack said you went to town.'

'It was okay... Auntie Vic bought me a load of clothes. I tried to tell her not to, but she insisted.'

'Oh.'

'I'm not really sure what to do with them all. I'd be so embarrassed if I had to go out in them. I didn't know how to tell her.'

I frowned. 'What do you mean? What kind of clothes?'

'Like, miniskirts, really tight ones, and short satin dresses, the kind you'd go to a club in. She said it was time my wardrobe matched who I really was and showed off the fact that I'm a woman now.' I could hear her cringing as she said the words. 'She was being really weird about it. I was too embarrassed to tell her it's not really my thing. You know I hate showing off my legs – they're so pale and skinny.'

'Holly, there's nothing wrong with your legs, but nobody has the right to tell you what to wear. Put the clothes in a bag and leave them in my room. I'll sort it out when I get back. And

I'll take you out to buy some things you *do* feel comfortable in, okay?'

My voice sounded calm and reassuring, but beneath my serene facade, I was raging. How dare Victoria try to force Holly to do something she wasn't comfortable with? How did she think she had the right to tell my daughter she needed to grow up? She had overstepped the mark, and it seemed she just wouldn't stop pushing her boundaries with my family. It had to stop.

'Okay, Mum. I will, and hopefully you'll be home soon, right?'

I glanced up as McCormac waved at me from the desk, then gestured for me to end the call. 'I have to go, darling.'

'But Dad's coming now – he really wants to speak to you! Here.' I heard the crackle of the phone being handed over, and then Mike's voice.

'Lisa? Thank God. I've been trying to—'

The line went silent, and I looked up, seeing the smug smile on the detective's face, his finger on the button of the wall-mounted phone, pressing hard as he severed my connection to my husband.

I couldn't stop the tears from spilling over this time. It was too much. I had been so close to speaking to Mike, letting his deep, soothing voice remind me what I was capable of, what I was fighting for. I needed him, needed to feel the love in his words, to know it was all going to be okay, and I hadn't even been allowed that. Who knew when I might get another chance? Certainly not today, at any rate.

McCormac stared at me in silent challenge, as all the words I wanted to yell bubbled dangerously close to the surface.

With slow, measured movements, I placed the handset back in the cradle, the action taking more strength than I knew I had in me. I took a deep, steeling breath then turned to him, my expression blank, my tone neutral. 'I'm ready to go back to my cell now.'

I watched his eyes flash with frustration and dislike, and then he turned, stalking away from me, yelling at a grey-haired PC to take me back. I held my head high as I returned to the airless box to wait once again.

THIRTY-SEVEN

VICTORIA

The table was piled high with mounds of Russell's clothes, neatly folded and sorted into stacks, some to donate, some to sell. I'd decided not to keep anything, not wanting to let myself be overly sentimental about a favourite shirt or jumper. I couldn't imagine him holding on to any of *my* clothes if the shoe were on the other foot.

There was a pulse of adrenaline running through my veins as I scooped the neatly folded piles into bags ready to take to the charity shop, as if at any moment he could walk through the door and catch me in the act. After so many years of living under his scrutiny, checking with him before I made any changes and hearing the word *no* fall from his lips time and again, I felt rebellious, and a little frightened in being so assertive. It felt too soon, disrespectful somehow, and yet, I knew it would never feel like the right time to pack away his life and admit our marriage – our life together – was truly over. As hard as it was to think about, if I was going to stay living in the house we'd shared, the house he'd had full control of, I would have to find a way to make it feel like it was really mine. The first step was to get rid of everything he owned and make a fresh start.

I'd been in touch with the insurance company, and with the lump payment I was due to receive from Russell's life insurance policy, I could afford to do whatever I wanted with the place. I could redecorate to my taste. Knock down walls and make it open-plan. Get rid of all the antique furniture he'd been so enamoured of and choose new things *I* liked. I had options now. If I felt like it, I could even move somewhere else, somewhere bigger, nicer – a real fresh start – but going anywhere else was the last thing I wanted to do.

I carried the bulging bags through the house, opening the front door and looking across the road to Lisa's house, thinking of Mike and the kids, how much they needed me right now. And how much I got out of being a help to them. It gave me such a buzz to be a part of their lives. To be able to cook a meal, give a hug and feel as if my presence made a difference, no matter how small. It was a pleasure I hadn't thought I would ever get to experience.

I looked at my watch, waiting for the taxi I'd booked earlier this morning to arrive, the bags piled high around me as I stood on the driveway trying not to look at Russell's Audi coupé, not wanting to think of him spending his Sunday afternoon polishing and waxing it until it gleamed, whilst I cooked and cleaned, wishing we could go to the pub or a restaurant for once. He'd been so flashy with his money when we met with other people, but when it was just the two of us, he'd watched every penny, preferring to save for material possessions he could show off rather than opening his wallet to make memories with just the two of us. But I didn't want to think of that now. Instead, I let myself drift off to the delicious memories I'd made yesterday.

I had loved taking Jack and Holly out by myself. Buying them clothes with Russell's cash. Listening to them talk over lunch, never once feeling like I didn't belong. I couldn't help but note how different I felt about Holly now, and I'd had to work hard to ignore the unanswered questions whirling in my head and concentrate on enjoying the day. I couldn't let those intrusive thoughts slip in, let myself picture those images that made me sick to my stomach. I knew it was only my imagination running wild, and I wouldn't let myself go down that road.

But despite the pleasure I'd got from our day out, I hadn't been able to push Lisa from my mind. I couldn't stop myself wondering what she was doing, what she might be saying. What else the police might have found and when they would call me to tell me what they knew.

When I'd suggested to Mike that Lisa might not be as innocent as he thought, he'd recoiled at the merest hint of an accusation. But I could see, as the days passed and the investigation continued, that he was beginning to have his own doubts. It was too much of a coincidence. The missing car. Lisa home alone with no alibi. The fact that they still hadn't let her go.

The taxi pulled up on the drive, and I forced my mind away from the confusing, frightening thoughts that seemed to swarm through my head at every opportunity. I pasted on a smile, gesturing to the bags by my feet. The driver, a good-looking man in his thirties with tattoos up both arms, jumped out. 'In you get, love. I'll chuck these in the boot.'

I thanked him and slid into the back seat, leaning against the cool leather. The driver got back in. 'Where are we off to then?' he said, flashing me a smile.

'Cats Protection on Turner Road first please.'

He nodded and pulled out of the driveway. I was grateful when, instead of making small talk, he turned the volume up on the radio, saving me from having to keep up the act.

It was only a few minutes' drive to the charity shop, and I asked him to wait for me as I took the bags inside, a sick pleasure at the memory of Russell's dislike of cats hitting me as I handed over the expensive designer clothes to the volunteers at the counter. I'd chosen to sell on his best suits and shoes, but the rest of his wardrobe was crammed into the bags. I could only imagine the colour his face would have turned if he could see his Gucci shirts hanging on a mannequin in the window beside a poster of a kitten in a basket.

I headed back outside, climbing into the waiting taxi. 'Can you take me to the police station on Harold Street now please?' I asked, feeling a swarm of butterflies take off in the pit of my stomach.

'I certainly can. Going to hand yourself in for being too beautiful?' said the driver, flashing a wink in the rear-view mirror.

'Flatterer,' I replied, smiling back, though inside I was cringing. Why did he think I wanted to hear that? There was nothing nice about being ogled by a man twice your size whilst sitting in the back of his car, completely at his mercy. I was angry at myself for not telling him just that, but years of habit forced my true feelings to remain locked inside.

I had never been able to speak up when it came to the opposite sex. The analytical side of my brain knew it was a result of my childhood years, the absolute need to please my father, be what he wanted in the hope that he might throw me a scrap of the attention I craved so deeply. I'd moulded myself into this quiet, meek, unobtrusive little girl and, little by little, had succumbed to the act. I couldn't help the desperate need for men to like me, desire me, think of me as a woman they would be lucky to have. It was why I had never been able to tell Russell when he was wrong, or speak up when I disagreed with him. Why I let him dress me up like his own little doll. I was scared he wouldn't stay with me if he knew the real me.

It was only very recently that I had come to the realisation that nobody in my life had truly loved me, because I'd never been brave enough to show anyone who I really was. I hadn't trusted anyone to show them inside my heart and soul, to let them see any part of me that I didn't consider worthy. If I had, Russell would have left me for dust years ago.

I sat silent and uncomfortable in the back of the car, trying to appear relaxed as I watched the route, hoping the driver would take me where I had asked rather than somewhere else where he could lock the doors and force me to have sex with him. A photo on the dashboard showed two kids, tawny heads, big smiles, and I held on to a shred of hope that he was a good dad, a decent man. My chest loosened a little as we followed the main roads in the right direction, eventually pulling up outside the main doors of the police station.

'You want me to wait for you again?'

I shook my head, smiling. 'No, thank you. I'll be a while,' I said, though I wasn't sure. I didn't want to get back in the car with him again though.

I paid and got out, and he drove away without a backwards glance, leaving me with an uneasy sense of guilt at how harshly I'd judged him from one little comment.

I ran my fingers through my hair, checked my make-up in the little mirror attached to my phone case, then, with a deep breath, walked up the three concrete steps and into the police station.

I'd never been inside one before. There was a feeling of being watched, of needing to stand up straighter, be on my best behaviour that came from being around so many people who had the power to arrest me. I swallowed, trying not to appear nervous, and approached the front desk. A woman was asking if her purse had been handed in, tears streaming down her cheeks as she begged them to check again.

'It has a handwritten note from my dad inside it,' she explained. 'I don't care about the money. I just need to get that back. It's the last thing he gave me before he died. You have no idea what it means to me... Please, please help me get it back.'

Her words dissolved into sobs, and from where I stood, I could see the racking jolt of her shoulder blades through her thin cardigan.

I took a step back from her, my spine stiffening at her vulnerability, her complete lack of embarrassment at falling apart in a room full of strangers. It was alien to me that she could be so raw with her emotions. It was something I couldn't have done. It was upsetting to see, and I felt for the female officer at the desk, knowing how slim the chances were of the purse being found. I stood, uncomfortable and awkward, glancing at the people around me as I waited for my turn.

Finally, the woman left, still sniffing, balling a handful of tissues to her streaming nose. I sensed her look up at me but quickly glanced away, not willing to see the pain in her eyes. As I took her place, I smiled warmly at the PC on the desk, hoping to reassure her that I wasn't about to make her day any harder.

'Hi, you have someone here in custody, Lisa Grey. I was hoping I might be able to see her?' I flashed her my most winning smile, knowing I was asking a lot, but she barely glanced up, her head already shaking her refusal.

'Nope. I'm afraid social calls aren't on the menu.'

'No visitors at all?'

'That's right.'

It was what I'd expected to hear, but I was still disappointed. 'Okay, I understand. Could I give you a message to pass on to her then? It's important.'

'I'm sure it is, but it'll have to wait until she's either bailed, charged or released. I'm not a messenger and I have more than enough to do.' She nodded to the queue of people that had formed behind me without my noticing and gestured for me to step aside.

A teenage boy with a scar on his top lip moved forward, effectively knocking me out of my place. I opened my mouth to argue, but when he began shouting at the officer, slapping his hand on the counter, demanding his brother's bail, I quickly closed it and backed away.

'Did I hear you asking after Lisa Grey?'

I turned to see a woman wearing a grey suit and carrying a briefcase standing at the back of the queue, her dark brown eyes fixed on me.

'Yes, I was hoping to see her.'

The woman left her place in the line and nodded to the door. I followed her outside.

'Sandy Adamu,' she said, holding out her hand for me to shake. 'Lisa's lawyer. You're a friend?'

'Yes.' I nodded. 'And neighbour.'

She frowned. 'Not... not Mrs Fox?'

'Yes. Victoria.'

The warmth vanished from her expression as she stepped back, folding her arms across her body. 'I'm sorry, I can't discuss the case with you. I just thought I heard you say you had a message for Lisa.' She was already walking around me, heading back to the door.

I grabbed her arm. 'Wait! I'm not fishing for information. I know she's innocent,' I said, my voice hushed so as not to cause a scene. 'And I do have a message.'

'I really should get back inside.'

'Please. You don't have to say anything else. I don't expect you to talk to me. Just listen and tell her what I've told you. Please?' My hand was still on her arm, as if I might have to hold on to her to stop her from walking away.

Sandy twisted her mouth then gave a short, decisive nod. She propped her briefcase on the low wall behind her, opened it and handed me a blank notepad and a pen. 'Write it down and I'll make sure she gets it.'

'Thank you,' I breathed. I took the notepad with a rush of gratitude. 'That's all I wanted. Thank you so much.'

THIRTY-EIGHT

LISA

'You look awful. Did you sleep at all?'

I shook my head as I watched Sandy sit down opposite me, pushing a paper cup of coffee across the table. I glanced at it but didn't move to pick it up. I had enough anxiety pumping through my veins without adding caffeine into the mix. Sandy didn't seem to take offence at my silence though. I expected she was used to far worse treatment in her line of work than anything I'd put her through.

'So, I've spoken to them at the desk and I think we're in for another long day. DS McCormac walked past when I was checking in, looking very chipper. I imagine you'll be called into the interview room in the next hour or so,' she said, folding her arms across her ample bosom. 'I'm hoping you're going to keep your cool. I know how much he pushes your buttons – he's an expert at that. *And* I know how tired you are. But the less you give him, the better.'

'I know.' I sighed. 'It's just so draining. I want to go home so much – it's all I can focus on. Knowing I'm stuck here...' I shook my head, unwilling to get into my sadness with her now. I had to stay strong.

I took a deep breath and picked up the coffee cup, digging at the cardboard rim with my fingernail. 'Did you know Mike was here yesterday and they refused to let him see me?'

She shook her head. 'No. But even if I had, I couldn't have done anything about it. There's a no-visitor policy while you're in custody. You aren't entitled to see him. Oh, that reminds me. I have a note for you.'

My heart leaped. 'From Mike?'

'No. Victoria.' She pulled a face. 'She was at the front desk when I got here asking to see you.'

'What? Why?'

'Said she needed to tell you something.'

She rifled through her briefcase, producing a purple-covered A5 notepad. She flipped it open to the first page and slid it towards me.

'I assume she wanted to show her support, but I can't see why it couldn't have waited. I have to say, it's a first for me having the victim's wife turn out in support of the chief suspect.' She reached back into the briefcase, pulling out a small box and flipping it open, taking out a pair of small gold hoop earrings and putting them on. 'She made it sound urgent; it was the only reason I hung around waiting for her to write it.'

'You read it?'

'I might have glanced at it.' She shrugged. 'I'm your lawyer, not your postwoman.'

'I can't get used to the lack of privacy in here. It's horrible.'

I pulled the pad towards me and scanned the neat writing on the page.

Lisa,

I'll make this quick. I hope you know I'm here for you and your family. Russell and I have always wanted the best for you all, and that hasn't changed. I'll be here for Mike and the kids while you can't be. I'll make sure they have dinner on the table. I'm taking Jack to get his hair cut tomorrow, and I've washed Mike's polo shirts for work, if he decides he wants to go back before you're able to come home. Please concentrate on yourself and don't worry about us. The boys will be fine. I know you fret about Holly, but we both know she's not a child any more. Your girl is safe with me.

Vic xx

I looked up, my eyes wide. 'What the hell does this mean?'

'I assumed she was trying to help?' Sandy said. 'She seemed nice, given the unorthodox circumstances.'

I shook my head, a tremor working its way down my spine, a sudden nausea hitting me, threatening to bring up the slice of toast I'd forced down earlier that morning. This wasn't reassurance. It was a threat. A hidden message, coated in honey to disguise it. Everything I had done, the secrets I had tried to keep, it was all in vain. She knew about Holly.

I pushed my chair back from the table, rising to my feet. All this time, I'd thought I was doing the only thing that made sense. I thought I'd been protecting my family, letting DS McCormac arrest me, keeping my silence. But now I realised, as long as I was here, I couldn't stop Victoria from weaving her way in amongst them. They needed me there. I just had to hope the truth would stay hidden, that my release wouldn't open up a whole new can of worms, but it was a risk I would have to take. I couldn't stay here a moment longer.

There was a knock at the door, and PC Hewitt, a ratty-looking man with an angry gleam in his eyes, poked his head round the door. 'They want you in interview room two in fifteen minutes.' He closed the door and left without waiting for a response.

Sandy looked up at me, confused. 'What's going on? You

need to calm down before we go in there or you're going to fall apart.'

I shook my head. 'No,' I said, making up my mind. 'There's not going to be another interview. I think it's time I gave you my alibi. I want to go home.'

'Mike, do you want gravy with this?'

I pulled the golden-crusted pie from the oven, relieved that it hadn't burned. I was aware of how average my cooking skills were in comparison to Lisa's, and I felt a strong need for my food to live up to the standards Mike and the kids were used to. A part of me felt a certain need to compete, to have them say how delicious everything was and, for a moment, forget how worried they all were about Lisa.

Mike, sitting on a bar stool, his phone clutched in his hand, didn't even look up. He'd been quiet this afternoon, the wind taken out of his sails as he wandered around the house as if he couldn't decide what to do next. He was realising, I thought, that this could be it now. Slowly absorbing the reality that his wife might not be coming back. I could see it in his eyes, the way the fire seemed to have been replaced by something else – a ghostly, broken light that made him look suddenly older.

When I'd turned up with a bag full of groceries, Holly had let me in without a word, and Mike hadn't questioned it when I'd made my way into the kitchen and begun making dinner. It had become almost routine now, and I knew, despite his silence, he appreciated the act. It was obvious to anyone that he didn't have the energy right now, and it kept my mind off Russell, Lisa, Holly, my empty house, my newly widowed state. I liked being busy.

I made gravy, using the instant granules I'd bought at the supermarket and hoping they wouldn't complain as I poured it into Lisa's blue ceramic gravy boat. I spooned peas and carrots onto the plates and then, half wanting to insist that everyone come and admire the pie I had made from scratch, I cut into the pastry and doled out generous chunks. I'd served a plate for myself too. It felt natural to sit down with them to eat after I'd gone to the trouble of cooking, and besides, I wanted to stay as long as I could. Dinner around the table was the best time to hear how the kids were really feeling and talk to them about the things they'd been fretting over during the day. Jack had gone to school, despite Mike telling him he didn't have to yet, but he'd insisted he couldn't sit around waiting and worrying, and I was sure it was for the best.

Holly, on the other hand, had barely left her room, and the brief glimpses I'd seen of her had shown a pale, tear-stained face, her slim frame dressed in oversized pink pyjamas that made her look more like fourteen than seventeen. I was trying not to be offended that I hadn't seen her wearing a single item of clothing from our shopping trip. It was only natural, I supposed, that she would cling to the familiar right now.

I opened the fridge, pulling out the bottle of white wine I'd bought for Mike and me to share, and smiled at the memory of the day out.

I had been going back and forth in my mind trying to figure out what had really taken place behind my back. The more I watched Holly, the more ridiculous I found the idea of her with Russell. Had the look I'd seen on her face actually been fear for Lisa, worry that I might expose her affair to Mike? Had she witnessed the two of them together and decided to protect her mother's secret?

I had seen Lisa and Russell in the café together. Witnessed a level of emotion pass between them that couldn't be easily explained away. It had been so clear to me that the two of them had something between them.

It was when I was choosing dresses, passing them over the curtain of the changing room for Holly to try on, feeling fit to burst with joy at getting to do something that felt so maternal, that I suddenly felt as if I were on the precipice of everything clicking into place. Jack had gone across the road to the gadget shop, and it was just us girls. Holly, always so coy, had opened the curtain, holding out the red mini dress I'd just handed her. 'This isn't really me, Auntie Vic.'

I had smiled, seeing the doubt in her eyes as she folded her arms round the baggy T-shirt she was wearing, her frame thinner than ever beneath it. Had Russell wanted *me* to be thinner? I couldn't imagine him not making a point of it if he'd thought I needed to lose some weight. It wasn't beneath him to make a snide remark if I served a bigger portion for myself than he deemed appropriate. But was Holly's more modelesque form the reason he'd strayed? I clicked my tongue, pushing down a wave of confusion and jealousy, trying to tear my gaze away from her perfect glass-smooth skin, her silky naturally blonde hair.

'Maybe not,' I agreed. 'But I think it would look gorgeous on you. And it would really show off your figure.'

I wanted to see her as the woman she was turning into, see this other side to her that she'd kept so well hidden. I needed to understand. If I were to watch her strut out of the changing room in heels and a siren-red dress, it might be the light-bulb moment I needed to let me finally see her in a different light – as my husband might have done. And if I couldn't, if it still didn't click, then I would have my answer. But to my frustration, she'd steadfastly refused to try the dress on, and I'd been left to wonder: what if?

The thought that it was Lisa was hard to bear, and yet it would make my actions over the past few weeks far more justified. Understandable even. But still, there was a part of me that wanted it to be Holly. Teenagers were selfish. Stupid. Careless with other people's feelings. I remembered just how much the world had seemed to revolve around me when I was her age. I could forgive Holly for being led astray by an older, more sophisticated man, and I was only too aware of how selfish my husband had been. What Russell wanted, Russell took.

But Lisa... Lisa had everything I'd ever dreamed of. If she'd risked it all for a sordid affair with my husband, it would be unforgivable. She would have destroyed everything I had worked for. And if she had done that to me, a life spent behind bars would serve her right.

FORTY

LISA

'Why the hell didn't you tell me this before? I could have got you out of here the first day!'

Sandy's face was a picture of confusion and frustration as I sat back in my chair. I couldn't say I blamed her. I knew my behaviour seemed to be verging on insanity when I had a get-out-of-jail-free card hidden in my back pocket. But I had my reasons.

I stared at her, tight-lipped, and she shook her head. 'Fine, never mind, you're obviously not going to explain any of this to me. I'm only your bloody lawyer!' she huffed.

'Sorry. It's complicated. I didn't feel I could tell you before. But this is enough to get me out of here, right?'

She gave a snort and shook her head, still in disbelief. 'I'm going to call each of the women now and hear what they have to say. If they can back up your story, then that's eight witnesses to attest to the fact that you were not only nowhere near the scene of the crime, but that you were miles away at this woodland retreat. It's solid. Even DS McCormac won't be able to find a way to break through an alibi as strong as that. Which is why he's going to wonder why you didn't use it earlier.'

'Like I said, it's complicated. But you'll get me home?'

She flashed me a grin. 'By dinner time. You'll be sleeping in your own bed tonight, Lisa.'

She picked up her briefcase, making for the door. 'You know, I'm not supposed to say this, but I actually thought you might have done it... Not that it would have made a difference to how I treated you, you understand. It's my job to defend you. But I really thought—'

She broke off with a shake of her head and gave a little laugh as she walked out, leaving me sitting alone. I could hear her chatting with the PC outside the door and knew he'd be in any minute to take me back to my cell – I presumed I would have to go back there for a while at least while they verified my story.

I was shocked at her words, though not as surprised as I might have been. There had been something in the looks we'd shared, when she told me to keep my mouth shut and give them nothing, that had alluded to it, but to hear her admit out loud that she really thought I was capable of a crime like this made chills run up and down my spine. If *she* could think it, no wonder DS McCormac had it in for me. I pictured the shock on each of my friends' faces when they got the call. No doubt I would be inundated with messages when I got out of here.

Friendships, for me, had always been secondary to my family. A bonus but not the main part of my life. I'd been lucky that when I got pregnant with Holly, I had gone to a fantastic Bump and Me group, where I'd met some amazing women. We didn't see each other on a weekly or even monthly basis, but we shared a deep bond and knew we could always call or use the group message chat we'd had running since it became an option. And ever since our children were tiny, we'd organised a yearly mums' retreat – though for those first few years, the babies had come along with us. We would leave our husbands to fend for themselves, leave all the stresses of real life behind, and book a lodge somewhere in the countryside where we could sit around a bonfire drinking wine, talking and just being free to say whatever was on our minds.

This year, life had been particularly busy, and what with one thing and another, I'd mixed my dates up and completely forgotten it was happening. I hadn't realised until Mike and Jack had already left for their camping trip and I'd glanced at the little organiser I kept in the kitchen drawer, sure that I was forgetting something. I'd almost called to say I couldn't make it – it had seemed like too much hassle to go with no notice – but when Holly had said she was going to a sleepover with her old school friends, it had seemed silly to miss it just to sit in an empty house by myself. And it had turned out to be a good decision. If I had stayed home alone, I wouldn't have the word of eight women to back me up now and swear there was no way I could possibly have been anywhere near the accident that night. I would be lost.

I put my head in my hands and let myself breathe a shaky sigh. I was going home.

I was trembling as I made my way up the driveway, my eyes fixed on the living-room window, hungry to catch a glimpse of Mike or the children. I'd been ready when Sandy had come to tell me the good news that I was finally free to go. I'd been sure she would come.

Not that the day had been smooth sailing. Just as she had predicted, DS McCormac had been utterly incredulous when faced with my rock-solid alibi, which I'd seemingly plucked out of the blue. He'd had me brought back into the interview room, where he'd spent the best part of the day demanding to know why I'd kept it from him, determined to find some hole in my story that would enable him to keep me there. But Sandy – strong, steady Sandy, who'd been ready to support me whether I was guilty or not, who had been my voice when I could only parrot 'no comment' until the words ceased to make sense – knew my rights, knew he had no way to keep me there with the statements from my friends pouring in in droves.

I couldn't pretend I hadn't felt a tiny smidge of smug satisfaction when I'd seen the look on his face as I waved goodbye, following Sandy out the main doors. She'd kindly dropped me back home, since I'd left without so much as a purse, and though I could tell she was as bewildered by the turn of events as McCormac was, she seemed genuinely happy to be helping me walk free.

My fingers tingled with anticipation at the thought of my family just steps away. I couldn't wait to surprise them. I wished I had a hairbrush with me, or even a pack of baby wipes to get rid of the smell of the cell – the plastic-coated mattress, the lemon-scented bleach that had been poured into the toilet, making my head swim and my belly churn. I wanted to wash away every last reminder of that place, and I would. But for now, they would have to take me as I was.

I knocked lightly on the door, bouncing on my toes as I waited. As I stood there, hopeful and impatient, I couldn't help but cast a glance over to Victoria's house. Was she in there? Was she watching me right now? The thought was stupid, no doubt brought about by overtiredness, making me paranoid and silly. Even so, I snapped my head back, feeling like I didn't want to be caught looking her way.

I knocked again, louder this time, my fist rapping on the glass, and was rewarded with the sound of footsteps. The door swung open, and there was my husband, dishevelled, unshaven, his hair thick with grease, his eyes swollen and red rimmed, but in that moment, I thought he was the most beautiful man I had ever laid eyes on.

'Oh my God!' he gasped.

He lunged forward, scooping me into his arms, burying his face in my neck as I gripped him as tightly as I could.

'How...? What...?' He was sobbing, I realised, and I pulled him closer, my hand moving in tight circles along his spine, unable to speak, to cry, just so relieved to have him in my arms again. And then Holly and Jack were behind him, alerted by his noisy sobs.

'Mum! Mum, you're home!' they yelled over each other, shoving their way forward into the hug, both desperate to be close to me. I couldn't hold them tight enough, couldn't stretch my arms wide enough, but that didn't stop me giving it my all.

Finally, we untangled ourselves from each other, faces stained with tears, and somehow moved in convoy into the living room, where we all squeezed onto the big blue sofa together, unwilling to be parted again.

'Are you really home? For good?' Jack asked.

'For good this time.' I glanced at my daughter with what I hoped was a reassuring expression. 'I think it's over now. My lawyer said they're talking about joyriders. They think some teenagers they saw on the CCTV footage must have stolen my car and Russell got hit as they drove away. They don't have a clear image of them though, so it's pretty unlikely anyone will be brought in, but I don't think they'll be back here again.'

She nodded but said nothing, and I reached over, squeezing her hand.

'God, I missed you all. You have no idea what it means to be back in my own home. I've always loved this house, and now I don't think I'll ever take it for granted, even for a minute. I can't wait to get back in the kitchen and start cooking again.'

I heard a creak in the doorway and looked up, frowning, my entire body stiffening as I saw Victoria standing there, my favourite apron tied around her hourglass waist. I felt my blood turn to fire.

'I bet you can't,' she said, flashing a sickly-sweet smile. 'I've done my best to keep them all fed. I don't have your skill in the kitchen, Lisa, but they haven't starved, so...'

'What are you doing here?' I shook my head, looking from Victoria to Mike. 'It's nine o'clock at night.'

I knew my tone was cold, accusing, but I didn't care. Why was she here? She hadn't known I was coming back. How long might she have stayed if I hadn't come home tonight?

'Oh, is it?' She smiled again, clearly not picking up on the tension radiating through my body. 'Time seems to fly when I'm here. I just get busy cleaning or sorting the laundry or chatting, and before I know it, the sun's gone down and everyone's yawning. I hadn't realised quite how time-consuming taking care of a family can be. You make it look so easy, Lisa.'

'Yeah, she fell asleep on the sofa last night, didn't you, Auntie Vic?' Jack said.

I looked at him sharply. There was an undercurrent to his tone, as if he were trying to communicate that he wouldn't be keeping any secrets for her. He smiled at me, and I saw warmth reassuringly present in his eyes. It made me feel like he'd been looking out for the family while I'd been gone. Where Mike was too laid-back to notice or care if she outstayed her welcome, Jack was sharp. It made me wonder what else he might have seen.

I pressed my lips together, rising to my feet. 'Really? Well, you must be tired. You'd better be getting back to your own home. I'm sure you've got things to do.'

'Oh, it's no trouble. I've enjoyed helping out.'

'I'm sure you have. But I'm back now. It's been a tough few days, and I would like some time alone with my family.'

My tone was clipped, and I didn't bother to smile. Mike had obviously encouraged her far too much in my absence, relying on her to take on my role, as if I were entirely replaceable. *He* should have done the cooking and sent her packing, but he would never be rude, not in the face of someone acting under the guise of a good deed. It was clearly going to be up to me to put a stop to her role-playing as the mother to my family.

I could feel Mike, Jack and Holly watching me from the sofa, but I didn't break eye contact with Victoria.

She opened her mouth, and I was sure she was going to argue – insist on staying to help me settle back in or some unnecessary nonsense to keep her from having to leave – but I didn't have the patience.

'Do you need me to walk you to the door?'

'I...' She glanced behind me to Mike, hoping perhaps that he might speak up for her. When he stayed silent, she gave a nod. 'Right, yes, of course. You must be exhausted. There are leftovers in the fridge if you're hungry. I'll just grab my bag from the kitchen.'

She stood awkwardly by the door for a moment, as if she were waiting for me to say something else – thank her or change my mind. Instead, I sank back onto the sofa, cuddling into Mike, starting a conversation with Jack and Holly that left no room for intrusion. I heard her leave the room, and then, after what felt like an eternity, with her banging around in the kitchen, the front door opened and closed. I glanced through the window, watching her cross the road back to her own house.

Mike nudged Jack with his elbow. 'Right, you two. Why don't you pop upstairs for a bit and give me and your mum a chance to catch up.'

Holly's eye caught mine, and I smiled. 'Go on. I'll be up in a bit to have a shower. I'll come and have a chat then, okay?'

'Yeah, you need to wash the jail smell from your hair.' Jack leaned in, giving an exaggerated sniff, then kissed me on the cheek.

'Good to have you home, Mum,' he said, ruffling my hair playfully, though I could see just how much he meant it.

Once they were gone, Mike pulled me into his arms again, his hands clamped firmly around my waist, as if he was privately making a promise to himself to stop anyone from taking me away again.

'I know you must be exhausted,' he said gently, 'but you probably need to apologise to Victoria tomorrow. That was a bit harsh, sending her off like that. She's been a real help while you've been away.' He made it sound like I'd been on holiday.

He continued, his words measured, and I knew he was trying not to upset me so soon after I'd made it home. 'She really stepped up when we needed help.'

'Well, *I'm* here now. And you would have survived without her, I'm sure. You're more capable than you give yourself credit for. I heard you came to the station to fight for me?' I smiled.

'Not that it made the slightest difference,' he said, his expression darkening.

'It did. When they told me you'd been there, I was so angry they had kept us apart. But then I just felt glad to know you were close, even when we couldn't be together. It helped. It gave me strength and stopped me from falling to pieces.'

I leaned into him, kissing him, a feeling of rightness and relief spreading through my body. 'It really did help.'

I stood outside Holly's bedroom door, listening to the sounds of Mike banging pots and pans in the kitchen, having insisted on making me dinner. I'd told him I didn't fancy the leftover pie Victoria had made. The idea of her in my kitchen, cooking for my family while I was locked in a cell, made me feel funny – an uneasy sense of anxiety that came from still being unable to place her true intentions. I couldn't shake the thought that she'd had something to do with my arrest. The way she'd been acting, the little hidden smiles and her sudden refusal to leave Mike and the kids alone, made me more and more convinced that she'd done something to make the police come after me. Her face when she'd walked into the living room to find me surrounded by my family had given nothing away – no jealousy, no irritation that I'd come back – but she'd had time to compose herself in the kitchen before making her entrance, and I got the feeling she was very good at hiding her true feelings.

Mike, as excitable as a puppy with a bone, hadn't batted an eyelid when I'd refused her food, claiming he was happy to make whatever I wanted to eat. I could tell he needed to do it, to expend some of the nervous energy in his system. Any other time he would have grabbed his surfboard or his hiking boots and headed out the door, pushing his muscles to work until they burned and he was no longer fizzing with adrenaline. But tonight, he wouldn't leave me. Not that I'd asked him to. I wanted him here, all of us together under the same roof. Instead, I'd set him the task of cooking a meal, hoping it would help focus his mind and calm his restless body, for now at least, though I wasn't holding my breath that it would actually be edible. Cooking wasn't really his strong point.

I desperately wanted to shower and change my clothes, but not before I'd spoken to my daughter. I'd seen the look on her face and could tell she was frightened. She didn't believe this was all over, and I couldn't blame her after everything she'd been through. Watching them take me away had left a scar on her heart that I was sure would never fully heal, but I was determined to make her see that she had nothing more to fear.

I knocked gently on the door and heard her invite me in.

'Hey, sweetie,' I said quietly, so as not to alert Jack that I was upstairs. I needed a moment alone with my girl first.

I pushed the door closed to give us some privacy. She was sitting on her bed, her long legs drawn up to her chin, her back curved against a pink mohair cushion.

She looked up at me and smiled, though it was obviously an effort. Her eyes were rimmed with dark circles, and her face was so pale it almost appeared translucent. 'Are you okay? Were they awful to you there?' she asked.

I shook my head, clambering up beside her on her double bed and pulling her close. 'They were fine. The detective was a bit of a jobsworth, but nothing awful happened. It's just dreadfully dull: lots of sitting around and waiting for someone to call you.'

Holly snorted. 'You don't have to lie to me, Mum. I'm old enough that I don't need you to sugar-coat the truth for me. I can handle more than you think,' she added quietly, looking down at her knees, her fingers pinching and releasing the white cotton duvet cover.

I pressed my lips together, forcing back a wave of emotion, the tears pricking at my eyes. I knew only too well how strong she was. How brave. She and I had never been able to keep secrets from each other. Since she was tiny, she'd insisted on knowing what her dad and brother were getting for Christmas, and to her credit, she'd never once spilled the beans, darting little smiles at me when they were out of the room, pleased to be in on their surprises. I knew she could be trusted not to say anything, but I'd never have believed she could keep secrets from me.

I stroked her hair back from her face, knowing she was so close to telling me the thing that had burdened her heart for some time now but hadn't been able to say out loud.

'I know,' I agreed softly. 'You *are* strong. And you're not a child any more. The truth is, I was scared. But I never believed they would keep me there. I kept telling myself I was coming home to you, and in the end, I was right.'

'But what if—'

I cut in. 'It doesn't help anyone to focus on what-ifs, darling. Life is unpredictable, and there's only so much we can control. The rest just happens to us, whether we want it to or not. All we can do is make a choice on how we're going to react to adversity.'

She glanced away, as if she wanted to argue.

'Holly,' I continued. 'You know you can talk to me about anything? Anything at all. I *mean* that. I will always be on your side, I promise.'

She looked back so suddenly I caught the expression of hope on her face and held my breath, waiting for her to speak.

'You can't *always* be on my side,' she said softly. 'I make mistakes too, Mum. I... I'm not as perfect as you like to think I am.'

I shook my head, playing with a strand of her hair. 'I never thought you were perfect, darling. You're *human*. Beautifully and fallibly so.'

I smiled as I remembered the mischief she'd got up to as a child.

'You're the girl who switched the oven off when I was cooking Christmas dinner for twelve the year you turned seven. You're the girl who forgot to do your English homework then tried to pass off Edgar Allen Poe's "The Raven" as your own work, without realising your teacher would recognise it as one of the most famous poems of all time. You leave half-empty mugs all over the house, and you sleep through your alarm at least once a week. But none of those things make me love you even a drop less. And whatever mistakes you might have made... big or small,' I added, seeing her roll her eyes, knowing she was thinking I couldn't possibly understand her, 'no matter how awful you think they might be,' I continued softly, holding her gaze, trying to connect, to show her how much I really did know her, more than she could ever realise, 'it won't change the fact that I am your mother. And I am *always* on your side.'

I leaned forward, pressing a kiss to her forehead, before sliding off the bed. I could feel the tightness in my throat, the pressure building in my head, and knew I was going to burst into tears any minute. There was so much more I wanted to tell her. That the way she was so hard on herself wasn't fair. That some things weren't black and white. But I couldn't trust myself to keep talking without breaking down, and I didn't want her to have to comfort me, not right now. I wanted to give her time to absorb my words without worrying about *my* feelings, about protecting everyone else from saying what was on her mind.

'Thanks, Mum,' she said shyly as I walked across the room to the door.

'I mean it,' I answered simply.

I left the room, heading to the bathroom and turning on the shower, before sinking down to the tiled floor, pressing my face into a towel and finally letting the tears come.

'Oh, sorry, excuse me,' I apologised, having bumped into the blank-faced teenage boy coming out of the community centre.

He grunted, barely looking up from his phone as he continued walking across the car park to a row of bike racks, where he unlocked the chain around a black mountain bike and, phone still firmly clamped in his hand, jumped on and pedalled away, his eyes only half on the road. It made me nervous for him, sure that it was only a matter of time before his reckless disregard for traffic caused an accident. It was hard not to think of Russell, his last moments before the car made contact with him, how he must have felt in that split second before he hit the ground. I watched until the boy disappeared then looked back down at my own phone – the reason I'd been distracted enough to walk into him in the first place.

Morag had called three times since breakfast, and each time I'd muted the ringtone and watched until the screen went dark again. She'd left a voicemail after the first call, demanding I get back to her with news on the investigation, berating me for not keeping her in the loop. It was obvious that now, with the funeral over, she'd transferred her focus to the police and their efforts in her need to get justice for Russell.

I couldn't blame her for that. I knew she needed to keep her mind busy in an attempt to avoid facing her grief, but I didn't want to be dragged into it. We had never been close. She had made it abundantly clear that she didn't think I was good enough for her precious boy, and that she didn't like me, and now that he was gone and we'd got through the funeral, I felt my obligation to have to answer to her had lifted. It was remarkably freeing, to see her name pop up on my phone and know I wouldn't call her back. I wouldn't have to sit with her hard, beady eyes boring into my head at Christmas this year. Wouldn't have to wait anxiously for Russell to find out I'd been anything but the perfect daughter-in-law to his mother.

It wasn't like she needed me anyway. There was nothing stopping her from calling DS McCormac and making her own enquiries. I just wouldn't be her go-between. She would only use it as an excuse to take out her frustration on me when she didn't get the answers she was looking for and the case got shuffled to the bottom of the pile. And judging by Lisa's sudden release last night, it seemed that was the way the case was heading. I still didn't know how I felt about that...

I closed my eyes against the memory of hearing her voice drift down the hallway, the excited screams of her children as they engulfed her in a protective bubble, instantly forgetting all about me. I hadn't been able to suppress the momentary flash of jealousy at how easy it was for her to get that overwhelming, unconditional love from them. I couldn't imagine how it must feel to see the sparkle in their eyes and know it was all for her.

I had been so overcome with wanting, the envy making my grip on the knife I'd been putting away tighten, my heart thumping hard against my ribs, that I'd had to take several minutes to breathe through the emotions before I could trust myself to go and join them all in the living room. I felt so conflicted over my response. Had I thought there was a chance she might not come back? That Mike and the kids would need me to be there in her place? I had to admit the thought had entered my mind. I'd pictured Lisa being held behind bars, trapped, knowing that I was with her children, her husband, stealing her life the way she had stolen mine. I couldn't deny that my actions had been motivated by revenge more than once in recent weeks. All I wanted was to stay. To be included. And I wasn't ready to give that up.

My house, when I'd left them to go back to it last night, had been cold, dark and eerily empty.

Unable to face going to bed alone, to sleep in the bed I'd shared for so many years with a husband who had never truly loved me, I had sat in the darkness of my living room, my eyes trained on the warm squares of light radiating from the windows across the road, picturing Holly and Jack cuddling up to Lisa, Mike pouring her a glass of wine. As I saw the lights go on in the children's bedrooms, I'd imagined Mike wrapping his arms around Lisa. The way he would stare into her eyes, really connecting, not just going through the motions as Russell had always done with me. I couldn't imagine Mike being anything less than a loving husband.

As I had stared hungrily at their house, wishing I could think of a reason to go back that didn't make me come across as unhinged, I'd found myself thinking of the two of them together. Mike would be gentle. Considerate. He would kiss her neck. He would undress her, sliding his fingers down her buttons one by one. He would talk to her, smile and whisper how much he needed her, how much he'd missed her, and as he rose above her, stripping off his shirt with one hand, never letting himself fully release her from his hold, she would feel like the only woman in the world.

I had sat alone in the dark, thinking, imagining, picturing

them, my breath shallow with longing, and for the thousandth time, I had wondered if Lisa had any idea how lucky she was.

When I'd woken this morning, curled up in the armchair, my neck stiff and sore, I'd known I had to come up with a way to keep my connection with the whole family. If Lisa was off the hook and ready to step back into her role, I would be pushed out if I didn't act fast. I couldn't let that happen. It had to begin with her. If we could build on our friendship, become closer, then my presence in their home would be a natural and easy habit to form. If she accepted me there, *wanted* me there, everything would be okay.

I'd felt a coldness from her the past few times I'd seen her, and though I knew part of that was down to the stress she'd been under, and the awkwardness that it was *my* husband she was accused of hitting, I also realised that she was someone who liked her own space. She enjoyed her private little moments with her family, liked to relax without the pressure of entertaining, and my visits made it hard for her to feel at ease. What I needed to do was to help her see me as part of the furniture, build that easy relationship between us, and I couldn't think of a better way than the two of us doing the thing she loved most together. If I couldn't succeed in getting closer, it would be all the more difficult to figure out how to make her pay for what she'd done to me. And I was determined that one way or another, she *would* pay.

I muted my phone, slipping it back in my bag, then walked through the double doors of the community centre, heading over to the desk. A woman was just finishing her conversation with the receptionist, and as she turned away, our eyes met and I realised with a sinking feeling that it was Russell's cousin, Beth. I hadn't recognised her from behind – if I had, I'd have turned and walked away before she clocked me, to avoid having to make uncomfortable small talk with her. She'd had her hair cropped short, the back of her tanned neck pink from having caught the sun, and she'd lost weight since I last saw her.

'Victoria! Hi,' she exclaimed, taking my wrist between her palms and squeezing lightly. She had a look of sickly-sweet sympathy in her eyes, and I slid my hand from her grasp, stepping back, not wanting her pity.

'Hello, Beth. How are you?' I asked, trying to keep the conversation formal, light.

'Oh, never mind that! How are *you* doing, you poor thing? I was there, you know. At the funeral. I was hoping to catch you afterwards, but I had to rush off to pick the little one up from pre-school. I was supposed to go to the wake in Mum's car, but I had to get a cab in the end. Poor Dylan had a bit of separation anxiety, and I didn't like to leave him there when he wanted me.'

'Oh… right. So you got a taxi from the crematorium then?' I said, watching her nod as my mind moved to that flash of brown hair, the woman I had so hoped was Lisa stepping into the car, the blinding sun making me squint. Even though it had made no sense, I had held on to the idea that it had been her. It had comforted me somehow. Made it feel like she cared, if not about Russell, then about me. That she wouldn't want me to be alone at a time like that.

'Yep. Cost a fortune, and they didn't even bother to bring a car seat. What kind of help is that? But I doubt you want to hear about my little niggles. You've got bigger things to worry about,' Beth said, giving me a sad little smile.

I had a sudden urge to slap it off her face, wishing she hadn't bothered coming to the funeral, making my head spin with all the what-ifs that had come from seeing her there.

I glanced past her to the desk, not bothering to say anything else.

The silence quickly became awkward, and Beth looked at her watch. 'Well, I suppose I'd better get on. I hope you're okay,

Victoria. If you need anything, please let me know. Although I am awfully busy. Mum life, you know?' She gave a smug little laugh and then, squeezing my arm briefly, dashed past me and out the doors with a cheery 'Bye then!'

I breathed in deeply, trying to squash down the irritation she'd ignited in my belly.

'Can I help you, love?' the receptionist asked, peering at me over the rim of her glasses.

I swallowed my anger and tried to focus on the reason I was here, my plan giving me the strength to continue.

'Yes,' I said, flashing a wide smile. 'I was hoping you might have a couple of spaces left on your cookery course for me and my friend. The one that starts next week? I'd love to sign us up.'

The house smelled delicious. The weather was far too hot for a stew, but I didn't care. I'd spent the morning mixing and rolling, making dumplings to go in the rich beef and potato stew that was simmering on the hob, needing the ritual of making a meal I knew by heart – the epitome of comfort food.

As I dropped the soft creamy-white balls into the bubbling sauce, pushing them under the surface with a wooden spoon, I tried to ignore the anxious tightening in my belly at each and every noise I heard. Mike going in and out of the front door, putting the recycling out; Jack jogging up and down the stairs with no idea that his thundering footsteps made the breath catch in my throat, my whole body trembling in anticipation of another arrest. Logically, I knew they wouldn't come for me again. But that didn't mean it was over. DS McCormac wasn't going to drop the case unless he was forced to, and until that day came, I knew I would always feel this gnawing sense of dread.

My phone beeped, and I closed my eyes, my fingers squeezing the wooden spoon in the pan tight enough to make them tingle, the hot steam curling around my hand, scalding against the soft skin. I took a deep breath then opened my eyes, slowly, almost mechanically, reaching over to pick it up. I felt my shoulders relax the moment I saw Amy's name on the screen.

Last night, having showered and eaten, I'd found my phone in my bedside cabinet drawer, where I'd left it. When I switched it on, I'd been inundated with messages from the women I'd been on the retreat with. They'd all had an unexpected call from my lawyer, and now they wanted hard details. They'd each had to speak to the police too, to give official statements. I knew I owed them the full story, but I'd felt sapped of energy and hadn't been able to find the words to reply to any of them. I wanted to thank them, to tell them it had all been a misunderstanding – a formality I'd been caught up in – but the messages had come too fast and I'd been overwhelmed. Now, I scanned Amy's message and sighed.

We're so worried about you, Lisa. If we don't hear from you by tonight, I'm coming over with Shana to check on you. Please, if you can, text or call. And if you need anything, let us know. xxx

'Everything okay?'

I glanced up to see Mike standing in the doorway, a frightened expression on his face, as if he was waiting for me to share more bad news.

Quickly, I placed the phone back on the counter and forced myself to smile. 'Yep, everything's fine. Just Amy asking if I want to go for a drink with her and the girls later.'

I hated myself for telling the lie. I hadn't explained anything about the alibi to Mike, knowing he would find it impossible to understand why I hadn't used it straight away. He would ask too many questions – questions I just wouldn't be able to answer.

'You should go,' he said, instantly relaxing. 'A night out is just what you need. I'm sure your friends have been worried about you.'

He crossed the kitchen and kissed me, then turned, dipping a spoon into the stew and blowing on a chunk of steaming beef. 'God, I've missed your cooking. Victoria tried, bless her, but nobody can cook like you.'

I tensed at the mention of her, seeing an opportunity to ask what I'd been wondering. 'Was she here a lot while I was... you know?'

He touched the tip of his tongue to the spoon and then winced, blowing cool air on it again. 'She was a star. You have her to thank for the house looking so good. I was in bits; I couldn't have managed nearly so well without her help.'

'Help with what?' I couldn't keep the irritation out of my voice.

'She cooked dinner. Cleaned up. Did the laundry. I did tell her she shouldn't be worrying about us when she's just lost her husband, but she insisted. And if I'm honest, I didn't push too hard, because it saved me from trying to manage everything.' He tested the meat again and then shovelled it into his mouth, his eyes half closing as he chewed. 'Delicious. Oh, that reminds me, I saw her outside a minute ago.'

'Who?'

'Vic. She was just coming back from town. Said something about the two of you doing a cookery course at the community centre. Here.' He reached into the back pocket of his shorts, pulling out a leaflet.

'Intermediate cookery course,' I read. 'What is she trying to say? I was trained at the Morgan Hotel Culinary School. Why would I need a class on how to' – I scrolled through the list – 'bake your own bread? Make the perfect roast?' I looked up at him. 'I don't get it.'

He shrugged. 'I don't think she means it as an insult, Pixie. She was saying how she wanted to learn more and thought it might be fun. Something the two of you could do together. I think she's signed you both up, so you might need to have a word if you're not up for it.'

I raised my eyebrows. 'She signed me up to this? Without even asking first?'

He put down the spoon, finally realising how on edge I was. 'What's upsetting you so much, Lis? If you don't want to go, just tell her. I'm sure she won't mind.'

I shook my head. 'That's not the point. Don't you find it strange, I mean, how much she's been here? How intense she's being? She was never more than a neighbour before all this happened, and now suddenly she's cooking my children's dinner and signing me up to night school.'

He shrugged. 'She was more than a neighbour. The kids call her Auntie. She's been over to dinner. We've been to hers to eat.'

'Casual barbecues,' I said, not wanting to admit how close we had been. Mike was right, but the friendship had always been with both her and Russell, and with him being such a loud character, all these years on, we had never really got to know Victoria in her own right.

'And *she* started the Auntie nickname,' I continued. 'I was just too polite to correct her, and it stuck. It seemed harmless at the time, but now I'm not sure I was right to let it go. I know we've always been friendly with her and...' I paused, not wanting to say *and Russell.*

I took a breath, trying to collect my thoughts. 'We *were* friendly. Close neighbours perhaps. But she's acting like family, and she isn't that.'

'She's just lonely.' He frowned. 'You're usually the first person to offer a kind word or smile to someone who needs it, Lisa. What's got into you? I'd have thought you'd be brimming with gratitude after everything she's done for us, especially given that you were under investigation for killing her husband.'

I blanched, and he pursed his lips, shaking his head, realising he'd mentioned the elephant in the room.

He sighed, softening his tone. 'All I'm saying is, there aren't many people who would do what she's done for us this week. She's just being kind, trying to find things to keep herself busy and out of that empty house.'

I turned my back on him, stirring the stew, seeing that the dumplings had now doubled in size.

'I don't want to sound ungrateful, and I know that's how it's coming across, but I just... I don't think that's it. Not all of it. I think she—' I broke off, not sure *what* I thought. Did she want to steal my husband? Pull the rug from beneath me and take my place, become the mother she thought my children needed? Or might her motive be about getting revenge? Getting closer so she was in a better position to strike. Did she know something she wasn't letting on? I wasn't sure. All I knew was that she was making me uneasy. And it was time to put a stop to it.

FORTY-THREE

I crossed the road, not wanting to step inside that house again, afraid that the memories of Russell would be too much for me to bear. I didn't want to see his things, smell the musky scent of the expensive aftershave he always wore, imagine him there. Too much had gone on to ever make me want to spend time in that house again, and yet I didn't want to invite Victoria to come to me. This conversation needed to be quick. I wanted to re-establish our boundaries, let her know she needed to back off now, give us some space. It was just too much, her constant visits, and the way she looked at Mike made me sure she had an ulterior motive.

I sucked in a breath, gathering myself for what would certainly be an uncomfortable conversation, and rapped on her door, ignoring the gnawing trepidation in my belly.

The door swung open, and Victoria greeted me, a wide smile on her face, her eyes bright and sparkling, as if she were delighted to see me. It made me uneasy. She was so practised at hiding her true self, I could never be sure what was real and what was an act.

'Lisa, hi! I was just on my way over to see you. I got these gorgeous berries at the market this morning and thought we could make some sort of crumble out of them. Or maybe something else? I don't know.' She shrugged with a deferential smile. 'You're the expert. Did Mike mention the course to you? I thought it might be fun, you know? Something to do in the evenings together.'

I gave a frosty smile, unwilling to be drawn into a conversation over why she thought I might need cooking classes. 'Actually, Vic, can I come in for a sec? I need a word.'

She hesitated, her hand on the door frame, glancing briefly over her shoulder as if she wasn't at all pleased with the idea of my coming in, but then she gave a nod, stepping back. 'Of course. Shall I put the kettle on? Or something cold perhaps?'

'No. Thanks, but I can't stay.'

'I can always come to you if you're in a rush trying to get the house sorted. I did what I could while you were... well, you know. But it's never the same when someone else does it, is it? I expect I put everything back in the wrong places, didn't I?'

'It's fine,' I said, not wanting to think about how violated I'd felt when I found my clothes folded into neat piles, slotted into the wrong drawers. I'd asked Mike about it, hoping he'd just been too distracted to put them in their usual homes while I'd been gone, but he'd admitted he hadn't touched the laundry, that Victoria and Jack had done the majority of the household tasks while Holly hid in her room and he tried to cope without me. Victoria had been through my laundry basket, through my bedroom drawers, and God knows where else, and he hadn't considered it might be something I would object to.

'That's actually what I wanted to talk about,' I said, following her into the kitchen. It was a stuffy room, painted in burgundy, furnished with a heavy dark wooden table and chairs that looked old-fashioned and uncomfortable. I recalled Russell bragging about finding them in an antiques shop somewhere, how pleased he'd been with them, though I'd thought privately that he'd been fleeced.

'Oh?' she replied, raising a questioning eyebrow.

I pressed my lips together, watching as she poured herself a glass of iced tea from the fridge.

'You sure I can't tempt you? It's home-made. Your recipe. I hope you don't mind me borrowing it?'

I shook my head. 'No... thank you,' I said, moderating my tone, though I felt like I'd been slapped. That recipe had been in a book made for me by my grandmother before she passed away. A book I treasured, kept on a shelf in the back of my kitchen cupboard where it wouldn't get cooking grease or dust on it. To hear that Victoria had been rifling through it, helping herself to family recipes without so much as asking first, made me wonder what else she'd helped herself to.

'Anyway,' I continued, clasping my hands together, trying to stay calm, 'like I was saying, I wanted to thank you for stepping in and being there for my family when I couldn't.' I placed a subtle emphasis on the *my*. 'Mike said you really helped him out.'

'Oh, it was my pleasure. You know I love you guys. You're family to me, and families pull together in tough times, right?'

I scratched my arm, feeling awkward. 'Well, thanks,' I said stiffly, not sure how to respond. 'But it's been a really difficult week, and now, we just need some time to reset, you know? Just the four of us, I mean. Time to be together and process everything that's happened. We appreciate all your help, but I'm home now and...' I paused, seeing the way her face had frozen, the smile no longer reaching her narrowed eyes. I took a breath and continued. 'There's no need for you to help out any more.'

She nodded slowly, and for a moment, I thought it was going to be that easy.

'I get it,' she said. 'Time to reacclimatise is a good idea. I hear you. I have a few things I need to organise anyway. Why don't I give you a couple of days to get back on your feet and then I'll pop round to see how you're doing at the weekend? I can bring the information about that course, and I told Jack I'd help him with his history homework too – I was top of my class in school and he's doing the Tudors. It was always my favourite period to read about.'

I shook my head. 'That's kind of you, but we can manage. We've got all the textbooks.'

'I don't mind. Honestly.' She smiled, brushing my concerns away with a flick of her hand, as if she wasn't hearing what I was telling her.

I didn't know what to say – I had so wanted to part ways on a civil note, but she was leaving me no choice but to be rude, something I had always shied away from.

'But *I* do. Look, I'm sorry, Vic, maybe I'm not being clear, but a few days isn't what I meant. Prior to Russell's accident, other than quick chats on the driveway, we socialised with you maybe a handful of times in a year, and now...' I shook my head, feeling my fingers tremble at the confrontation I'd been forced into. 'Now, not a day goes by when you aren't at our house. It's too much. Far too much. We need our privacy, our family time, and I'm sorry for your loss, but, I mean, don't you have friends, family who can support you through this?'

'You... you don't want—' She broke off, folding her arms tight across her chest. 'I thought *you* were my friends?'

'We *are*,' I said, though I could hear the lie on my tongue. The truth was, we might have chatted and socialised as a foursome, but after everything that had happened in the past few weeks, the way she'd changed – or perhaps just shown her true colours – I had come to the realisation that I didn't want her in my life. Didn't trust her enough to ever consider her a true friend. She was a chameleon, constantly changing herself to be what she thought other people wanted. *I* could see it, even if Mike, Holly and Jack were fooled by her act. She'd slipped up too many times, showing her hand in front of me, and now I didn't feel like I could ever see past the insincerity in her character, no matter how much she smiled and said the right thing. And even if I could, she was a constant reminder of Russell. His death. My arrest. With her in our lives, we would never be able to move forward. His ghost would always be there in the dark corners of the room, an uneasy presence – a memory we could never forget. It was the last thing I wanted.

'We'll see you at the harvest fair on the common, I expect. And it's not like we won't bump into each other. We do live opposite each other.'

'The harvest fair? That's in two months' time.'

'I'm just saying, we need space.'

'Who does? *You*? Because Mike and the kids were singing a different tune all this week. They want me around.'

'Well *I* don't!' I yelled, shocking myself with the sudden outburst. 'I'm not going to go on a cookery course with you! I don't want you in my house! I don't want you with my husband! And I don't want you near my fucking kids! Do you know what your husband did?' I demanded, slamming my palm on the wall beside me. 'I bet you do, don't you? I bet you turned a blind eye, just like you always did with him. Do you know the kind of man you married, Victoria? What he did to her? Because I can't stand it, and every time I look at you, I see him and I hate you for it!'

I was shaking, I realised, shocked with myself for saying any of those things. I hadn't meant to. I'd thought it was locked up, so secure in the vault of my heart that it would never break free.

I pressed my hands to my mouth as if I could force the words back in, but it was too late. *That* had been it, I realised. The root of that lurking suspicion. That off feeling. Had I been too afraid to ask the question in case I got an answer I couldn't bear to hear? Had I suspected all along that she knew exactly what kind of man she had married and had stepped back, turned her face away while he went after Holly? She was so focused on appearances, on making sure her home, her clothes, her marriage couldn't be scrutinised. And, I realised now, if she had known his true colours, she might have gone to the ends of the earth to brush it under the carpet. She would hate to admit he was anything less than perfect, whatever the cost.

She placed her hands on the counter, nodding slowly as if a question she'd been pondering had finally been answered.

'So, it *was* Holly.' She clicked her tongue. 'For a while, I thought it might have been you, but I guess not. I'm not sure which is worse. To be betrayed by the girl who's as good as a daughter to me or by my best friend. Although you've made it abundantly clear that we don't share the same ideas on what constitutes a friendship.'

I stared at her, shocked at how calm she was in the face of my outburst, at her use of the words *best friend*. I had no idea she had thought of me in that way. She was a neighbour to me. *Mike* was my best friend.

'Betrayed?' I repeated, choking on the word, watching her expression turn smug, as if she'd caught me out. 'What the hell are you talking about?'

'It makes more sense that it was her. I should have realised it from the start,' she muttered, looking down at the floor. 'I thought you were mad to sleep with Russell when you had Mike.'

I blanched, my skin breaking into a thousand goose pimples, the thought sickening. 'What?' I gasped, reeling from her words.

'But then I never thought *she* could really do such a thing. Not so sweet and innocent after all, it would seem. I wouldn't have believed she had it in her. To hurt me like that. To look at him that way. To try and steal him from me. And did you *really* think he wouldn't break her heart?' She gave a sharp, cold laugh that sounded mocking and harsh. 'Russell might have been many things, but he would *never* have left me, not even for her.

It was always going to have to end between the two of them. I am his *wife*,' she said, conviction ringing in her words. 'I love Holly, but I would never have stepped aside, watched the two of them head off into the sunset, leaving me behind like a used tissue. My marriage vows meant something. They're binding. Till death us do part. And despite all his flaws, Russell felt the same.'

She closed her eyes and took a deep breath. When she opened them, her face was impassive, carefully blank.

'Look,' she continued, her tone softer now, 'I'm sorry she was naïve enough to believe he would give her the world. He was good at spinning a story, and I don't blame her for falling in love with him. But I'm not sorry she didn't get to live happily ever after with *my* husband.'

'You think—' I broke off, my eyes wide as I realised that she either didn't know or wasn't prepared to admit the truth. 'You've got it wrong.'

'I found her underwear in his office.'

'No!' I shook my head.

'Don't tell me this is news to you. That your darling Princess Holly dared to keep her sordid affair a secret from Mummy? I *know* you knew about this, Lisa. You should have told me. A good friend would have put a stop to it, not gone behind my back and—'

'He raped her! There was no affair! Russell raped her!' The words rang out, leaving me breathless, my stomach churning painfully. The only sound I could hear was the blood pumping in my ears.

Victoria stared at me, her mouth falling open as if she was genuinely stunned. Her reaction was surprising to me.

Finally, she spoke, her voice measured, quiet. 'You're lying.'

I shook my head. 'No,' I whispered.

'He would never!'

'He did.' I pinched the bridge of my nose, trying not to cry as I relived in my mind the moment I had found out – a hyper-colour memory that blinded me multiple times a day.

Victoria shook her head. 'He might have seduced her. But rape? No. You're wrong.'

I stared back at her, my eyes unwavering. 'He raped her, Vic.'

She searched my gaze as if she were trying to work out if this was some trick. If I could be wrong. I saw her confusion slowly morph into shock, disgust as she finally absorbed my words, accepted the truth. Her hand flew to her mouth as she stepped back heavily against a polished wooden sideboard. 'When?'

I swallowed, not wanting to discuss it but knowing she needed the truth now. 'Seven weeks ago.'

'Not when I was in hospital?'

I gave a tiny shrug. She'd been admitted with concussion, having fallen down the stairs. The disgust on her face made me sure she was matching up the dates. The cogs seemed to turn in her mind, her eyes unfocused as she shook her head, rewriting the past she thought she knew.

'So...' she murmured. '*Holly* did it. She killed him because he hurt her, and you let them arrest you because you were protecting her. It all makes sense now. Why it was your car. Why they found your scarf. She's always borrowing your clothes. And you would give up your freedom to save her in a heartbeat. I knew something was off...'

'You don't know what you're talking about. Holly didn't do anything!'

'Oh yes I do. And I bet if the police bothered to dig around, they would find that her alibi isn't nearly as solid as yours.'

'You wouldn't go to the police! After everything she's been through...'

She paused. Shook her head. 'No,' she said, a slow smile creeping across her face. 'That's not what I want.'

'What *do* you want, Vic? Because I'm sick of this. I need it to be over. So does Holly. When Russell died, she was given a second chance at freedom that she might never have had. You can't blame her for needing that – she's just a child! I'm sorry you lost your husband, but he wasn't a good man, and you said yourself, it wasn't much of a marriage. Maybe he didn't deserve for his life to end that way, but he made a choice and those were the consequences. So tell me what it's going to take for you to let her move on. What do you want from us?'

'Family. *Your* family. That's what I want.'

I stepped back, ice flooding my veins, the fears I'd carried for so long finally voiced out loud, confirming everything I'd suspected. 'What?' I breathed.

Victoria stepped closer, a smile playing at the corner of her pretty mouth. 'You came here asking me to leave you alone. I'm not willing to agree to that. I want to be an auntie to those children. I want to be part of their lives. Invited to dinners and parties. Picnics and pub lunches at the weekends. I want to take Holly and Jack on days out, and drink wine in your garden with you and Mike. I want what I've always wanted. A proper family.'

'So get your own!'

'Tried that. Why do you think I married Russell, if not for that very thing? All I ever wanted was something real. You don't see how lucky you are, having a husband who adores you. The children – God, they're so funny, so clever. There's nothing that can compare to it, a noisy, loving family. The talks around the table. The in-jokes and innocent teasing. You've never had to struggle to feel accepted, but not everyone gets that. Russell promised me the world when he married me. Promised he'd give me all the things I'd ever dreamed of. Unconditional love. Children. A happy home. But he didn't mean it. He wanted the trophy wife, my attention just on him. Stretch marks and breast milk, Lego on the living-room floor didn't fit his idea of perfection. He never even tried to find out who I really was. Just told me who he wanted me to be, and I did it, because I thought he'd relent on the children eventually.' She gave a wry laugh.

'When we met you, I was so excited to see a pregnant woman on the street. I thought if he could see how beautiful you were, how incredible you looked whilst growing a child inside you, he would change his mind. That he'd see how gorgeous your kids were and want his own. And he did start to soften, or at least I thought he did. But every year, he insisted on a bit longer, a little more time.'

She shook her head sadly. 'I couldn't have known I'd go through early menopause. That he was wasting time we didn't have until the chance was stolen out from under me. He took everything. Crushed every hope I ever had. I didn't want a lot, just the things *you* take for granted.' She sighed. 'My fertile years are long gone, and I will never trust a man again. Russell spent the whole of our marriage grinding away my confidence, and to be honest with you, I didn't have much to begin with. No, that door is closed for me now.' She shook her head, her eyes meeting mine.

'But,' she continued, 'I can be an auntie to *your* children. A sister to you. A friend to Mike. I love you all. Them, you. Don't you see that, Lisa? I *love* you. *You're* my family now. And if you let me be a part of it, you won't regret it.'

I was stunned. In all the years I'd lived opposite her, I had never known she was longing for a child of her own. I'd learned early on in life never to ask a couple about their reproductive plans – that some subjects were best left unmentioned – but privately, I'd been guilty of assuming that neither Russell nor Victoria wanted the disruption to their lives that came with babies. Even so, despite her heartbreaking confession, I still felt uneasy. There was the hint of a threat behind her declaration of love, and as awful as I felt for her, it didn't change the fact that in latching on to my family, she had made me feel uncomfortable in my own home. All this talk of being a part of it... it felt intrusive. *Obsessive.* My gut was screaming at me to cut ties now. I couldn't ignore that her fixation with us had become unhealthy.

'And if I say no?' I asked, clasping my hand tight around my wrist as I spoke.

She sighed. 'Don't make me say it. I'm not asking much and—'

'Vic... if I say no?'

She shrugged, turning away as if she couldn't bear to look me in the eye. 'Then I'd hate to have to ruin her life. And yours.'

'You mean, you would go to the police. Tell them to go after Holly,' I said, my voice flat. 'You would really do that, after what he did to her? You can't love her as much as you claim if you would go after her like that!'

I saw her shoulders slump, her back still facing me as she stared out the kitchen window at some unseen spot in the distance. For a moment, she didn't speak.

'I *do* love her,' she said eventually. 'But if I can't be with her, with all of you, what else can I do? I'm not strong like you, Lisa. I never have been. I've spent my whole life being squashed, and I'm sorry if that means I have a few flaws in my character. I know how it sounds. Really, I do. But I can't help the way I feel. For the first time in my life, I know what I want and I'm not willing to take no for an answer.' She turned to me with a sheepish expression on her flushed face. 'Can you really blame me for using what leverage I have to achieve what I want?'

I stared at her, seeing the conviction in her eyes, knowing she meant every word and realised I wasn't free after all. I was her prisoner now.

FORTY-FOUR

VICTORIA

Lisa was looking at me with an expression of absolute horror, but I held her gaze, trying not to let her see how rattled I was. One word played over and over in my mind, though I tried to shove it away. *Rape. Rape. Rape.* It took every tiny drop of my strength to retain a facade of self-control, when all I wanted to do was drop to my knees and scream. I couldn't bear it. When I'd had my brief moment of suspicion that the other woman might in fact be Holly, it had never even entered my mind that whatever had happened between her and my husband had been anything other than consensual – a seduction on his part of course, but I'd never considered her as anything other than a willing participant. She was young, yes, but not much younger than I'd been when I had met him. I had pictured her filled with excitement at his attentions, blinded by infatuation to the point that any sense of morals or decency was forgotten.

It had been sickening that he could look at her in that way after watching her grow from a sweet, angel-haired baby girl to the woman she was now, but the emotions I had felt then were nothing compared to the revulsion I felt now. I wanted to vomit.

To tear off my skin in order to rid myself of the crawling sensation, the horror of what he'd done hitting me over and over, forcing my mind to picture what my sweet, darling Holly must have felt when my own husband had turned on her so unforgivably. To think I had been married to someone capable of such a thing. I had known he was a man with many faults. A man who liked the finer things in life, liked to be seen as the best. Who liked control. But even so...

Hands shaking, I picked up my glass, taking a shaky sip of the sweet iced tea, hoping the sugar hit would give me the strength to keep my composure. I didn't want Lisa to see me crack. To pity me. I could see how much I had frightened her with my ultimatum, and yet I couldn't bring myself to take back the words. Because I meant them. I knew it now more than ever. With Russell gone and the perfect image of my marriage in tatters, I had nothing left. I needed her family.

Lisa's voice was brittle when she finally spoke. 'Holly deserves a clean start.'

I looked up from my glass, meeting her pale face across the room. I noticed she hadn't moved from the doorway, making it clear she had no intention of staying long.

'He's dead,' I said, my voice hollow. 'How much cleaner can it get?'

'You're a reminder of him. Surely you can see that, Victoria? You must have noticed she isn't the same around you any more. She's forced to remember him every time she looks at you – we *all* are. Do the decent thing and walk away.'

I placed my glass down, modulating my breathing, trying not to let on how angry her words had made me. 'You make it sound...' I took another breath, determined to speak with decorum, slow, steady. Russell had always hated it if I became shrill. 'You make it sound as if *I'm* at fault for what happened. I am not the one who hurt her.'

'Maybe not.'

'What's that supposed to mean?'

She fixed me with a look that shocked me, and I saw real hatred behind her eyes. It hurt. I didn't want her to look at me like that. Didn't deserve her venom.

'You can't tell me you never suspected he was capable of it,' she said quietly. 'I find it hard to believe that you could be married to a man for so long, sleep beside him in bed night after night, share dinners and conversations, live under the same roof, and not know the kind of person he was. You must have known he had this side to him. That he wasn't safe to be around children – *my* children!'

'Of course I didn't!' I gasped. 'You really think I would just brush something like that under the carpet? You *know* I would do anything for Holly. I would give my life for hers!'

'I don't know anything of the sort. You're delusional if you think that, Victoria. You threatened me with handing her in to the police not two minutes ago!'

I shook my head. 'Because I have no other leverage and you're trying to brush me off like a dead fly. You can't do that to me! I'm not Russell. I didn't hurt her.'

'Did he do it to you?'

'What?'

'Did he *rape* you?'

Her tone was hard, as if she was devoid of any sense of empathy, and I cringed away from her fury. I stared at her, my mouth dry, my heart pounding. 'He was my *husband*.'

She folded her arms, not breaking her stare, and I felt like squirming away, hiding from her probing gaze.

I took another steeling breath and looked down at the counter. 'I think you should go now. We both need to cool off.'

'Answer the fucking question, Victoria! Did he rape you? Did you know what he was? Did you know that you had married a monster?'

There was anger in her expression but also something more,

I realised. Concern, perhaps? Or was it pity? I opened my mouth to deny it, to tell her my marriage was perfect up until my stupid husband had made the choice to go after her daughter, but the words stuck in my throat, my eyes closing as I felt the unwelcome prickle of hot tears, the golf-ball-sized lump wedged deep in my throat. I had always known he was a man who liked to dominate. I couldn't deny that. Yes, there had been rules... so many rules I had to follow to meet his high standards. I'd bent to his will when it came to how I dressed, what I ate, who I talked to even. I had told myself that he was an alpha male. Wasn't that what everyone wanted? To be taken care of by a strong, confident man? Wasn't that what all the romance novels were about these days? I was lucky. But that word... *rape*.

I squeezed my eyes tighter shut, picturing the nights he would crawl into bed after a day of putting me down, telling me how I had shown him up, how I looked cheap and fat, was useless as a wife, how I should be grateful I had him because nobody else would put up with me. I had lain in bed feeling hurt, ugly, worthless, and when he'd rolled on top of me, I had felt sick, my body stiff and unwilling beneath his, his touch enough to make me recoil into the mattress, wishing I could be anywhere else. I had never dared to speak the words, to tell him no, but there were so many times I had tried to push him away, only to be held tighter, my wrists forced above my head, my wishes ignored. I had never considered myself a victim of abuse. Of rape. And I didn't want to now.

'He was my *husband*,' I spat, repeating the mantra, gritting my teeth, turning away from Lisa to grab a bottle of Russell's whisky from the bar. I spun the lid off, pouring a large measure into a tumbler, drinking it back neat in one go. The heat hit the back of my throat, a spicy burn, and I doubled over, coughing hard.

Lisa, though, was relentless in her interrogation. 'And he

was *my* friend. As good as an uncle to my children. But that still didn't stop him, did it? I know he wasn't the perfect husband, Vic. You know that too.'

I looked back up and saw her face soften for a brief moment. Was *that* how she saw me? How everyone saw me? As a victim? Weak? Pathetic? I had done everything in my power to keep up appearances. To give the impression that my life was successful. That I had the house, the husband, the looks. That I was someone who had value. But it had all been in vain.

'Your husband was a rapist. And I think he did it to you too. I think if you'd been strong enough, you could have saved her.' She shook her head, and I saw a tear slide down her pale cheek. 'God, I wish you'd come to me, Vic. I wish you'd asked for my help.'

'Stop it!'

'I would have believed you. I would have—'

'I said stop it! Stop talking! I don't want to hear it! Shut up, shut up, shut up!' I screamed, rage and shame coursing through my veins, my world shattering around me as I realised the truth of what I had been living with all these years.

He wasn't just a controlling man. He was an abuser. And I was his victim, something I had never wanted to admit to. I couldn't bear to be seen that way. And I couldn't stand that Lisa might be right. That I could have helped Holly. I had done everything to be the perfect wife to him, never letting myself dwell on the fact that he was taking advantage. Hurting me. Breaking me down so I would never leave him. He had destroyed me, piece by piece. And now, he had hurt the girl I loved most in the world.

I let out a bellowing scream, clutching the neck of the whisky bottle tighter in my fist, then whirled around, sending it hurtling across the room. It hit the wall with deafening force, spraying glass across the kitchen, the smell of alcohol filling the air. Lisa stood frozen in the doorway, and I turned my back on her, unwilling to see the look of horror on her face.

'Go,' I whispered. 'Now.'

I heard her suck in a breath and, a moment later, the fast retreat of her footsteps followed by the slam of the front door. I was alone.

FORTY-FIVE

LISA

I hadn't been snooping. I was an overprotective mother – that much I was willing to admit. I hated if Jack came home ten minutes past his curfew, my mind running through every possibility and taking me to the darkest of places. I made my children put Savlon on when they cut themselves like they were still five years old, and I was never at ease when they weren't safe under my roof where I could see them. But as much as I loved to keep them wrapped up in cotton wool, trying to prolong the years I got to take care of them before they flew the nest, I had never betrayed their trust. I believed in children having their privacy – something I'd valued myself as a teenager. I forced myself to let go, let them make their own mistakes, as hard as it was, but I couldn't deny, it was easier with Holly because she was still so young for her age. She, unlike her brother, had never given me much cause to worry, save for her tendency to stop eating.

So I hadn't been looking for secrets that day, hard as that might be to believe. The notepad had been slotted amongst a pile of paperbacks on her bedside cabinet, and I'd just flipped it open to see if it was from the creative writing course she'd dropped out of after only a few weeks, thinking I might pop it in the drawer with the rest of her old school work. She'd yet to decide on another course to sign up to, and though I knew Mike was keen for her to go back as soon as possible, I thought the year off to consider what she really wanted to do would stand her in good stead when she re-enrolled for the coming September.

It had been lovely having her home so much over the past eight months, and I knew I would miss her company when she went back. I wondered if the reason the notepad was out was that she might be reconsidering her hasty decision to leave the writing course.

After scanning a few lines, I had automatically slammed it closed, realising it was her diary, then stood in the middle of her room, my heart pounding, my hands sweating as if I'd done something terrible. One word had glared out from the page, though I couldn't imagine why I would have seen it there. Why would my daughter be writing about such things? I must have imagined it. My mind was playing tricks on me. Perhaps it was a fictional story after all, though instinctively I'd been sure it wasn't. I'd gripped the notepad tightly, knowing it was wrong to look again, but I had to know for sure.

Slowly, I opened it to the same page, and there it was. Written in Holly's beautiful writing, though I could tell her hand must have been shaking as she wrote. One word that made my breath catch and my stomach drop. *Rape*. Why would my sweet young daughter, who'd never even held hands with a boy, never been on a date, be writing about such an awful subject?

I scanned the pages, reading so fast I had to force myself to slow down as I skipped through the passages, missing the details. Finally, I looked up from those awful words to find I was sitting on her bedroom floor, soft rose-coloured carpet beneath my legs, though I had no memory of choosing to sit down. I looked at the date and saw the entry had been written two weeks previously. A fortnight she had held on to this corrosive secret. Two weeks of her keeping quiet, going through hell, and I hadn't known a thing.

Russell, the man who'd been friendly and warm to us from the day they'd moved in opposite – a man older than her own father – had raped my baby, and she'd never said a word.

The shock hit me, and I dropped the diary, grabbing for Holly's pink waste-paper basket, throwing up until my throat was raw. I'd made her come to their barbecue last weekend. She'd tried to talk her way out of it, and I'd been tired and irritable and thought she was being selfish when Russell and Victoria had gone to so much effort. She'd begged to go to a friend's house and have a sleepover there instead, but I'd forced her to come, secretly worried that she wouldn't eat if I let her out of my sight. I remembered feeling like she was trying to get out of having to finish a big meal and feeling frustrated with her.

I'd made her sit across from him, thank him for the lovely food he'd used his bare hands to place on her plate. And I'd been angry that she was so sullen and ungrateful, embarrassed at her manners, though Vic had waved off my concern. Why hadn't I questioned why she'd suddenly lost her appetite again? Why she was so resistant to coming when she'd never shown any hesitation to be around him in the past? How had I been so blind as not to see what was right in front of my face?

As I realised what I'd put my daughter through, how smug he must have felt sitting there across the patio from her, the power he must have thought he had over her, I had wanted to kill him. To scream at him, demand that he tell me why. He had known her since she was a baby, for Christ's sake! But more than that, I wanted to get in my car, drive to the playing field where she was having her hockey practice and pick up my little girl. I wanted to wrap her in my arms and tell her it was okay. If not now, then later. It *would* be okay. Somehow, we'd make it better. But I could do nothing. I was frozen in a realm of impossible choices. It wasn't fair for me to force my sympathy and comfort on her. Not if she wasn't ready for me to know. This was *her* story. *Her* pain. I could end up doing more harm than good in my clumsy attempts to help her.

And as much as I wanted to hurt him, skin him alive and watch him burn for laying a finger on my daughter, I knew it would only bring the whole story out, and in doing so inflict more pain on Holly. And right now, *she* was all that mattered. I would find a way to help her, to get her to open up to me. But until she was ready, I would wait. I would do nothing but be the mother she needed. It was all I could do.

FORTY-SIX

'Honestly, it's fine. I want you to go,' I said, picking up Jack's raincoat and eyeing the darkening sky, hoping he and Mike weren't going to come back too drenched. They both stood uncertainly on the drive, looking between me and the Land Rover, clearly unsure what to do. It had been my suggestion that the two of them head off to hike the Seven Sisters for the day. Their love and attention had been everything I could have needed on returning home from the police station, but now I was beginning to feel claustrophobic, and there were only so many cups of tea I could drink. I could tell they were both trying so hard to take care of me, but being stuck indoors didn't suit them. A day romping over the clifftops, stopping to poke around in rock pools and dip their feet in the ocean, having fun without worrying about me, was exactly what they needed.

'I'm not ill,' I insisted, smiling at Mike as I pushed the mac into Jack's hands. I tried to keep the wobble out of my voice, hoping to gloss over the unease I felt at being left home alone. Holly had gone to town with a friend, and though I was glad to see her doing something fun, pushing herself to enjoy her usual routines again, I couldn't help but worry about the secrets she was holding close. And being alone in the house didn't sound overly appealing to me.

Any other time, I might have gone out to the Green Flamingo, but I was too embarrassed to show my face there just yet. I knew the owners would have questions, having had the police in there asking about me – about Russell. The memory of seeing him there that day, the cocky smile on his face, the absolute confidence that he could get away with what he had done made anger swell inside my chest, my pulse racing faster. It had been two or three days after I'd read Holly's diary, the first time I'd seen him since finding out what he had done to her, and I hadn't been at all prepared. I had so desperately wanted to respect her privacy, let her choose when to tell, but that left me in a situation I didn't know how to deal with. I couldn't confront Russell, and yet the thought of even looking at him, breathing the same air as him, made me sick to my stomach. When he'd called my name, waving over the hedge, I had frozen, hoping he would just keep walking, have the sense not to poke the mother bear, but when I'd ignored him, he'd forced himself into my line of vision, and despite my resolve not to out Holly in any way, I had experienced such a visceral reaction, I hadn't been able to stay in my seat.

I knew he'd seen the hatred in my eyes. I had watched his face morph from friendly neighbour to something else. Seen the exact moment he had realised I was no longer in the dark about his awful secret. There had been fear in his eyes, and a stubbornness, as if he thought he could brush it all away with a smile and a hug – convince me I was mistaken. But I couldn't let that happen. Couldn't have him anywhere near me. So I had run. Eventually I would have to go back and settle up. Maybe have a coffee and a cake and wait for the awkwardness to subside. But not today.

I was almost tempted to jump in the car and go with Mike

and Jack, but I wanted to be here when Holly got home – and besides, it really did look like it might pour down.

I glanced over to Victoria's house, unable to stop myself from wondering if she was watching us out here. I had seen the moment of realisation in her eyes when I spoke those awful words yesterday. I knew it was cruel, that I was forcing her to admit things she wasn't ready to face, and a part of me was ashamed for how I had spoken to her. But I'd had to know for sure that she wasn't complicit in what her husband had done to my child. I had to see the truth in her eyes, and perhaps I'd got more than I'd bargained for. Her horror and shock had been wholly genuine, I was certain of that. I knew now that whatever he had done to her, she hadn't ever considered the possibility that he would be a danger to anyone else. Despite my anger, I felt sorry for her, hating that I hadn't known what was going on, hadn't been able to support her, but I wished she would realise there was no way we could be friends after everything that had passed. It was too hard. Too raw.

If only she would move away, start again somewhere fresh, but I knew she wouldn't let the matter lie. I had seen the determination on her face when she'd told me she wanted to be a part of my family, and every time I replayed her words, I felt sick, terrified at what she might do in her unhinged state. Holly's freedom was everything to me, and Victoria knew it. And no matter my feelings on the woman, I would fold my hand if it meant protecting my daughter.

'You're sure you don't mind?' Mike asked, though he was already wearing hiking boots and had a bag full of crusty ham rolls and home-made flapjacks on the back seat.

He took a step closer, his big arms wrapping around me, pulling me tight against him. 'I feel like I should be with you. What if that man comes here again?'

I pressed my cheek against his chest. 'I told you, it's not going to happen. DS McCormac isn't coming back.' *Unless I give Victoria a reason to send him here*, I thought, closing my eyes briefly.

I kissed him quickly, then stepped back. 'Go, both of you, before I change my mind and get you doing something far less exciting. Like cleaning the bathroom!'

'That's all the encouragement I need,' Jack said, winking as he hopped in the passenger seat. 'Love you, Mum.'

Mike squeezed my shoulder then nodded, walking around to get in the driver's seat.

'Love you too, both of you. Don't go through any long grass – I don't want you both covered in ticks when you get back here.'

Mike slammed the door, blew me a kiss, then backed off the driveway fast, as if he needed to go before he could change his mind. I waved as they headed up the road out of sight, then sighed. I resisted looking back towards Victoria's house. I didn't want to acknowledge her presence, give her the satisfaction of knowing she had me rattled. Instead, I turned, walking back inside and heading into the kitchen, the smell of warm butter and cinnamon from the early-morning batch of flapjacks still lingering in the air.

I poured myself a coffee, popped a slice of the flapjack on a plate and slid onto the padded bar stool at the counter. It was a ritual I was familiar with, something I did all the time, and yet sitting here in my own kitchen, able to enjoy the scalding-hot coffee in a proper mug, held between my palms, choose when and what I ate, made me acknowledge how close I had come to losing those freedoms.

I had always been grateful for my life. Being able to stay home with my children and watch them grow, to be a home-maker, loving the little routines and rhythms of my days, the simplicity that came with taking care of the people I loved. I hadn't let it escape my attention that I was in a position of great privilege, though over the years it had meant living frugally, simply. But now, having nearly lost it all, I appreciated it all the more. The comfort of being in my nest, the knowledge that tonight I would make a meal, sit around the table with my husband, our children... Things were far from perfect, but still, I was grateful.

I'd been so wrapped up in counting my blessings that the creak of the floorboards in the hallway made my head snap up, my heart suddenly beating faster. I sat frozen, listening hard, wondering if I might have imagined it. I gripped the cup tighter, the hot ceramic pressing painfully against my skin.

And then I heard it. A footstep. Unmistakeable. I wasn't alone.

All the warmth and security I had been feeling vanished in a split second as instantly my thoughts turned to Victoria. It had to be her. She had broken in, made up her mind to take the matter into her own hands. She had made it abundantly clear that she wouldn't stop until she got what she wanted. What sane person would insert themselves into someone else's family the way she hoped to do?

I slipped off the stool, quietly as I could manage, my hands still wrapped around the scalding coffee, as if I might use it for a weapon – throw it or something. I could taste fear on my tongue and knew that if she was here in my house, it could only mean something bad was coming. I took a breath.

'Who's there?' I called, hearing the scratchiness in my throat.

Another creak. And then the air rushed out of my body as my daughter appeared in the doorway. Her eyes were rimmed with red, her pale cheeks tear-stained, thin arms folded across her narrow chest.

'Holly! Oh my God, you frightened the life out of me!' I gasped. 'I didn't hear you come in.'

I placed the coffee cup down harder than I meant to, splashing its contents over my fingers. 'Damn.'

I grabbed a towel and dried my hands, then turned to her. 'Sweetheart, I thought you were out.'

I wanted to mention her tears but didn't know how to bring it up without making her feel uncomfortable. Did she *want* me to ask? One of my children coming in hurt or upset had always been a trigger for me to comfort them in the past, but I couldn't be sure that response was the right one any more. From the moment I'd read her diary, I had second-guessed my every action. Being a parent, knowing how to handle overtired toddlers having a meltdown, how to remind them of their words when they spoke without thought for the feelings of others, those things had always come naturally to me. But now, I was lost in the woods without so much as a torch to guide me, and I knew one wrong step could spell disaster.

She bit her lower lip. 'I... I would never have let you go to jail, you know. You *do* know that, right?'

I raised an eyebrow, shaking my head in confusion. I felt a premonition about what she would say next, and though I'd wanted her to open up to me for so long, I wasn't sure I was ready. I felt like I couldn't trust myself to get it right, say what she needed to hear. I should have read up on what to do, should have spoken to a therapist or something. Now, with tears streaming down her cheeks, a determined, resolute look in her eyes, I wanted to hold out my hands in protest, stop her from speaking. Buy myself longer to prepare. I didn't want to mess this up.

'Holly, what are you talkin—'

'You must think I'm such a coward,' she continued, speaking over me. 'When did you realise I was the one who did it? I knew... as soon as they came to the house. I thought they'd come for me, you see, but then you let them take you. Walked out without so much as a word, didn't even try and defend yourself. And I knew then, you were planning to take the blame for me. You always know, don't you? I never have been able to hide things from you.' She looked down. 'I was a coward,' she whispered. 'I know you think that.'

'Holly, don't be silly. I would never think that about you.'

'Well, I was. But it wasn't because I didn't want to go to jail. It was because if I had owned up, the whole story would have come out...'

She squeezed the tops of her arms, the action narrowing her frame, making her appear even more tiny, then raised her face slowly, her gaze meeting mine. It was all I could do not to look away, the pain in her eyes breaking my heart in two.

'And then the whole world would know what he did to me,' she finished, her voice barely more than a whisper.

I could feel her watching me, testing her suspicions, and couldn't hide the anguish I felt from crossing my features.

She nodded, seeing the truth written on my face. 'I knew you'd figured it out,' she said softly. 'And I love you for trying to protect me. But I need you to understand that, scared as I was, I wouldn't have let them put you in prison for what I did. That night when you came home, I had already made up my mind to go to the police and tell them everything. I was scared, but it wouldn't have stopped me. I promise, Mum. I wouldn't have let you take the blame for me.'

'Holly,' I said. 'I don't want this to stay on your conscience. It was a mistake. A reaction. It wasn't your fault, and it doesn't make you a bad person.' My voice rang with conviction. I didn't know if I was being reckless, telling her these things, if a therapist would go about it another way, but it was what I felt to be true and it was all I had. 'It was a mistake. And you aren't to blame. I mean that. You can't let this ruin your whole life. Promise me you'll let it go. That you'll forgive yourself.'

She looked down at her feet, and I saw they were bare, her toenails tiny half-moons with the remnants of a glitter polish I'd put on for her myself. I remembered the moment. It had been before I learned the truth. But after Russell had... I bit my lip, feeling sick at the thought of me going through the motions, giving her a quick pedicure before getting back to the housework. We had talked about this and that, but I'd had no idea of what was really going on in her mind. The trauma she had been through. She'd put on an act, and now, I couldn't help but think she had done it to protect me, because she knew it would be devastating for me to hear what he'd done to her. Was it because I loved her so much that she hadn't been able to confide in me? Had my need to protect her made her feel like she was letting me down when I hadn't been able to?

She gave a long, deep sigh. 'Was what *he* did a mistake too? Am I supposed to forgive him? Or was he bad deep down?' She shook her head and I saw the tears begin to flow freely down her cheeks again. 'Did I do the wrong thing, Mum? Or did he deserve what happened?'

I stared at her, not knowing how to even begin to unpack her question, to give an answer I had no right to give. I couldn't find the words. Couldn't speak. Instead, I held out my arms, and to my relief, she rushed forward, hugging me tight, as if she were still my baby girl. I breathed in the smell of her head and wished I could make the world a better place for her.

'He's gone now,' I said softly into her hair. 'That's all I know. And he'll never hurt you again.'

EPILOGUE

One year later

'More wine, Vic?' I smiled, topping up her glass, trying not to mind that she was sitting so close to Mike as she talked animatedly about her mishaps in yet another cookery class she was taking – without my company. It seemed she had fallen in love with the kitchen, just as I had, and now she'd progressed from casual evening classes at the community centre to an adult education course at the local college. I couldn't help but hope she would meet someone at one of these classes, but she never mentioned so much as a new friend, let alone a romantic partner.

She paused her anecdote now to smile up at me. 'That'd be lovely, thanks, Lisa. I'll come inside and help with the dishes in a minute.'

'Oh, don't be silly,' Mike piped up. 'You're a guest. You might have held the fort last year when Lisa had her little holiday,' he joked, 'but you really don't have to now.'

'You always say that. And do I ever listen?' She smiled. 'Honestly, Mike, I like doing it. I want to help. It makes me feel useful. And by now, I'm practically one of the family.' She punched his arm playfully, breaking into that tinkling laugh of hers.

'Well, you can't say I didn't try.' He sat back, stretching his long, tanned legs out in front of him. 'You may as well get me another beer while you're in there then,' he said, his cheeky smile infectious, making me grin despite myself.

I walked away from the two of them, back to the patio table, pouring myself another glass of wine and sipping deeply. Holly, having invited two friends from *her* new college course – this time animal management – was talking with them over on the decking at the back of the garden, pausing between sentences to take big bites from the cheeseburger on the plate balanced on her knees.

She was coming out of her shell more and more as each week passed. She still hadn't spoken outright about what happened between her and Russell – at least not to me – and we'd never again touched on the topic of how he'd died since our talk when she'd sworn she would have owned up before things went too far, but there had been snippets of conversations, little offerings she'd brought up about how she was feeling, how certain things triggered her into a state of panic, reminiscent of the two awful nights he'd left his mark on her – the rape and the night he'd been killed.

She still wouldn't walk home alone after dark, wouldn't be alone with any of Mike's friends when they visited, and she couldn't bear to go inside Victoria's house – something I wholeheartedly supported her in. She had been hurt deeply by Russell's actions. The fact that she had trusted him and he had hurt her so badly made it hard for her to really feel safe with any man, aside from Jack and her dad. But although I could see that she still had healing to do, she had been so much stronger than I had ever anticipated. She hadn't let what Russell did ruin her.

I knew she'd joined several online support groups and was finding solace in meeting other people who had experienced similar traumas, sharing coping strategies and advice, and though I couldn't be sure, I guessed she was more comfortable in going into the more difficult details of her rape with these faceless strangers. I could understand that. I knew she would find it a struggle to hurt me with those words – that I would live her pain as if it were my own. And this wasn't about me. She needed the opportunity to talk without censoring herself and had instinctively gravitated to other sources of support.

Even so, we had talked a lot more about deeper subjects in the past year than we ever had before – about life, philosophy, emotions and healing – and though we never delved close to the nucleus of her pain, she'd begun to talk at the dinner table about how nobody had the power to make you feel something. How life was a roller coaster and negative experiences would inevitably come your way, but even though we might be powerless to stop certain things from happening to us, one thing we *did* have control of was how we reacted to adversity.

Mike had teased her, saying she'd gone 'all woo-woo', asking when she was heading off to India to live in a monastery in the mountains, but I had told him to leave her alone, secretly smiling at how determined she was to move forward. I'd offered to pay for professional therapy sessions for her, intending to use the tiny pot of savings I'd put aside over the years, but she'd refused, and though the offer was always open and she knew it, I had a feeling she wouldn't take me up on it, and that was okay. She was so much stronger than I had ever given her credit for, and somehow, seeing this over the past year, watching her hold her head high, sign up to a new course, make new friends and move on with her life had forced me to stop seeing her as the little girl in need of wrapping in cotton wool. She was a woman in her own right now, and I had so much respect for her.

I hid a smile as Jack strolled over to the little group, flirting shamelessly with one of Holly's friends. I couldn't help but think that for all the ways he and his dad were similar, he didn't share Mike's lack of awareness when it came to the opposite sex. There was no way Jack would miss an opportunity to ask a girl out, the way Mike had done with me, smiling and turning back to his tools the day we met. He'd told me later that he'd had no idea I was even interested, though I'd blushed scarlet the moment he looked at me. His head was too wrapped up with adventure, projects, *life*, and as much as I hated the way Victoria seemed to flirt with him in her coy, doe-eyed manner, I knew I had nothing to worry about. Not from Mike's side anyway.

I stood by the patio table, waiting for Victoria to come back out with the promised beer for my husband, then, once she was seated opposite him again, I picked up the wine bottle, batting away a fly as it buzzed in my face, and headed inside to pop it in the fridge for later. As I closed the fridge door and turned to look through the kitchen window, I couldn't help but think of how different things might have been now if Russell had survived that night. If I had never found Holly's diary. How broken my daughter would have been knowing he was still a threat. Would she have confided in me? Or would the secret have destroyed her?

I breathed in, letting my thoughts go to that night. The rain, the dark, the taste of rum on my lips...

My alibi had been rock-solid. With Mike and Jack away on their trip and Holly insisting she was going to stay over with her old school friends, there should have been nobody home that night. I'd been shocked when Holly had come downstairs with a packed bag, not expecting her to want to sleep away from home, given what I knew. But then it had struck me that it might be better for her to get away from this house. That she must feel suffocated by being so close to where *he* lived, picturing him across the road.

The realisation had made me determined to find a way to talk to her about it after the weekend was over, but for that night, I had let her go, and then, finding myself home alone, had called Melissa and got a lift up to the forest retreat with her, where I'd spent several hours drinking cheap red wine around a bonfire and listening to my friends sharing their news. It wasn't until everyone started heading inside the lodge to go to bed that I realised I'd left my phone at home. And it was then that the niggles began to creep in. The fear that Holly might have called to ask me to pick her up, or worse, that she had come home to find the house empty.

Everyone had fallen asleep quickly, but not me. I had sat in the dark worrying for what felt like an age before making up my mind. Not wanting to cause a fuss or ruin the night for the others, I had borrowed Melissa's car keys from her bag without asking permission first, making sure not to wake anyone as I quietly slipped out of the lodge. The fear had made me sober up, and I drove carefully as I made the forty-minute journey back home. I'm still not sure what prompted me to change my route, adjust my plan, but five minutes from home, I suddenly made a decision, my gut calling to me somehow, I suppose. I pulled over into a side road, knowing I could cut across the unlit park and reach the back gate to my garden unseen. Something inside me was screaming danger, though I couldn't be sure what. Holly wouldn't be there. But what if she was? What if *he* was? I couldn't say why I felt the need to hide my arrival, but I did.

As I stepped out of the car, the first fat drops of rain began to fall, a deep rumble of thunder moving overhead, the night muggy and electric.

Beneath the moonless sky, I could hardly see the path, and I walked as fast as I dared through the park, stumbling now and then on unseen obstacles – sticks discarded by distracted toddlers and loose pebbles worked free from the dirt. I kept close to the hedges, my belly flipping with nerves at what might be lurking in their depths.

From somewhere not too far behind me, I heard the scream of an urban fox in the throes of mating and quickened my pace, regretting my hasty decision to come this way. It seemed suddenly over the top, and I felt sure I had worked myself into a state for nothing. I should have just parked outside my house.

As the narrow entrance to the alleyway that led behind my row of houses came into view, my stomach lurched at the thought of walking down the long, dark stretch, unable to see what dangers might be lurking just ahead.

A flash of lightning lit up the sky, making me jump, but as it illuminated the world for a moment, I confirmed that there was nothing there but the stack of tyres Greg from three doors down had piled up by his gate, and a few broken pot plants that had blown off Margery's back wall and smashed.

Another rumble of thunder boomed like a sonic blast above me, and the rain became a solid sheet of water, plastering my hair to my head, running down the back of my jumper. I broke into a run, letting myself in through the gate and then pulling my keys from my bag to unlock the back door, diving into the kitchen to escape the torrential downpour.

I stood in the silence of the kitchen feeling scared and stupid and wondering what I had expected.

Without flicking on a light, I walked from room to room, tiptoeing, though it felt ridiculous. When I reached Holly's bedroom, the curtains were wide open and the room was empty. I should have felt relieved, but I couldn't. That awful, clawing sense of unease lingered on deep within my gut.

I had been about to head out of the room when I saw the window had been left slightly ajar, the rain pattering in, hitting the pale pink wallpaper. Crossing the carpet to close it, I glanced outside and frowned. My car was missing from the drive.

I racked my brain, the effects of the wine from earlier making me feel foggy, tired, as I tried to recall where on earth I could have left it if it wasn't on the drive. The road was dark, the street lights having been switched off at 1 a.m. under the council's new environmentally friendly money-saving policy, but as I stared out of the window, there was another blinding flash of lightning and I saw the shadowy figure of a man walking along the pavement, unsteady on his feet, oblivious to the weather. Something about the way he moved, the curve of his shoulders beneath the long, tailored coat, made the tiny hairs rise on the back of my neck.

It was less than a second later that it came. The dazzling glare of headlights. The high-pitched screech of tyres. The car – *my* car, I realised – seemed to emerge from nowhere, as if it had been hidden the whole time, the driver lying in wait. It swerved sharply to the left, veering onto the pavement in what could only have been an intentional manoeuvre. The man just had time to glance over his shoulder before impact. I saw it coming and gripped the windowsill, my eyes squeezing shut automatically, though I forced them open, needing to see to believe it was happening.

He was tossed into the air like a rag doll, and I knew instantly who was in the driver's seat – knew exactly who I would find lying broken out there in the street.

I watched, trembling, as my Mondeo sped off down the road without ever once touching the brakes, and felt sick at the thought of where it might be heading. For a minute or two, I stood frozen at the window, watching to see if anyone else had heard – if lights from the surrounding houses would flick on, doors be thrown open. When nothing changed, I spun away from the sill, heading through the house, pausing only to open the cupboard under the stairs and grab my black winter parka from the hook, slipping it on, wanting to shield myself from view, though it was far too muggy a night to need it, even with the rain pelting down out there. I retraced my footsteps through the back door and out into the dark alley beyond.

There was no hesitation this time as I ran along the narrow pathway, my heart thumping hard, adrenaline creating a strange absence of fear. There was only a deep, unshakeable understanding of what I had to do now. How I had to protect her, no matter what.

I came out of the opposite end of the alley at the corner of the road – a grassy verge, a horse chestnut tree shielding me from view and offering some protection from the storm. And there he was, lying in the mud on his side, his leg bent at an unnatural angle. Even in the dark I could smell the blood, and it made me want to run, but I couldn't. Not now.

Looking behind me to check I was still alone, I pressed my lips tightly together and walked slowly towards the figure, pulling my hood up as I did. I jumped back as I realised his eyes were open. And he was looking right at me.

'Lisa,' he croaked, his gaze intense, forcing me not to look away. 'Lisa, help me... call an ambulance – please!'

I stood above him, my heart threatening to burst out of my chest, the blood roaring in my ears. Slowly, I lowered myself down to crouch beside the top of his head. From this position, I could see the white glare of bone poking through the skin of his thigh. There was a cut on the side of his face, and he was breathing rapidly, but I couldn't be sure if it was because of the pain of his leg or something more serious – internal injuries perhaps. Would he die from this? Or would he recover... after all he'd put her through?

I couldn't believe it had come to this. That it was *my* daughter who had caused such horrific injuries to the man who had been our neighbour for all these years. I couldn't have imagined there was any part of her that was capable of going through with something so calculated, premeditated – no matter what he might have done to her. And yet, I knew it was true. My fear of bringing up the subject and telling her what I knew, my inability to be there for her when she needed me most, had led her to feel so alone, so terrified, that she had taken matters into her own hands. Had I found the courage, the words, we could have gone to the police. We could have told the world what he had done. Made them see what a monster he was, ruined his reputation, and Holly would have known she wasn't alone. But now... now it was too late for any of that.

'Lisa,' he said again, his tone pleading.

I stared down at him, numb, empty. It felt as if it were someone else wearing my coat, crouching over him with a cold, blank expression. That I was watching from some faraway place where none of this was real. It was like being trapped in a dream; all my emotions felt dulled, diluted.

'I can't feel my fingers,' he said. 'I think my arm's dislocated. *Please*, you have to call someone. Get Victoria. I need Victoria.'

I stared into his face, picturing him looming above my daughter, taking what she wasn't prepared to give, and suddenly, it was all so clear.

I reached into the pocket of my coat, pulling on the leather gloves I hadn't worn since last winter; then, checking I was still hidden by the boughs of the huge tree, I leaned in closer, pressing both hands over his face, pinching his nose as hard as I could and tilting my weight forward, cutting off his air supply completely.

I looked up at the stormy sky. His left arm was flailing, trying to grab at me as he thrashed his head from side to side, desperately seeking a breath of air that I wouldn't allow him. Rain pelted my face, biting against my skin, blurring my vision. I couldn't look down. Didn't want to see – to have that memory etched in my mind for ever – though the reality couldn't have been worse than the pictures my imagination formed in their place.

If I'd glanced down, perhaps I would have seen that my

scarf had fallen out of my pocket, but hindsight is a wonderful thing.

It felt like hours before he finally stopped moving, but still I held on. I had to be sure. I could not let him live. Not now. Too much had happened. Holly wouldn't survive it – I knew that with absolute certainty. And now that I was faced with the choice, I knew I wanted her to be able to live in a world where her rapist didn't exist. To not have to constantly look over her shoulder, wondering when or where he might pop up, imagining his voice everywhere she went, never fully safe or secure. If he lived through tonight, who knew what would happen to my daughter. How she would cope knowing that her attempt to free herself from the man who had hurt her so badly had failed. I wouldn't let her go through that.

Finally, still unable to look at what I'd done, I stood up, walked back down the alley and not home but instead across the park to where I'd left Melissa's car. On the way, I tossed the gloves and my coat into a bin outside a house, already out ready for rubbish collection in the morning.

I got in the car, and without allowing myself to think of where Holly might be now, what I had just done, I cranked up the heater to try and dry myself off, a fruitless attempt to dull the tremors rocking through my core, then drove back to the forest lodge, arriving just after two in the morning. As I slipped in through the door, something inside me clicked and I realised what a mess I had made. I needed an alibi that couldn't be questioned. Everyone was fast asleep. What if the police asked them for evidence to prove I hadn't slipped away?

I walked into the kitchen and pulled the ice-cube drawer from the freezer, tipping the contents into the blender and reaching for the bottle of rum on the counter. I took a deep, burning swig straight from the bottle, then another... another. Finally, I flicked on the lights.

'Wake up, ladies!' I yelled, shaking the sleeping bodies of

the women I planned to use to my own advantage. 'Tomorrow we have to get back to real life. But tonight, we're free. I'm making piña coladas! Want one?'

Amy rolled over, bleary-eyed, then stretched and broke into a slow smile. 'Why the hell not? You're only young once!' she exclaimed, reaching for the bottle in my hand and taking a mouthful, wincing as the rum hit the back of her throat.

I forced my face into a smile as they dragged on jumpers and grabbed glasses, their chatter distracting me from the pounding thoughts and vivid images in my head. Before I knew what was happening, all nine of us were drinking ice-cold cock-tails around the rustic wooden kitchen counter. I stood sipping my drink, listening to them laugh, craving home, my own bed, the safe, warm arms of my husband, wishing there had been another option. I had done something terrible, something that could never be taken back, but I'd had no choice. I'd had to protect Holly. Any mother would have done the same.

When the police had arrived at my door the following week, it had almost been a relief not to have to wait for them any more. I had already made up my mind what I must do. I had to continue to shield my daughter. I would take the blame. Let them see me as the suspect, do whatever it took to keep them from turning their focus on Holly. And if it had come to it, I would have kept my mouth closed for ever, let them put me behind bars without ever once bringing her name into it. I would have sacrificed my freedom for hers in an instant.

It had only been when I had feared for her safety, known Victoria was getting steadily closer, felt terror at the thought of what she might have planned, that I had known I had to give up my alibi and claim my freedom. As mothers, we have to make tough choices every day, and sometimes all you have to go on is your gut. Mine was telling me I had to get home, be where I could take care of my family and stop anything else from hurting my children. In the end, it had worked out for the best.

I looked back out of the kitchen window now, hearing Victoria's tinkling laugh as she touched Mike on the knee, encouraging him to continue with whatever story he was telling, no doubt one she'd heard before. All things considered, putting up with her company wasn't the worst thing in the world. I had killed her husband after all – not that she knew the truth. It was simpler to let her hold on to her belief that it had been Holly, a story she seemed to understand, having accepted the horrible truth of what Russell had done to her. In her mind, Holly was a frightened girl who had made a decision in the heat of the moment, and somehow, despite it all, there seemed to be no trace of resentment in Victoria's attitude towards her. It was clear to me that Victoria was relieved he was gone, though she had refused to acknowledge out loud what she now knew to be true. That she was as much of a victim as my daughter had been.

I had spent countless hours thinking over my actions that fateful night, wondering if I should tell Holly the truth of what had happened after she had driven away. She too believed that she was responsible for taking Russell's life, and I worried the guilt would tear her apart. But as the weeks had passed and I'd seen her coming out of the fog, becoming a stronger, more secure version of herself, I had made the decision not to share the truth with her. I didn't want her to feel guilty, to feel she'd forced me to do something I didn't want to do, and I knew that her empathetic, sweet nature would mean she would blame herself for giving me no other option but to take that path. For making her mother into a murderer, because she *would* see it that way. It was a burden I didn't want her to bear.

And strangely, there was a larger part of me that didn't want to take away the power she'd seized for herself. She wasn't a bad person, and I felt sure I had raised her with enough self-acceptance to truly believe that. She had retaliated, yes, wanting to rid the world of an evil man, but in doing so, she had released a new-found sense of confidence deep in her own core. She wasn't afraid of the world any more, and I wouldn't take that away from her by revealing that I had finished the job she had set out to complete. She and Victoria could both stay in the dark for ever as far as I was concerned.

To Victoria's credit, she had kept her word, and Holly's secret, never sending the police back our way. She'd told me that someone from the station had called a few weeks after my release, apologising for the fact that the case had been shelved, the finger pointed at joyriders they had no hope of catching.

I had been grateful to her for telling me and made sure to slip it into conversation at dinner, seeing the relief in Holly's face, knowing she had worried they would come back – this time for her. A mother never misses these little signs. It had been a gift for Victoria to let us breathe again, one she hadn't had to give. The fact that she treated Holly like a daughter, despite everything she knew, made me look at her in a different light. I could see now that she wasn't a sinister seductress looking to step into my shoes. She was just a lonely, lost woman needing something to grasp hold of. And *we* had become her purpose.

I walked back outside, pausing in the sunshine by the back door, smiling at the scene. My happy, thriving children. The husband I loved more and more with each year that passed. And Victoria. She saw me looking her way and paused her conversation to smile with genuine warmth in my direction. I would never think of her as a friend. But it was clear that she was a part of our lives now, and nothing was going to change that. And she had proven herself a loyal ally at the very least. She could have destroyed my family, but she'd chosen not to.

I raised my glass, and she did the same, offering a silent cheers, renewing the pact we'd forged. It was a small price to pay for her silence and my daughter's freedom.

A LETTER FROM SAM

I want to say a huge thank you for choosing to read *The Guilty Mother*. If you enjoyed it, and want to keep up-to-date with all my latest releases, just sign up at the following link. Your email address will never be shared, and you can unsubscribe at any time.

www.bookouture.com/sam-vickery

I'm often asked if my characters are essentially me. If I'm just writing my darkest thoughts and secrets onto the page, and the answer is: it's not that simple. In this story, I found myself relating to both Lisa and Victoria, empathising with their deepest emotions. Haven't we all experienced that gnawing loneliness that drives Victoria at one point in our lives? Craved more connection, something real and raw and true? Her need for Lisa's friendship, her family, is one that stems from the simple desperation to be accepted wholly for who she is, but in her quest for those relationships, she loses herself, her boundaries become blurred, she makes choices she might not have made in different circumstances.

And Lisa's absolute dedication to protecting her children was one I felt in my heart. When it came to losing her freedom, there was no choice to make. It was just what she knew she had to do, and she never even questioned it, never considered a different path.

I loved writing these characters, knowing they both had

secrets they couldn't share. Lisa's being how far she had *really* gone to protect her daughter, a secret she kept, even after the final pages had been turned. And Victoria's, a secret she concealed even from herself. Her revelation that she was the victim she'd never wanted to become, that her husband had abused her, coerced her, raped her was as much of a shock to her as it had been to Lisa. And despite the threats she made, the power she held over Lisa, I couldn't help but feel she wasn't the monster in this story after all.

I hope you enjoyed reading *The Guilty Mother* as much as I enjoyed writing it. If you did, I would be very grateful if you could leave a review. I'd love to hear what you think, and it makes such a difference in helping new readers to discover one of my books for the first time.

I always enjoy hearing from my readers – you can find me on my Facebook page or get in touch through my website,

www.samvickery.com

Until the next time,

Sam

 facebook.com/SamVickeryWrites

ACKNOWLEDGMENTS

I have been surrounded by so much support during the writing of this story and I am so grateful for all the talented, hard-working people who have played a part in getting this book into my readers' hands. To my fantastic editors, Susannah Hamilton and Jennifer Hunt, whose guidance brought so much to this story, thank you. I have learned so much from you both.

To my publicist, Sarah Hardy, for organising blog tours and sharing this story with the world, thank you. To Aaron Munday, the very talented designer who provided me with such an incredible cover, thank you! To Kim Nash, Noelle Holten, Jane Selley, Laura Kincaid, along with all the incredible team at Bookouture, thank you.

I began planning this book whilst battling morning sickness and the exhaustion of early pregnancy, and completed it some eighteen months later with a baby attached to my breast and in even more of a fog. It has taken a long time to get from start to finish with this one, but despite the challenges, thank you to my sweet baby Caspian, for showing me I had room in my life to be even more productive, and for reminding me that family always comes first.

To Jed, Viggo, Aurora. My loves. Always thank you.

And of course, to my wonderful readers, thank you for your continued support, your gorgeous reviews and for enabling me to continue to write these stories. I hope you've enjoyed this one.

9 781837 903504